T0354380

The
Canyon's
Edge

Nancy Nielson Redd

 www.trafford.com
North America & international
toll-free: 1 888 232 4444 (USA & Canada)
fax: 812 355 4082

DEDICATION

To Bob, my husband of sixty-plus years. Without your love, support, and encouragement, I wouldn't have my education, my writings, my art, a lifetime of cherished memories, or our children, Steven and Lynne, and their families. Thank you for this life and love we have shared.

ACKNOWLEDGMENTS

M any thanks to many people: to my daughter, Lynne Coulter, and my granddaughter, Jordan LaBarr, for being my beta readers from the beginning. Both English majors and voracious readers, they have been a valuable resource. Thanks to the critique groups I have joined: Dr. Howard Carron's group at the Southwest Regional Library in Gilbert, Arizona, and to the Desert Sleuths' critique group of Susan Budavari, Merle McCann, Sally J. Smith, Maria Grazia Swan, Terry Cipriani, and Steve Fleishmann in Scottsdale. All have given me much needed advice. A special thanks to Sally J. Smith for her professional editing. She caresses one's work with a human touch while kicking butt with her no-nonsense attitude. Thanks! I needed that! Also, thanks to Kay Shumway for his spectacular photography of the Southwest's high desert country. Great appreciation and thanks to Gilbert Arizona police officers Kim Kelly and Sy Ray for their expert advice on police procedure. Thanks to all the dedicated professionals at Trafford Publishing and to Greg Crawford and Evan Villadores. Their help was always there at the touch of my email.

PROLOGUE

Two hours before sunup, Doria, a middle-aged Navajo woman, drove an old Ford pickup along the steep graveled road out of Navajo Canyon. She kept her speed at fifteen miles per hour, both hands on the wheel and eyes straight ahead. After she had turned onto the smooth pavement of Highway 95, she relaxed, put her foot down and increased the pace to forty-five miles per hour.

Doria and her parents were on their way to Willow Water at the southwestern edge of the Navajo Reservation. Neither her mother nor father spoke English or knew how to drive. Her father, revered Navajo medicine man Hosteen Hatathlii, also known by his English name of Joseph Singer, had been hired to perform a Blessing Way rite at the Willow Water trading post.

She parked in front. The Anglo trader stood waiting on the covered porch.

The three stepped out of the pickup just minutes before the sun slipped up over the horizon where the streaked clouds of an April sky foretold a brilliant sunrise and possible rain.

The medicine man carried a traditional woven basket filled with corn meal. He nodded in recognition of the trader. Without speaking, he faced the rising sun in the east, lifted the basket, and began to chant. The massed clouds caught the sun. Etched in coral, they highlighted a spiritual moment. Shafts of sunlight limned the cedar trees, sagebrush, and tumbled rocks of the sandy desert. In the northwest lay the benign presence of Navajo Mountain, sacred to *Dineh, The People.*

The medicine man turned south, west, and then north. He walked around the fenced trading post, singing, and flinging corn meal in alternate tosses to the left and right.

Wrapped in Pendleton blankets, Doria and her mother followed him, as did the trader. The women carried additional baskets and a cotton bag filled with more corn meal.

After the exterior of the trading post and the sky above it had been blessed, a crowd of Navajo men, women, and children gathered, laughing and talking. Once inside, all talking stopped and the singer's high, keening chant filled the central room.

Dressed for the traditional happy blessing in age-softened Levis, a red velvet shirt, heavy silver jewelry, and well-worn moccasins, his presence lent a formal dignity to the occasion. A blue bandana knotted around his forehead identified him as a ceremonial singer.

Moving around the room, he scattered small finger-pinches of sacred corn meal and sang in a steady rhythm. The crowd of about forty people followed him. The Blessing Way insured that harmful spirits would stay away from this gathering place of *Dineh.* Should the trader neglect the blessing, no Navajo would shop there.

The chanted benediction lasted a mere thirty minutes. When finished, the singer presented the basket he used to the trader. Bits of corn meal still clung to the weave.

"*Hyeh-he, Hosteen,*" (Thank you) the trader said. "*Niizhonii.*" (Very good.) "*Toqui peso?*" (How much do I owe you?)

With an eloquent shrug, Joseph Singer said, "*Toqui bi-ye-e?* (How much is it worth?)" It was worth the future of the business. He knew that the trader couldn't pay much, and the trading post was essential to his people, so his expectations were humble. In payment for his long, early morning journey and his prayerful song to invoke good spirits, the ceremonial singer earned one hundred dollars, a filled gas tank, two quarts of oil, a substantial breakfast shared with friends, and admiration and appreciation from the trader and all of his customers.

After the ceremony and subsequent business came the early morning feast of Navajo fry bread and mutton stew for everyone. In anticipation of sun, tables had been set up on the shady side of the building.

Instead towering black clouds, now gathering in the northwest sky, threatened rain.

"*Yah-te-hey! Yah-te-hey!*" (Hello, how's it going?) Old friends who had gathered silently for the Blessing Way ceremony now greeted each other as if they hadn't met for days. Although they hurried to beat the weather, they still ate with pleasure, mopping up the stewed mutton juices with golden orbs of fry bread and finishing with more fry bread drizzled with honey.

As Doria drove her parents back to their hogan, she talked to them about her daughter.

"Tiahna wants to go to school to be an artist. She has Victoria now, and she's living with Rubio in Sedona. I want her to take nurse's training instead of art school, but I don't know how we can pay for either one. What should I do, *Shazhe-e, Shamah*?" (My father, my mother.)

She said nothing more. After several miles of traveling in silence, her father began to chant. All the way down the rough road into Navajo Canyon, he sang as if to himself. When they reached the hogan at the bottom, he stopped singing and began to speak. Even then, his words were few. "Go to see Tiahna's father. Tell him your story. He will help."

In the moonlit hours after midnight, Rubio and José waited in a crumbling adobe house a few miles west of Nogales on the Arizona side of the border. Rubio nodded in rhythm to music only he could hear through his earbuds. Dogs barked and branches, moving in a predawn wind, scratched against the house. Clumps of Tamarack flourished where nothing else survived in the alkali-crusted soil. Half hidden in the tall bushes, a dark blue pickup with a camper shell on the back blended into the night.

About three-thirty, José heard the sound of an approaching engine. He tapped Rubio on the shoulder and beckoned with a jerk of his head. They went outside to stand in the shadow of the house. Rubio carried a suitcase he set on the ground while José scooped up a handful of alkali dirt and put it in the pocket of his jeans. Within minutes, a dust-covered van drove into the yard.

Eight men, seven women, three teenage girls and four children climbed out into the light of the full moon. The driver, who emerged from the cab wearing baggy trousers, loose shirt, and huarache sandals, sported a handlebar mustache. His actions belied his casual, laid-back appearance. He moved with swift precision, wasting no time or energy.

With a black metal case in each hand, he ignored his passengers and walked straight to the pickup in the bushes. After switching on a small flashlight, he opened the hood and clamped the cases into metal straps secured behind the engine. He took a tube of petroleum jelly from his pocket, smeared some on the cases and then picked up a handful of soil to dribble over the gel. When he finished, the cases looked like the rest of the engine: greasy and dusty. He eased the hood shut, holding the release catch.

While the driver carried out his role in the exchange, Rubio and José stepped out of the shadows. Rubio handed the driver the suitcase while José moved the desperate group of Mexicans toward the concealed pickup. He spoke Spanish to the men in a low voice. The women and children huddled together, the children staring up at him with solemn faces.

When José heard the driver's returning steps, he opened the back of the pickup camper. The women and teens climbed in. The men lifted the children up then crowded in themselves. The van driver walked in wide avoidance of them to his van and drove away. The three smugglers, commonly called coyotes, knew the drill.

José got in the passenger side. Rubio plugged in the iPod buds and drove north. To avoid Border Patrol and drug-sniffing dogs, he took the rough, rutted back roads through the almost trackless desert. Swinging to the beat, hanging loose, he grinned and gave a cheerful thumbs-up to José. Everything had gone without a hitch. The border was a sieve and always would be, tailor-made for save-the-world types and the transfer of drugs.

Just before sunrise, Rubio stopped. José got out and lifted the hood with practiced efficiency. He leaned in over the engine on the driver's side, pulled out the black case strapped there, and removed four small baggies of powder from the dozens it contained. He closed the case, strapped it back in place, and sifted some of the sand from his pocket over it. On the passenger side, he did the same. He straightened up, wiped his hands on his jeans and slammed the hood.

With a broad grin creasing his face, José handed four bags to Rubio and stuffed four into his pockets.

"Damn, we got a good thing goin' here, José. Easiest money I ever made," Rubio said.

They completed the two hundred fifty mile trip to Sedona by noon. Rubio followed old secondary streets through town to a nondescript strip mall. He opened the camper. "Wait here. Somebody'll getcha *uno momento. Bueno suerte*, good luck!"

Both young coyotes walked across the parking lot to a small dry-cleaning shop at the end of the strip. Inside, Rubio handed a ticket stub to the proprietor and received two envelopes in return. Rubio and José each thumbed through his envelope and then shoved it in a pocket. Again, no conversation. Outside, they stopped in front of a pet store window and watched several puppies tumble and play. In a few minutes, a man walked from the dry cleaners to the pickup they had just left, got in, and drove away.

"Where will they go now?" José asked.

"Maybe to Father Quejada. He helps some of them, or up through the Rez," Rubio replied. "And then up through southeast Utah to I-70. They could end up anywhere east of there if they don't have a wreck, or get caught at some checkpoint or other."

José nodded.

Rubio whistled "La Bamba" as the two continued beyond the end of the strip mall, up a rocky hill behind it, and into an older residential neighborhood. They went to separate cars parked in front of one of the houses. A woman opened the door of the house, looked out, waved then shut the door. Rubio backed his car out of the parking spot and raced down the street without a backward glance.

José had secretly recorded every word and every relevant sound since the day before when they left Sedona for Nogales. Now, he drove to a house in a different part of town where another Hispanic man waited. José removed a keychain from his pocket and handed it over. Attached to the keychain was a hidden flash drive capable of seventeen to twenty hours of recording time which he had switched off when Rubio slept. He also handed over the envelope of cash and the four baggies of cocaine. José and the undercover cop shared a high-five and a satisfied grin.

ONE

Six months later

I drove from Page to Flagstaff then down through Oak Creek Canyon toward Sedona under heavy clouds and intermittent rain. My cell phone displayed "no service" all the way through the canyon. Just as well. The winding road forbade its use. I pulled off at the West Fork trailhead hoping to make my call to Char, but still no go.

While parked there at the side of the road, breathing in the rainwashed air, a sense of peace settled around me. The rain decreased to scattered drops. To stretch my legs, I walked up the creek bank into a shadowy seclusion of trees and ferns, soaking my jeans and shoes in the process. I didn't care. The soothing sounds of burbling water helped me release tension my body had held for months. It was like shedding a heavy coat and boots on the first day of spring. I felt more relaxed than I had in ages. With some reluctance, I turned and went back to my car.

As I approached Sedona, the clouds became sunstruck billows of fire, creating another extravagant Arizona sunset. When the clouds began to darken again, I called Char, my best friend.

"Hey, Char, I'm almost there. Dinner's on me. You pick the place."

"Great, I'm so glad you're coming, Maggie," Char said. "When you get to the gallery, head out back to the studio. I'm there now getting ready for the workshop."

I am Maggie McGinnis, and I arrived in Sedona with the first lighthearted gladness I'd experienced in months. Even the October clouds didn't dampen my spirits. All the way from Page I listened to smooth jazz CDs. My mood mellowed out with every mile I put between me and my lonely home.

Char's *Galeria de Luz* was situated near a few similar galleries but stood by itself on a lovely, tree-shaded property just off Highway 179. Her studio was behind the main building. I parked and walked back to it, stopping in the open doorway when I heard voices. Char stood talking to a stunning young Navajo woman. I stared for a few moments, unable to take my eyes off her.

Her beauty appeared natural; I could discern no makeup. Their conversation seemed to involve the colors of the traditional Navajo skirts and blouses spread on a table before them.

Char held a deep pink velvet blouse up against the turquoise top the young woman wore over a purple satin skirt. She squinted for perspective as artists do. "I think the American Beauty Pink," she said. "It's perfect with the purple skirt and will paint so well."

Still unnoticed, I agreed with her.

Char turned to lay the velvet blouse on the table and saw me. With a delighted cry, she hurried over and hugged me. "At last. I'm so glad to see you." She stepped back, placed her hands on my shoulders, and appraised me with her artist's eye.

In unison, we said, "You're so thin," and laughed together.

Char turned away. "Come, Maggie. Meet Tiahna."

Tiahna displayed her shyness with a slight smile and a lowered glance.

"Tiahna is the model for our workshop," Char explained. "We start Monday. Are you ready?"

"If anybody can teach me to paint, it'll be you," I answered.

Char and Tiahna took a few minutes to finish choosing her outfit and then Tiahna said, "I have to pick up the baby from my mom." She turned to leave.

"We won't need you to pose until Tuesday morning, Tiahna," Char called after her. "Tomorrow I'll give instructions to my class, and we'll do head sketches. So if you're ready by eight thirty on Tuesday, that'll be great."

Char locked up her painting studio. Rita, her manager, would lock up the gallery at closing time. We went to dinner at Savannah's where we enjoyed the warm ambience of low-lighting and wood beam ceilings, and watched the sunset beyond Thunder Mountain through a lovely arched window.

Opting for their turf and surf specialty, I enjoyed the food while Char moved hers around on the plate. We talked nonstop the way longtime friends do. While we were there, Char's husband, Victor, called.

"Okay. Will you meet us at the gallery?" Char asked him. "I have to go there to set up a backdrop for class on Monday morning." She turned to me. "Maggie, do you mind following me there?"

"Not a bit, I love your gallery, and I want to see your latest work."

When we came out of the restaurant, the rain had started again. I followed Char back to the gallery. Even set on high speed, my windshield wipers had a tough time wiping the downpour away.

I thought about Char as I drove. She'd been uncharacteristically quiet, letting me do most of the talking. She seemed tense to me, but there wasn't anything specific triggering that feeling. Unable to pin it down, I dismissed it. Her life was probably quite hectic at present, what with staying on top of things at the gallery while getting ready to conduct a workshop.

Saturdays are always busy in the galleries of Sedona, but they still close early. There was no moon and, ironically, the *Galeria de Luz* was intensely dark. I pulled in, parked beside Char's car, and stepped out into a puddle.

While I was reflecting on the amount of muddy water that had soaked into my shoe, Char came up beside me and said, "The storm must have knocked out the lights."

"Hmm, that's strange. The lights down the street are on." I looked up but couldn't see the tops of the power poles.

It was literally pitch black around the entrance to the gallery. Even on an ordinary night, the picturesque ceramic lanterns hung by the door and placed at ground level along the walkway gave only a dim light. Now, they gave no light at all.

Something crunched beneath my feet as I made my way toward the gallery. "Is that glass?" I asked. "Broken glass?"

Char sounded frustrated. "Oh, damn. It's the lightbulbs. Someone has broken the bulbs out of my lights." She fumbled in the dark with the door lock.

To get out of the rain, I moved toward where I remembered an immense tree whose branches covered half the courtyard. Heavier than the drumming of the rain came the sound of water splashing nearby. In my mind's eye, I saw the fountain that sat next to the big tree.

As I took my last step to get under the branches, I stumbled over something lying in my path. I landed with a muffled thump. "Oh, damn!" Whatever was under me was soft but unyielding. "What is this?"

It reeked. I gagged but fought it back. A few seconds passed. With trembling hands, I touched wet fur, hairy ears, and then cold, hard, bare legs that felt human. Dread swamped me. A dead dog? A body? I gasped and struggled to move back off it.

I heard Char stumble toward me in the darkness. "Maggie, are you all right?" Then something landed on the paved courtyard with a thud, followed by the sound of smaller items scattering. Her purse?

"Oh, crap!" was the only warning I had before she landed on top of me. Her weight pushed my face down into the wet dog stink. Whatever lay beneath me hadn't moved. It was stiff, and if it ever had been alive, it didn't seem to be now.

"Oh, my God, Char, help me up."

"What did you fall over?" Char said.

"It feels like a dead body."

Just then, Victor arrived on his Harley. As his headlight swept over us, I caught a quick glimpse of a man's bare legs sticking out from under a hairy pelt.

Char got to her feet and reached down to help me. Stiff, curved fingers snagged the sleeve of my jacket. Hysteria rose in my throat. I tried to scramble back. My snagged jacket forced me to stop and yank it away from the unyielding hand.

"What are you two doing over there?" Victor aimed his headlamp at us.

Char and I faced each other in the dim glow. The look on her face, a mixture of shock and disbelief mirrored my own feelings. I swallowed hard, afraid I might throw up after all.

"Victor, come here. Hurry." Char's voice shook.

Victor brought his flashlight, flinching when he saw the body. "Oh, dear God." It was almost a prayer. He helped Char first then me to stand up. Char took hold of his flashlight and directed the beam at the ground where her purse lay, the contents scattered around it. She dropped down and began to gather her belongings.

"Victor, I think . . . can you tell . . ." I could barely speak. "Is that a real person under that—what—dog skin?"

"I can't find my keys." Char clutched her purse against her and stood, still fumbling inside it.

Victor shone his light around the courtyard, stopping on the studio door. "They're in the keyhole. You girls go call the police and let me see . . . Oh, God . . . What in hell's going on here?"

Char and I went inside. She turned on lights both inside and outside then called 9-1-1.

I pushed my sodden hair out of my eyes and looked at my watch. It was only six-thirty but seemed so much later. In my agitation, I had lost my sense of time. After Char hung up the phone, she brought me a hand towel. I used it to dry my face and head. She did the same then we stood side-by-side, nervously waiting for the police at the open front door.

Rain still pounded the courtyard. "Any evidence of our fall over the body will be washed away," I said.

"Yes," Victor agreed. "As hard as it's coming down, any evidence at all may be gone."

"Someone broke all the outside lights," Char said. "We couldn't see anything."

The first car to arrive carried a patrolman, who looked at the body. Without touching anything, he made a call. Within minutes, other police cars lined the street. The officer who appeared to be in charge greeted Victor and Char with familiarity, and then glanced at me.

Char briefly introduced us. "Detective Garcia Lopez, my friend, Maggie." He nodded and then turned to the body. Char whispered to me, "Garcia and Randa are engaged."

Hmmm. Good-looking guy. It surprised me a little that thought would cross my mind in such stressful circumstances.

A television crew drove up.

Two additional officers arrived to set up portable floodlights, which, along with the blue and red pulses from Detective Lopez's car, lit the grim scene—a horrible still life. The dead man lay face down with the skin of what might have once been a coyote covering his head and back. The animal's head was still attached, the fangs bared. Even without moving the body, we could see that the pads of the man's fingers and toes had been sliced away.

The police rolled him over.

Victor stumbled back a step. "Good Lord! It's José!"

"You know this guy?" Detective Lopez asked.

"Yes, I do. I did. He worked for the landscaping company that takes care of our yards here and at home. He's, I mean, he was a dynamite mechanic. He loved bikes as much as I do."

The detective stepped back under the eaves where it was drier and took out a small notebook. "Do you know his family?"

"No. We don't know his family. Why?" Victor put his hand over his eyes. "Oh. How in the world can they be informed of this if no one knows them?"

The two men stood looking down at the rain-drenched body. Char and I stayed back. I didn't want to stare at him; it felt like an invasion of his privacy, though he was beyond caring.

Detective Lopez ignored Victor's concern and turned to a young policewoman. "Sergeant, let's go inside and take preliminary statements from the Coopers and their guest." He led us inside to Victor's office, where Lopez introduced us to Sergeant Monica Slejak. Our stories, short and straightforward, didn't take long to record, and then Lopez told Slejak to return to headquarters to get our information into the computer and make copies for our signatures.

After the Sergeant had left, Detective Lopez lowered his voice confidentially. His words revealed thoughtful compassion, not just toward his fiancée's family, but toward José's family, as well.

"What I'm going to tell you won't be in the newspapers for a while at least," he said, "and I don't want you to say anything about it, either." He looked seriously at the three of us.

"Don't drive yourselves crazy thinking this had anything to do with you. I know this man, and I know his family. I don't think he died of natural causes, especially the way the body was staged. I'm sure this murder was connected to a police investigation concerning smuggling, both drugs and people. You've read about it in the newspapers. José was working undercover for us. He's undocumented, but since he was helping us, we started the naturalization process for his family."

My heart raced. Of course, I'd known the man couldn't do this to himself, but for the first time I considered the fact that I had stumbled into murder. Murder? Human smuggling? My God!

Char gasped. The color had left Victor's face.

"I'll go see his wife when we're finished here. They have two young kids, just babies." Garcia looked down and shook his head before raising his tired and troubled eyes to us.

My heart went out to him and to the young mother about to hear this terrible news. "Difficult news to deliver, even more difficult to receive. I'm sorry, Detective Lopez."

He nodded his appreciation, "Please call me Garcia," and then he sighed. "His wife's name is Maria." It was obvious he was shouldering the blame for the man's death.

"If there is anything we can do to help, please tell us," Char said. "This will be terrible for her." She rubbed her forehead and tears came to her eyes. Her cell phone rang. She looked at it and said softly, "It's Randa." We listened as she described the scene to her daughter.

Footsteps sounded in the hall. A uniformed policeman tapped on the open door and stuck his head inside. "The news stations want a statement. Anybody here up for fifteen seconds of fame?"

Garcia looked at us with a resigned shrug and stood. We followed him outside where the rain had decreased to a light sprinkle. Bright camera lights and a newswoman with a microphone waited by the door. When she heard it was I who stumbled over the body, she shoved her mike at my face, "Can you describe what happened here?"

I began to tell my part of the story, but before I could finish, Garcia launched into his announcement. She moved on, leaving me between words that trailed away to nothing as the microphone receded.

It was then that Randa arrived. I instantly thought of Char's worried phone call a few months before telling me about her daughter's accident in Oak Creek Canyon. Randa's most serious injury was a gash on the side of her head that they thought would leave a scar.

Victor had refused to let the doctors cut her hair away from the wound. Randa had fabulous hair like Char's—thick, red and curly—and she had Victor's blue eyes. She wore a shiny purple slicker and rain hat with no hint of her hair showing. I didn't see evidence of a scar or injury. Randa was small and slight with a pale complexion. She looked fragile next to her fiancé, the sturdy, good-looking Detective Garcia Lopez, who was tall and dark with tired eyes that looked as if they'd seen too much, too soon.

Randa stared down at the body, her eyes troubled. "What happened to him?"

"We don't know yet." Garcia turned her so she was looking at him instead of the grotesque corpse.

Her lovely presence underscored the bizarre scene. In the small, charming entry garden, the appalling enormity of murder assaulted every sense of humanity. The brutal destruction of life we'd stumbled upon and the casual way the body had been tossed aside horrified me. I had to agree with Garcia that there was something quite deliberate in choosing a high-end art gallery to dump the body. Even to me, it appeared obvious that this staged setup was meant to send a clear message, otherwise, why in front of Char's gallery?

I wished this man named José had not been stripped of all dignity at his life's end. He had family and friends who would grieve for him. I hoped his cruel death had been swift though I was sure he must have suffered.

My mind circled the scene. *Would Char have to cancel her workshop? Tomorrow, Sunday, she'd have a day to reorganize if necessary.* I became aware of the crassness of my thoughts and was ashamed.

Crass or not, people from several states had signed up for the workshop, and paid in advance. They would have arrived today or perhaps tomorrow to check into their hotels. Most of them no doubt flew into Phoenix and rented a car to drive north to red rock country. A lot of preparation and expense would likely have gone into the coming two weeks. Char already had many things clamoring for her attention, and now this.

I had so been looking forward to attending Char's two-week workshop in Sedona, an area I love, and to meeting people with whom to share my first efforts at wielding a paintbrush. I discovered the body and wanted to cooperate with the police, but I didn't want to miss out on the workshop. Even as I felt ashamed of myself for thinking of this, I still worried somehow this would upset the getaway I planned with such optimism, and had felt so lighthearted about.

I stood out of the way under the roof overhang and watched the crime-scene process, aware of a jangled-up disconnect from reality. This situation, so far removed from anything I had ever experienced, shook me to the core. I took deep breaths and let them out with a slow cadence while I counted from ten down to one, a self-hypnosis strategy to calm my nerves. It helped.

More serene, I watched Char and Victor, who were unaware of my scrutiny. The changed and charged atmosphere around them remained undefined.

Victor's erect posture and buoyant movements of the past were gone. His shoulders had a new slump. He looked burdened. Char's eyes reflected sadness, most noticeable in repose when she wasn't aware of being watched. Another change: they stood apart. The physical closeness, the quick glances of understanding that had characterized their togetherness were missing. *Maybe it is just momentary. Maybe tomorrow, they'll be their usual selves.*

I glanced again at my watch, nine-thirty. Must have been my nerves that made me keep checking the time because there was nowhere to go and nothing to do.

Char linked her arm in mine, "You've had a long day," and propelled me toward Garcia. She told him I was an innocent bystander and would be at her house for a couple of weeks if he needed to talk to me again.

He asked for my cell phone number and email address, cautioned me to be available for interviews then agreed to let me leave the scene.

As I turned toward my car, finally allowing myself to feel tired, Char hugged me and handed me a house key. "Try not to worry about this. Let yourself into the house and go to bed if you want. I don't know how long we'll be here."

Char's sensitive response to people and events was a quality I've long admired. It could be what made her such a compelling portrait artist. Although she had to be shaken by the horrendous discovery at her beloved gallery, she kept herself together all evening. She hadn't retreated to take in deep breaths as I had. I made a mental note to ask her secret.

At Char and Victor's house the rain had stopped; clouds had shifted, and the moon shone through. I thought about calling my children, Jennifer and Alex, but decided I didn't want to get them hyped up this late in the evening. Too, if I called, we'd be on the phone a while and I didn't want to miss the ten o'clock news. Since they grew up and moved out, it had been my habit to call them on Sunday afternoon anyway, so I decided to wait.

I unloaded my bags and carried them to the room I always use at Char's house. I loved it. One of her large oil paintings of Arizona hung on the wall opposite the door. All blue sky and golden Cottonwood trees, children and dogs playing among fallen autumn leaves, the painting was always the first thing I saw when I stepped into "my" room. Tonight, it hung a little askew. I set one bag on the floor, put the hanging bag in the closet, and straightened the picture.

I looked out through the sliding glass door onto the small patio replete with terra cotta pots of geraniums and grape vines snaking up over the latticed roof. Moonlight etched deep shadows on the patio floor and sparkled in rain pools. Across the patio, glass doors led into Char and Victor's room. It looked so peaceful, so normal.

Still wet and shivering, I sat on the floor at the end of the bed and turned the TV to the ten o'clock news. The murder led the broadcast. Victor spoke into the microphone, saying the victim did his landscaping work and worked on his bike, and always seemed pleasant and cheerful.

There were subsequent shots of Char and me. We all looked nearly drowned, with hair hanging in rain-drenched clumps. As I watched the newscast, I struggled to get my mind around the fact that I had stumbled onto a corpse. Who'd ever imagine such a thing?

Jangled and jittery with too much negative energy, I turned off the TV when the newscast moved to other news and hurried to get into the shower. Warm water, shampoo, and soap worked wonders. My cell phone was ringing when I turned off the water. My daughter's name, Jen, showed on the screen, along with four missed calls. The missed calls were from Jen and Alex. I guessed the murder had made the evening news statewide.

After I towel-dried my hair, I set up a conference call to tell the story just one more time.

Jen didn't even bother to say hello. "Wow, Mom. I just saw you on the news."

"Yeah. Looked great, didn't I?"

"Oh, yeah. Rain'll do that for you. So tell us about it. Are you okay?"

Samantha, Jen's two-year-old Sammi, said, "Nana, la looboo."

"Ah, yes, sweetheart, I love you too."

After we'd covered the television news, Jen said, "Daddy called. He wanted to know my plans for Thanksgiving and Christmas."

Alex said, "Yeah, me, too."

"What did you tell him?"

Jen said, "Just a minute. David is going to put Samantha back to bed." Silence for a few minutes on the other end, and then she continued, "I just told Daddy that Nana's was the only place for Thanksgiving and Christmas, but what did he have scheduled for Halloween or New Year's Eve?"

"Oh, Jen, bless you. What a perfect answer. How about you, Alex?"

"Mom, I didn't know what to say. I just said we'd planned to go to Susan's parents for Thanksgiving, and we weren't sure yet about Christmas. I'm not quick on the trigger with words like you and Jen are, but I love Dad, you know. It's hard because I can't imagine the holidays anywhere but with you, Mom." He drew a deep breath. "Dad did sound kind of lonesome."

Jen broke in. "I love Dad, too, but I thought he was just doing his duty, you know, checking in, making himself available for our holidays if we needed him. He knows holidays aren't the same without Mom. What would he do, take us all out for Christmas brunch?"

I bit back a smartass reply. "Thanks. You both know how much I love the holidays. Let's plan something extra special, okay?"

"The way we do it is *always* special," Jen said. "Don't change a thing. I want Samantha to grow up experiencing our traditional holidays."

Alex said, "Are you gonna be okay, Mom? You looked almost drowned on the news."

"Yeah, I'm okay. Don't worry about me. It was a bizarre experience, and I am wiped out. I'll call you, if not tomorrow, then in a day or two, when we know more about what will happen at the gallery."

My evening yoga routine, followed by deep relaxation and meditation, eased my jitters. I felt myself let go and, entering into silence, my mind became still and peaceful. In the silence, a question occurred to me: Were my jitters negative energy, or were they positive vibrations in a negative situation? After several minutes of listening in the silence, I decided to let that question float until an answer came to me. Or not. And then, at that deep level, I understood my energy had not been all negative. Instead, in an "ah ha" moment, I knew the vibrations were love and sympathy I felt for my friends and for the man whose life had been taken, along with the negativity of violent and unnecessary death. After that answer, I felt more able to cope with such a mixed bag of emotions.

Sleep eluded me. My head was crammed with thoughts of how life had led me into more than one situation I would never choose. Was something cosmic going on here? Some purpose for moving me into place to stumble over José's body? If I hadn't stepped under the tree, someone else would have found him later in the evening or the following morning. What was I supposed to do now, and what alignment of the stars had merged my path with a killer's? It scared me almost senseless until clarification came to me through the stillness. *I must be here for a reason. All I have to do is follow where it leads me.*

A couple of compelling reasons had brought me to Sedona. First reason: My husband, Ron, left me to wander the mountains and find himself, or so he said. He'd always wanted to be a mountain man, a Daniel Boone or a Hawkeye. From his explanation, I took it that life with a wife had evolved into a life too tame for him.

The sudden end of my long-standing marriage hit me six months ago. Damn him! He was the father of my children, so I tried not to call him names in front of them, but no matter how sensitive I wanted to be, I couldn't escape the fact that I thought he was selfish. I used "son-of-a-bitch" and "horse's ass" to describe him to myself. Both names fit his behavior, and that was a fact. He left me without a life partner, and not the least of my anger stemmed from the fact his departure also left me without a sex partner. I burned out on soul-searching during those months and badly needed a shift in perspective. So when the second reason presented itself, I jumped at it.

Second reason: When I called Char about the shocking turn my life had taken, she told me about the art workshop in October, and asked me to come and participate. The workshop would give me something creative to do with my hands, get my mind off my problems, and present opportunities to talk things over with my best friend. She said I should also plan on indulging in massage and treatments available at Tranquil Waters, the health spa her daughter Randa owned. Bless Char. It seemed to me to be exactly what I needed.

Lying in bed in Char's house, I admitted that right from the start I thought my vacation in Sedona would be all about me. Now, in light of the evening's events, my midlife crisis diminished to a more manageable size, receding to a small, dark cloud on my personal horizon. It was still something I had to deal with, but small potatoes compared to what José's family faced.

Ron and I had lived in Page, Arizona, for years where I worked in Human Resources as a counselor and personnel director. I loved my job, enjoyed counseling and working with people and felt rewarded by successful interactions. One of my best outcomes concerned an outgoing young woman named Casey, who came to work in my office as a secretary. Almost immediately, her supervisor discovered she couldn't spell the simplest words, *repete* for repeat, *cansel* for cancel. But Casey had a sociable personality and brought new life to the office with her friendliness. I hated the thought she might lose her job over her spelling problems and suggested we move her to Public Relations and put her on the event planning team. It turned out in the most positive way. Casey, her supervisor, and I were all thrilled.

My job could be stressful. It was never easy to tell someone their fellow workers could no longer work with them and that complaints about their attitude had come down to "improve your actions or leave." Our six-month work program was my best tool, even though we tended to employ catch phrases like "embrace change" and "things have a way of working out for the best," which sometimes sounded hollow.

These days I had empathy with those I counseled. When Ron left, change was the last thing I wanted to embrace. Since April, I spent hours trying to figure out how Ron and I could have grown so far apart that he had to leave. I never thought for a minute he'd been unfaithful. I believed him when he said he just wanted some space and thought he could find it in the mountains. The breakup of my marriage became a test of my character. My objectivity faded fast. I hoped the Sedona scenery and a chance to talk things over with an old friend would help me let go of my illusion that Ron and I had the perfect marriage. All along I'd thought of myself as Ron's "right" wife, and now found myself to be his "left" wife. It was hard to change my thinking on that.

Ron and I hadn't seen each other since he left. My anger fizzled out and left me heartsick and brain-dead from struggling with what I saw as undeserved rejection. Ron had to follow his heart and deep down I knew it, but that knowledge didn't make me feel any better. My self-esteem took a big hit, but my libido never diminished. So far I'd not sunk so low as to cruise the bars looking for love in all the wrong places. Was it possible to be a cougar and a counselor at the same time? I needed someone to want me but felt sad, and lonely, and old. This counselor needed counseling. I was hoping to find it in Sedona.

I shifted and squirmed in my bed and relived the discovery at *Galeria de Luz*. For most of the night, my mind ran in circles because I couldn't think straight. Even my deep breathing and counting down strategy failed. It bothered me the victim's young widow was now alone and undocumented in a country not her own. Illegal immigration had become a tangled nightmare in my beloved state of Arizona.

Morning came too soon. I gave up on sleep, got out of bed and performed my morning yoga asanas including the sun salutation. After my shower, I heard sounds outside and opened the arcadia door. Char and Victor sat outside on the patio with coffee and muffins, reading a couple of newspapers.

"Big spread in the papers today," Victor said. "Grab a chair and a cup and join us."

Yesterday's rain clouds had blown away during the night. The blue sky of Sedona in October, the sky I had so looked forward to seeing, greeted me as I stepped outside. On one hand, it seemed almost sacrilegious to indulge our curiosity and read about murder on such a shining Sunday morning. On the other hand, respect for the body we'd discovered and our natural curiosity demanded our attention.

The papers carried a photo of the victim and described him as an illegal immigrant. Supporting articles speculated about undocumented aliens who escape from drop houses in Phoenix where they're held against their will by *coyotes,* the criminals who smuggle them across the international border. The coyotes bring their *pollos,* or chickens, across the border for an agreed amount, but as soon as they're in the States, they hold the *pollos* hostage and demand more money from the families back in Mexico. While a direct connection was never made, the newspaper alluded to the possibility the victim, José, was an escaped *pollo.*

The critical question was why his body was left at *Galeria de Luz.* There was a photo of the gallery. Victor's, Char's and even my name were mentioned relative to the circumstances under which he'd been found. The lurid story, continued to a double spread on pages A6 and A7, made reference to undocumented workers, illegal smuggling, and the drain on Arizona schools and health care systems. It seemed to me the story was crucial because of its local aspects and attachment to *Galeria de Luz,* and the media capitalized on that connection. Not everybody found received so much coverage.

When we finished reading, Char stood. "The gallery is still cordoned off as a crime scene." She raked her fingers through her tousled mop of hair. "Garcia said he thought they could finish up there today so I can hold the workshop. Just in case they don't finish, I'm going to make arrangements to rent a studio at the Sedona Art Center until they do. So I'll be pretty busy today." She turned to go inside. "I don't know how long this will take, or if I can find anyone on a Sunday to help me make arrangements. Don't wait lunch for me."

TWO

A fter Char left, Victor and I picked up the coffee cups and muffin wrappers. "I have some repairs to make at the spa today," Victor said. "Would you like to go with me? You could relax in a hot tub, maybe have a massage?"

"That sounds perfect." There was the answer as to what I would do with myself today. "When do you plan to leave?"

"In an hour or so. I'll call Randa first and ask her when she'll be ready. I bought all the repair materials yesterday, so I'm set to go when she is."

"I'll take a walk then. It is such a gorgeous morning, I want to go out and breathe in some of this beauty."

I walked the streets of the neighborhood, surrounded by the red rocks of Sedona. In every direction, ancient stone outcroppings rose against the blue sky.

I had hours to fill. Maybe I should have stayed in Page until that afternoon. Who knew? Maybe my being there to discover José's body was fate, breaking me out of my own past and into a changed future.

Walking helped. After a while, I stopped thinking about my problems and myself and concentrated on deep breathing. I thought I was finished with the happenings at *Galeria de Luz*, except what I might hear about them from Char.

When I returned to Char and Victor's house, a car I didn't recognize was parked in the driveway. *Must be Randa.*

I stopped to admire the door of the house as I do every time I go through it. Char designed it. Heavy aged timbers framed glass and copper inserts. Sculptured native dancers, birds, and trees were interspersed in the panels of the door with stained glass blue sky, flaming cottonwoods, and burnt red *ristras*, those attractive Mexican-inspired strings of dried red chili peppers. I had forgotten to take the key Char gave me, so I rang the bell.

Randa answered the door and hugged me. "Good morning, Maggie. How are you feeling this morning?"

I told her I was fine and followed her to the kitchen where I found Garcia and Victor.

"Good morning, Garcia," I said. He nodded. He looked better than when I'd seen him last night. Less tired.

"Maggie," Randa said, "Mom asked me to come over to help you get settled. She'll be busy until she finishes getting her workshop set up. Garcia said her studio will be released and she can hold it there."

Until the previous night when she was covered in raingear, it had been two years since I'd seen Randa. At first, I thought she'd created a whimsical new hairstyle. Her hair, pulled over from the left into a splashed out effect, impressed me as contemporary and a bit on the wild side then I noticed it was combed that way to cover the injury from the accident. A lumpy, disfiguring scar protruded out from her hair in a downward trail about an inch into her right cheek. I must have gazed at it a moment too long.

She laughed, sounding a bit embarrassed, and patted her head with a delicate touch. "How do you like it, Maggie?"

"It's striking, Randa. Innovative."

She stroked her right temple. "Dad wouldn't let them cut my hair, so it's still kind of matted around my injury. I have an impressive stylist who helps me pick it out, strand by strand. She designs styles to help me camouflage the damage."

"She's very creative," I nodded my approval.

"I'm lucky." She smiled. Garcia reached up from where he sat to take hold of her hand. Their eyes met. "Not just for my hair. For my head. For my life. The doctors say I will always be scarred, but it won't be this awful looking after a few more plastic surgeries. Could be worse."

"Yes, it could have been much worse," Victor said. "We could have lost you."

Randa ducked her head, blinking away tears.

I turned to Garcia to change the subject. "Do you know how the investigation is going?"

"No, not really," he answered. "I do know the crime scene team doesn't think he was killed at the gallery, just dumped there. We're trying to figure out what message the killer was trying to convey by leaving the body in such a prominent place."

"Does that mean I'm not a suspect?" I said.

"No, you never were," he said. "Neither were Victor and Char, or Randa. There was no credible evidence to link it to any of you." Garcia raked his fingers through his hair. "I still think the fact that somebody left a body in the gallery yard is someone thumbing his nose at the police."

"I don't understand," I said. "Why Char's yard?"

"Because of Garcia's connection to them through me," Randa said.

"Oh." I turned back to Garcia. "Why not leave it in your yard, or Randa's yard?"

"Because I live in a condo," Garcia said.

"And I live out at the spa," Randa added.

"They could have left that poor man in the police yard," Garcia continued the narrative, "but they'd take a bigger risk of being caught there, and less chance of my understanding the impact of their statement."

"I'm still not sure I follow your reasoning."

Garcia drew a deep breath. "They know how prominent Char is. They know my connection to all of you, and that I wouldn't want to see you hurt. The way they did this involved some shrewd, sophisticated terrorism. Not hard to see that there's a message here."

"Who do you think 'they' are?" Randa asked

Garcia shrugged and shook his head.

I remembered then that he'd told us José was helping the police, so they were helping him become naturalized. "I've read a lot about the immigration problem," I said. "I just never thought I'd get this close to it."

"I know," Victor said. "I've read a lot of stuff, too. They've found smugglers use the migrants to camouflage the trail of massive shipments of drugs. They use those desperate people as decoys. If we didn't have so many addicts in this country, they'd lose their market. They are arrogant. They lure men who work for the minimum and have a family to support, and then toss them away when they screw up. And they always do screw up one way or another. They think they can do a little cocaine on the side or even sell a little, and it will never be noticed. A drug habit will always make itself known. The whole thing is an exercise in frustration."

Some years back, the governor of New Mexico had declared New Mexico to be a sanctuary state. A sort of sanctuary movement had also been afoot Arizona to provide water stations for illegal groups entering the country during the heat of summer. They might get through the border, but they wouldn't get far across the hot, sandy desert without water.

"Garcia says our agencies are underfunded and understaffed for the hordes of people and tons of drugs coming in." Randa sounded tense.

At this point, Garcia's cell phone beeped. He looked at it and said, "I've got to go." He turned to Randa. "Walk me to the door?" To Victor and me, he said, "See you later."

In our brief morning discussion, I learned more than I had expected. I felt too modern, too U.S.A., too sheltered. Could something be working on me this year, luring me out of my own increasingly uncomfortable rut?

Our conversation gave me a clue. The police knew what they were doing, so I didn't have to ask myself what I should do about any of that. I concluded that my involvement meant it was time for me to stop being so pathetic, so self-involved, and get real. The discovery of José's body smacked me upside the head, right when I needed it. My personal problems were tiny pinpricks in the overall scheme of life.

Victor, Randa, and I talked until the coffee pot was empty. I had already drawn conclusions that Victor and Char were not their usual selves. Now, I reflected that I'd always known Randa as a dynamo. At twenty-seven, she still looked small and soft and vulnerable, but she'd always been unerring in her style choices. Maybe because of the accident that had left her hair matted, the atmosphere around her was tense and wired, in contrast to the unstructured image she presented.

We sat in silence. I was thinking about the tangled web of circumstances, when Randa broke into my thoughts.

"Maggie," she said, "new subject. Have you ever been to a full moon drumming circle?"

"Yes. I go to a drumming circle in Page. I love it. Do you go to one?"

"Yes, I do. Tuesday night the moon will be full, and if we're lucky, the sky will be clear. For the past month, we've been constructing a labyrinth at the spa. This week, we're going to use it for the first time and have a full moon for our drumming circle. Why don't you join us? I've got a drum you can use."

"You know that full moon drumming started out as a pagan ritual?" I said.

"Not the way we do it. Depends on one's intentions. Our intentions are not focused on paganism or war or sacrifice. Our intention is to relieve stress. We drum to the rhythm of the heart."

I nodded. "I have my own little rituals for dealing with stress, but thank you, I'd love to come out to the spa and get in tune with the beating of my heart."

"Everyone I know who drums says it releases tension. Some even say it enhances the immune system. I was thinking after all you've been through since you got here, you could be feeling tense. Hanging out over the edge, you know?"

"Okay. I'm not quite hanging on by my fingernails, but I'm up for drumming by the light of the moon."

"Let's go get the repair work done, Randa," Victor said. "Do you still want to come with us, Maggie?"

"No, I've changed my mind, Victor. But thanks. I think I'll stay here and do some work on my laptop. I'll come out with Char later."

They left, and I stayed alone in the house. I opened my laptop and checked my email then opened my daily journal folder. Did I ever have a lot to tell my *Dear Journal*. As I started to write, a couple of questions in the back of my mind came forward. Was Garcia correct in his belief that the body in Char's gallery courtyard was to get at him? It sounded logical. And I wondered where Victor had been while Char and I had dinner together before we went to the gallery?

I shrugged off the questions. Char and Victor would never be involved with drugs, or human smuggling, or murder.

THREE

I t was mid-morning by the time I finished working, and I was still alone in the house. Another nature walk struck my fancy, so I dressed in blue jeans, a white T-shirt, and Reeboks and let myself out the front door. This time, I didn't forget the house key.

Rocks towered against the blue sky, and the autumn colors of oak and aspen blazed in the sunlight. Sedona's natural grandeur worked its magic on me.

Char had been like a sister through many decades of life's ups and downs. As true friends, we still disagreed, but our relationship survived in a comfortable acceptance of each other, warts and all.

And what was with Victor? Impulsive, friendly Victor—I'd known him since Char married him, and always liked him. But last night, I'd picked up strong impressions of nervousness, most of all from Victor. Granted, anyone having to deal with the police and news media in such a stressful situation would seem different, but this went beyond that. I hadn't wanted to pry, but I couldn't help wondering about the charged atmosphere. What was going on?

Victor gave the impression of uncertainty. Convinced I wasn't mistaken, I wondered if he were depressed or dealing with some other deep sadness. I couldn't think of any reason for him to live with a long-lasting sadness. Victor had always been the kind of guy who dealt with problems.

Just then I heard a motorcycle coming and turned to look. Victor's bike roared around the curve. I waved, and he stopped.

He swung his leg over the seat and stood up. A cat leaped from the wide motor housing on the Harley and rubbed against my leg.

I knelt to pet the cat. "I can't stay inside on such a day. Did you finish your repairs?"

"Yep. Come on. I'll give you a ride back to the house." He took my hand and pulled me up. Curious about how the cat rode with Victor, I took a look. A cushioned basket was attached in front of the driver's seat. The cat was protected behind the windscreen. That was the Victor I knew and loved—sensitive and thoughtful. The cat jumped back in the basket, and the three of us rode up the hill, breaking the neighborhood stillness with a roar. The cat looked comfortable. Helmets covered Victor's thick gray hair and my salon-highlighted brown hair. I clung to Victor's waist, aware for the first time of how his ribs stuck out. *Lordy, he's skinny,*

We swung in a wide circle into the driveway. "You might have to get debugged." Victor laughed and brushed something from my cheek. As we went in through Char's one-of-a-kind sculptured door, he said, "Char is still out organizing for her artists. Can I get you some coffee or tea or something?"

"Yes, please. Give me a few minutes and I'll meet you in the kitchen."

My room nestled into a corner behind the kitchen. I adjusted the painting that again had tilted a bit, and then looked through the arcadia doors. The light, filtered through the grape vines on the patio, gave a hideaway feeling to the interior of the room. I stepped outside to pick one of the few remaining bunches of grapes. Black Prince Seedless, Char called them. They were past their prime, but still plump. I washed them at a faucet at the edge of the patio and then went inside eating them and thinking, this house makes a statement: *"We made it!"* So what was going on within these walls, within these lives? Questions bugged me, and I couldn't just brush them away as Victor had brushed a bug from my cheek.

The changes I sensed in Victor unsettled me the most. He used to remind me of his motorcycle—fast and loud. When he was in the house, his footsteps or his music or his singing or his cooking or whatever he was doing broadcast his movements. *That's it,* I thought. *Victor is too quiet. I haven't heard him sing today or bang the pots and pans.*

Victor lived with supercharged energy. He always had. For the first time, his sexy energy was turned off. That was why he seemed so off-balance and edgy.

Victor didn't see me as I walked into the kitchen. He was at the table, staring out through the window into the backyard. The lines of his face were downturned; the defining word was *discouraged*.

The scent of coffee had beckoned me all the way down the hall. The teakettle was steaming and makings were on the counter. I picked up a mug. Victor swiveled toward me and turned on a smile.

"Hey, Mag," he said.

"Victor," I blurted out. "What's wrong? I've known you too long not to see you're worried."

He just looked at me with sad eyes. A dark red flush suffused his face.

"Sorry," I said. "I've embarrassed us both. It's none of my business." I turned away to pour hot water over a tea bag and stood for a moment with my back to him.

Then he said, "Uh . . . well, one thing . . . I'm going to have surgery in a couple of weeks, after the workshop."

"Oh, no." I carried my steaming mug to the table. "Nothing serious, I hope."

"I've put it off so long it's getting serious. I have hemorrhoids. They are so painful, I have a hard time riding my bike."

"Well, dang, Victor. Sorry to hear that. How long will you be laid up?"

Before he could answer, the front door opened and closed and a familiar voice called, "It's me."

"We're in the kitchen, Randa." He turned back to me. "I can't put it off any longer. I have a combination of internal and external problems. The doctor described them as looking like a bunch of grapes."

I had just taken a sip of hot tea and the image of the grapes I had just eaten caused a monumental snort and backed up the tea into my nose. The spray caught Victor right in the face.

He wiped his face; his wounded expression was my undoing. I put my head on the table to bring my mortified laughter under control.

"I am so sorry, Victor." I raised my head and looked at him. "I just ate some of Char's grapes."

"Good Lord, Maggie." He laughed with me, and then patted me on the back to help me catch my breath.

Randa walked in and looked at us with a puzzled expression.

"What's so funny?" she asked.

"Don't ask. You <u>honestly don't want to know</u>," Victor said.

With Randa in the room, our conversation took a new turn. I sipped my tea and looked up at her. From that angle, I could see the long line of her neck and the tightening of her mouth as unspoken feelings charged the atmosphere in the kitchen. Victor's surgery wasn't all that was going on with this family.

Randa's red hair, caught up by a giant purple clip, drifted around her head on the good side and fell over to conceal the damaged side.

"You look gorgeous, Randa Cooper," I said. "Like some famous movie star I can't think of right now."

"Maybe Alice Cooper?" she kidded.

She came up behind me and hugged me. "Are you coming to the spa for a massage?"

"Just try to stop me. Your mother tells me a massage is terrific for firming up one's . . . ah . . . resolve."

"Not to mention firming up one's other assets." She laughed.

"Char asked me to meet her at the gallery at noon. If she's finished her workshop arrangements, we'll drive to the spa together."

"It's eleven-thirty now," Victor said. "Do you want to ride down with me on the motorcycle?"

"No, thanks," I answered. "I'll take my car. That way I can come and go without bothering you or Char."

Randa said, "Don't forget there's a reception Friday at *Los Abrigados*." She turned to me. "We're all invited to meet some of the well-known citizens of Arizona. I don't know who'll be there, but it should be interesting."

Victor said, "Char will be honored at a reception in the spring. She's a famous citizen too, you know. You must plan to come for that." The strain in Victor's voice made me uneasy, as if my responses were too bright in the gloom of this house.

Randa's voice was edgy as well, bordering on rude. "I've got to run. See you at the spa."

"I've got a whopping big day, too. Lots of loose ends to tie up," Victor said to me. I hadn't asked about his day.

I parked down the street just as Victor's motorcycle roared in under the trees surrounding Char's gallery. *Galleria de Luz*, Gallery of Light, was housed in a Spanish-style building constructed to look old. The stone-paved courtyard was furnished with weathered plank garden benches beckoning the weary to sit a spell. The splashing of the fountain reminded me of the night before. Two uniformed police officers gathered up piles of loose yellow police tape. Gallery hoppers strolled up and down the street, in and out of galleries, laughing and chattering, pausing to look at the remains of the cordoned-off crime scene. Victor went to speak to the officers.

The courtyard looked and felt inviting and cool. Sunlight sparkled through the leaves. All signs of blood and violence had been washed away by the rain. Peace and serenity challenged my memories of last night. Without the yellow tape, no one would suspect anything had happened there. I hoped Char's business would not be harmed.

Victor joined me. "The gallery can open this afternoon. Char will be delighted."

We headed inside, but were blocked by a slouching young Mexican man talking in a low voice with a woman I assumed to be Rita.

"You know we don't have that kind of money, Ruby," I overheard her say before she realized we were there.

Char told me Rita had been her gallery manager for the past few years, but I had never met her. The last time I'd been here, two years ago, Rita had been on vacation.

"Hello," I said.

The young man looked at me with glittery eyes, and then turned to stand away from us.

The woman spoke to me. "You must be Maggie. I'm Rita. Sunday morning is not my usual schedule, but I came in to help Char."

Victor continued down the hall.

I nodded and started to speak to Rita, but she closed her eyes and drew a deep breath. *The young man must be her son. Who else could come into her workplace and upset her like this?*

She was polite but businesslike. "Char left word for you to come out to the studio. She'll be finishing up soon, and the police have said we can open this afternoon."

"Thank you. Victor just told me. That's a relief."

I walked through the familiar rooms of the gallery. None of my favorite paintings from two years ago were still on display, but there were new ones to love. My favorite new pieces were a brilliant ceramic vase combined with woven basketry and a piece of glass artwork.

At the end of the hall, I peeked into the office. Victor looked up before he glanced at his huge, turquoise studded watch.

"Char hasn't come in from the studio. Go on back."

I don't know if I went around looking lost or what, but everyone made sure to tell me where to go.

"Victor, who made the glass bowl and ceramic vase in the gallery? The colors are stunning."

"Oh, those were made by Tsosie Tsiniginnie. Have you heard of him? He's a modern young Navajo artist. Works at the Sedona Arts Center."

"Hmm. I love his work. See you later, Victor." I went out the backdoor and crossed the yard just as Char came out of the studio and locked the double doors behind her. A handsome Latino man accompanied her.

"Maggie, I'd like you to meet Tomás Avila, my *numero uno* assistant and right-hand man during workshops. He's married to Rita. They're both doing double duty today since its Sunday."

"I'm happy to meet you, Tomás. I just met Rita a few minutes ago."

"I'm glad to know you, too. Char has talked about your visit for weeks," he said. "Are you a Marguerita, too, like my Rita?"

"No. My name is Morgan."

"Such a strong and beautiful name for a beautiful lady." He was still holding my hand.

"You must be wary of Tomás, Maggie," Char warned just as Rita walked up. "He's a lady killer. All of my students adore him, and so do I."

"Tough *enchiladas*," Rita broke in. "He may be a lady killer, but he's all mine."

"Ah, my *empanadita*, Rita." He released my hand with a squeeze. "What's for lunch?"

"See? I've got him where I want him. He loves my Mexican buns." Rita winked.

Those two interested me. Tomás's flirting amused me, maybe because of that little bit of innate flirt in me. Dark and lean, aware of himself in an open, knowing way, he had a strong sensuality. Rita, well-padded in appearance, but flashy in personality also came across as aware and charming. She guarded him with forthright possessiveness. I asked Char about them as we drove away.

"Tomás is the stereotypical classic Latin lover. He just loves women. He's an accountant, sometimes teaches a class or two at the community college—business, Spanish. He comes from a close-knit family that immigrated several generations ago. He and Rita have five children, four grown and in their late thirties, and their twenty-year-old December son, Rubio. Family is everything to them. Either one would do anything, *anything*, for their children."

"We're all that way, aren't we?" I commented. "I'd do just about anything for my kids. If someone or something threatens them, I'm not sure to what lengths I'd go. I hope I never find out."

"Well, we both know that not everyone is that protective, but all the Hispanics I know make family their first priority."

"How long have they worked for you?" I asked.

"Rita has worked for me about six years. That was the first year I had a summer workshop. Rubio was just starting high school; I gave him a job running errands, cleaning brushes, that kind of thing. Two years ago, Rubio ran into trouble with the law. Drugs. Tomás showed up at the workshop to fill in for his son. Tomás got such a kick out of flirting with a roomful of attentive women. He was in his element. He's been here for the workshop ever since."

We drove past a Dairy Queen with an open-air Indian market. "Have you been to the Indian markets between here and Page?" Char asked.

"Yes," I answered. "I stop sometimes. Once I bought a cedar berry necklace."

"Tiahna's mother makes Navajo jewelry and sells it at that market there at the Dairy Queen." She pointed back at the one we'd just passed. "She's keeping Tiahna's baby there with her during the workshop."

"I thought Tiahna must be Navajo."

"Half-Navajo," Char answered. "Her family is from Willow Water. That's not far from Page, is it?"

"Right next door. She's beautiful."

"Yes," Char answered. "She has classic bone structure." After a moment, she added, "Victor is her father."

"What!" Caught off guard, I stammered. "*Our* Victor? *Your* Victor?" Char nodded.

"But," I stuttered. "Randa is five or six years older than Tiahna."

Char looked sadder than I had ever seen her. "Six. Remember the summer we spent with you and Ron at the lake in Page? Tiahna's mother conceived her that summer, but none of us knew about it until last year."

Stunned, I had trouble getting my mind around Char's revelation. What shock waves this must have unleashed in Char, in Randa, in Victor, and in Tiahna, who would have grown up half-acknowledged. Then I almost burst out with, "How could Victor keep on pretending to be Mr. Wonderful for twenty-plus years?" But my professional training kicked in. Char must have had her reasons for staying with him and trying to work it out.

"And now you paint her." I swallowed. "My God, Char. That must be so hard for you. For everyone."

"Maybe it gives me a sense of control." Char squeezed my hand on the car seat between us. She glanced over at me. Her eyes glittered with unshed tears.

At last I understood the strong, unsettling sensations coming from my dear friends. Char obviously needed to talk or wouldn't have plunged our conversation into the pain buried beneath the surface. And I'd been lavishing my sympathy on Victor. Go figure.

"How did you learn all this?"

"Well, you heard Tiahna mention she has a baby?"

I nodded.

"By the way, the baby is named Victoria. Can you believe that? When Randa heard that Tiahna had named her child after Victor, she went ballistic." Char pressed her lips together and shook her head. "Anyway, Tiahna had no means of support for the baby or herself except Aid to Dependent Children from the government. The baby's father is Rubio."

"Tomás and Rita's son?"

"Yep, the very same. He's around, but he isn't willing to share the responsibility. He's a living, breathing messed-up jerk." Char sighed. "But I'm getting off track. We learned about all this last year. Her mother brought Tiahna to our house one night. I'm not sure if Victor even remembered her after twenty years, but when she told him her name, he didn't deny her story. The woman came to ask him for financial help so Tiahna could go to art school."

"So helping her get an art education started before she had the baby?"

"Yes. I don't think she met Rubio until after she came to Sedona to go to art school." Char exhaled. "Victor wasn't legally obligated to help her at her age, but he felt morally responsible."

Silence settled over us. *Should I ask the questions that would prompt Char to continue? Oh, what the hell, let the questions rip.* "What did she say? How did she bring it out?" Char wanted to talk, and understood my need to know, as well.

She shrugged. "I answered the door and she asked for Victor. He was in the family room watching television. I invited them in and called to Victor. When he came into the hall, she just blurted out, 'I'm Doria, and this is your daughter, Tiahna.' Victor looked at me with a stricken expression. The blood drained away from his face. I thought he would have a heart attack. So right then I knew that it was the truth without his saying a word."

"And you agreed to give her help."

"Yes. But I have never felt such an awful drowning feeling."

"What about Randa? Is that the resentment I saw in her eyes this morning?"

"She's full of resentment and bitterness. At first it embarrassed her, and she wouldn't talk about it. She worried about my feelings and attacked Victor. She has always idolized him, and you know we spoiled her rotten. She doesn't speak to Tiahna."

"I don't understand all this, Char. Randa is resentful. You're hurt. Tiahna has got to be hurt or offended, or something, and yet you give her a job, you paint her. You invite her to Randa's spa, probably against Randa's wishes, and you make it very easy for Victor. None of it is Tiahna's fault, but it's still bullshit. What are you trying to prove?"

"I guess I'm trying to step over the bullshit, and be wise and tolerant," she said. "I have loved Vic for a long time. He's the only man I've ever loved. I thought I knew everything about him and that we had accepted each other's little oddities. This situation has just taken over our lives."

Char fell silent, her eyes on the road. After a few minutes, she continued,

"I guess I've been trying to show him, and myself, that I'm generous enough to understand and forgive. Rita doesn't like Tiahna, even though Victoria is her granddaughter. She told me to 'ignore the bitch' as she does. I don't think Tiahna is a bitch. That's just Rita talking. She doesn't mince words."

And I'd come to Sedona full of my own problems. Whooee! Whose situation was worse—mine with my failed marriage or Char's, still with a marriage to try to save but with this tangled mess of rampant emotions? Would including Tiahna in her daily life help her forgive and forget? As beautiful as the young woman was, her constant presence could only increase the smoldering resentments Char and Victor tried to hide. Randa demonstrated her animosity with minimal attempts to hide it.

We drove into the parking lot of the spa and stopped under the sign. The dry, pungent smell of cedar trees hung in the noon-warm air. The spa, built on several levels, fit into the hillside almost as if it had grown there like one of the twisted trees. It looked Oriental Southwest.

We walked in through a greenhouse entrance. Inside, the light filtered through hanging plants. At the head of a landscaped indoor fishpond, falling waters gurgled over smooth stones. Goldfish glided through the pool at the bottom of the waterfall. Victor's cat watched the fish from a sunny spot on the wide stair rail. It arched its back, purring under Char's long-fingered caress, then jumped down to follow us up the low, broad steps to the admittance desk. The atmosphere exuded a soothing calmness and normality.

I was wired after Char's revelations, but couldn't help admiring the attention to detail. The reception area was furnished with low benches against the wall. There was a mat-covered alcove to one side where two young men sat in lotus position. A slim Asian girl greeted us from behind a slate counter.

"Joon Li," Char said. "This is my good friend, Maggie."

The girl smiled and gave each of us a rolled bundle with a kimono, scuffs, a towel, and a locker key.

Just beyond the lotus-sitters, a sign reading *Massage Rooms* pointed the way downstairs. A side door led to the dressing rooms and showers then on to the gravel pathways ascending to the hot tubs and the cold plunge.

A few minutes later, Char and I, in kimonos and scuffs, walked up the hilly path to our tub. Spread across the cedar-dotted hillside rising above and behind the building, the wooden enclosures of the tubs and the plunge blended into the landscape. The pruned and shaped trees, the path of spaced flat stones in raked gravel, and the rustic wooden walls surrounding the hot tubs gave the yard the same serene, far eastern look of the front entrance. It was impressive and attractive but surprising under the wide blue sky of Arizona. We entered the enclosure where the fences gave ground-level privacy, but the roofless tubs themselves were open to the sky.

We eased ourselves into the tub, adjusted the jets, and then leaned back in silence and closed our eyes.

Char's voice broke the stillness. "I just felt I had to be civilized. What else could I do twenty years after the fact? Victor and I have had a loving marriage. He and Randa have always been close. That's what hurts the most now; they've lost that closeness. What would you have done?"

"Oh, Char, don't ask me. I don't know what I'd do," I replied. "But I have felt the strain. Victor is like an excluded man when he's with you and Randa." I stopped talking while I tried to untangle my thoughts. "Huh . . . if I'd known about all this, I might have excluded him, too."

"I know. In spite of trying to be so kind about it all, underneath I'm mad as hell. Vic had to help Tiahna and her mother. I know that, too. And it's been too long for me to act like a disillusioned twenty-year-old as I might have done if I'd known about this affair when it happened. I've tried to be generous, but damn it, I'd rather just kick and scream."

"So you gave Tiahna a job. You've seen her every day, and you've painted her with tenderness," I said.

"What can I say? I responded according to my gut reaction. I haven't discussed this with anyone else." Settled in the hot tub, Char closed her eyes again and sighed. "Ahh, the great unwinder." After a few wordless moments, she said, "Do you think I have been unreal and wrong?"

"Don't you think if you kept a little distance, it would be kinder to everyone?" I asked.

"Maybe. Yeah. I don't know, but I can't stop now. My workshop starts tomorrow." She drew another deep breath and let it out with a whoosh. "Maybe I'm kidding myself. I feel all jangled up when I paint Tiahna. It pains me that she's so beautiful, so easy to paint, but I can't back out now. She is a gorgeous model, but I've been thinking of not doing it again. It's too hard on Randa." She rested her head against the rim of the tub, her eyes still closed. "And it's hard on me," she admitted. After a moment and another whoosh of air, she said, "Must be hard on Tiahna, too, but she needs the money. In my misguided way I'm trying to help her."

I laid my head back and looked at the intense blue of the sky cut across by the white contrail of a jet. In contrast to that sign of modern life, the sunny, dry atmosphere of Sedona seemed to vibrate with an ageless air of mystery.

After a few moments of quiet, Char said, "I can't stop thinking about José. The killers must have known that finding him on our doorstep would scare the wits out of us."

"Have you learned any more about him, Char?" I asked. "I know Garcia thinks it was connected to an official investigation."

"All I know is that he thinks it was related to illegal immigration, and that issue gets bigger every day. The investigative teams don't advertise what they are doing," Char said. "I just trust that they are working at it all the time, but I haven't heard any more than you have about José. We miss him. He was such a skilled worker."

"Do you know anything more about his family?"

"Father Quejada gave them sanctuary and offered to sponsor them until they get their legal immigration papers. I don't know if his intervention will help, or if he knows about José's undercover work for the police and their involvement in his naturalization. A lot of people are angered by what they call his interference. He's told Jose's wife Maria she can work at the church when she feels able. Randa's been trying to think of ways she could give her work here at the spa."

"Randa's like you, Char. She has a decent heart."

The timer buzzed. Char raised her head and said, "How do you feel about a cold plunge?"

"How cold is it?"

"About fifty degrees, but it feels icy after the hot tub. Shocks you at first, but you feel so invigorated after you get out."

Wrapped in kimonos, we crossed the path to the cold plunge. The cat leaped up on the fence surrounding the plunge and sat polishing his nails as he watched us climb the steps then lower ourselves, gasping, into the chilled water.

A few minutes later, we walked down the path shivering. Char seemed to be relaxed for the first time since I'd arrived. Inside the main building again, we found Randa waiting for us.

"You look ready for a good rubdown, Maggie," she said. "Let me take you to the massage room."

We went down the stairs to a semi-basement. The back end of the room was built into the mountainside. Given the slope of the hill, the front end remained open with long windows looking out over a steeply slanting Japanese garden. We entered a room with half-closed blinds covering the windows. In one corner, a three-foot wide, two-foot high rock cut open to reveal a center of amethyst crystal nestled amid lush green plants. A hidden spotlight, focused on the crystal, gave it a sparkling glow.

Randa lit the candles placed around the room and turned on soft music. Joon Li came into the room and warmed her hands over the candles, then asked me to lie on the long table in the center of the room and cover myself with a sheet. Randa and Char turned to go.

Char said, "Joon Li has velvet fingers," as she closed the door.

Through the door, I heard Randa say, "Is Tiahna coming or not? Does she need a room and a masseuse?"

"No," Char said. "She isn't coming."

Randa's voice was tight, her tone curt. "Thanks for small favors. I don't like her in my space. I'll put up with her during your workshop. Don't ever say I didn't do anything for you, Mom, but please don't ever ask me to do it again."

Tension time for Char again. She murmured something and then Randa went on. "I'm going to the salon. We're going to design something for my hair as a trial run for the reception Friday night."

I willed myself to let it all go as Joon Li stroked my body with fragrant almond oil. My massage lasted an hour. Such a luxury. Soon, I began to dream—*when do we eat?* I decided on tacos or enchiladas after Char returned to the studio. With a margarita.

Just then the door opened and Char said, "We're having sprout sandwiches for lunch. Meet you upstairs."

"Sounds great," I lied. *Oh, shoot.* I dreamed tacos and got sprouts.

After my massage, I showered and washed my hair, blew it dry. It was like being a clean and empty vessel—warm, relaxed, and virtuous. Downright skinny. Starved. I returned to the foyer. Char wasn't there, so I sat down on one of the low benches. The cat brushed against my legs, purring. I petted him. Joon Li entered the room from the stairwell. "This is a very friendly cat," I remarked.

"Crazy? He's named for the crazy way he travels with Victor. They left here, and then came back while you were enjoying the spa."

The entry door opened. We all, Joon Li, Crazy, and I turned our heads at the sound. Randa appeared, framed by the greenery behind her. Her red hair gleamed, braided with turquoise blue netting wrapped around her head. The hair at the end of the braid splashed out and down like a fountain tied with the net into a bow that covered the matted right side of her head and temple.

"Your hair is terrific, Randa," I said. "I love it."

"Thanks, Maggie. You should watch the way people double take when they see what we do with it, and then realize why." She touched the damaged side of her head, and then called out, "Thanks, Dad!"

Victor stuck his head around the office door. "For what?"

"For saving my hair."

He looked at her over his reading glasses. "What a fight! They wanted to shave you bald."

Their cheerful exchange lightened the atmosphere. The best words I'd heard them speak yet, resonating like old times. Then Victor said, "Just don't put me through all that again." He waved and disappeared back into the office. The animated moment shattered behind his back.

Raw emotion twisted Randa's face into a frightful caricature, and she whispered to me, "What about what he put me through?"

I dreaded taking sides. Char saved me from it when she arrived from the direction of the showers. She stopped when she saw Randa's hair, unaware of Randa's masked anger at Victor.

She said, "I want to paint you, darling, just like that. Let me grab the camera and snap your picture against that backdrop. When can you come down to the studio for a sitting?" "Lunch is served," Victor called.

We went into the office. On a corner of his desk, he had arranged sandwiches and juice from the health food bar of the spa.

Char picked up half a sandwich thick with turkey, avocado, and sprouts and wrapped it in a napkin. "I've got to get back to the gallery to meet Chet Watson, one of my regular buyers from Texas. He does his Christmas shopping every year about this time. He loves flaming cottonwoods as much as I do." She took a bite and started for the door. "Can you come down later, Randa?"

"Not today, Mom. I've got appointments all afternoon. But we can do my hair this way again, maybe after the workshop?"

"Okay. We won't be so busy then." Char turned to go then turned back. "If you want to ride down with me, Maggie, you can get your car to go shopping or back to the house. I'm going down to the shower room to pick up my bag. Just give me a minute." She left, trailing small sprouts.

"I guess you met Tiahna this morning," Randa said.

"Yes," I answered, still not taking sides.

"Very impressive, our Tiahna."

"Randa, please don't," Victor said. He turned to me. "We're having a bit of family turmoil."

I just nodded. After my conversation with Char, I understood Victor's sadness.

My understanding, however, didn't help much. I felt like a cat on a hot tin roof wanting off. I said, "Uhhh . . . yeah. Char told me about Tiahna this morning."

My revelation met silence.

"I think you've all been super civilized about it." I blundered on. I now felt as if the cat had lost its footing on the roof and slithered near the edge.

"Thanks, Maggie." Victor cleared his throat. "I can't begin to tell you what Char's forgiveness has meant to me."

Randa's face closed and remained expressionless, but she blinked her eyes several times before she looked at me with an expression of naked appeal. Or maybe it was defiance. Hard to read. At that moment, Joon Li called Randa to the telephone and she left the room.

Victor looked whipped. Neither of us had much appetite. The now untidy desk was littered with half-eaten sandwiches, little sprouts everywhere.

Victor drew a couple of shallow, nervous breaths and said, "If you want to go shopping, or anything, Mag, I can take you. I'll clean up this mess later." Which mess did he mean? I wondered.

I thought he wanted to be alone without having to entertain me, so I said I'd ride down with Char. He nodded.

Tranquil Waters Spa lay nestled in an out-of-the way cul-de-sac in the hills between Highway 89A in West Sedona and Oak Creek Canyon. Surrounded by red rock monoliths, sagebrush, and cedar trees under pristine blue skies, the natural setting promised peace to the soul and rest to the world-weary. Still working hard to build the business, Randa lived in a small cabin on the premises.

As Char drove us back toward town, she said, "I can't believe you arrived just yesterday. So much has happened. It seems like you've been here for days."

"I know, seems that way to me, too, so I'm going to take that as a compliment."

"Oh, Mag, I didn't mean it the way it came out. I feel as if I'm in a time warp."

"Yeah, me too. I'll be glad to get started tomorrow on the art part of this trip."

"You can come and browse around the gallery while I meet with Mr. Watson if you want to."

"Thanks, but I think I'll go to Tlaquepaque. I always like to browse around there, it's so charming."

With its vine-covered arches, cobblestone walkways, and graceful sycamore trees, I always felt as if I'd stepped back in time when I walked into Tlaquepaque, which translated is "the best of everything." More a cultural experience than shopping destination, Tlaquepaque is archetypal Sedona¾restaurants, galleries, boutiques, wandering musicians. I strolled upstairs and down, listened to the splashing fountain, absorbed the explosion of color from the flowers, and then went to the Chapel, where I prayed. I wanted to include so many in my prayers: José, Maria, their two children, Char, Victor, Randa, Garcia, me, Jennifer, Alex, my grandchildren, and then I remembered something else I wanted to ask for Maria and her little family. I felt peaceful and satisfied when I left the small, cozy chapel and returned to *Galeria de Luz*.

Char and Victor stood saying goodbye to a cattle baron type in a white, ten-gallon hat.

"Thanks, Chet. It's a pleasure doing business with you. Your paintings will be shipped tomorrow."

Victor's social persona had slipped into place. He introduced me to their client, Chet Watson, laughing and joking with no hint of strain. "You're going to stay for dinner, aren't you, Chet?" he asked. "You wouldn't want to miss your Az-Mex fix!"

"Can't do it, Victor," Chet replied. "We're flying right back to San Antonio for a fundraiser. But I gotta tell ya, Tex-Mex beats Az-Mex every time."

"Boy, you got that wrong!" Victor quipped back.

FOUR

C har wanted to leave the house early on Monday morning. Since she had so many responsibilities related to the workshop and so much on her mind, I drove myself. That way she wouldn't have to worry about hauling me around, and I could come and go without being tied to her schedule. We agreed that I would go to lunch or happy hour or dinner on my own or with any of the workshop group I felt drawn to.

I arrived a few minutes early and sat on one of the benches in the front. A couple of workshop attendees were there before me. Others arrived in singles or groups until sixteen of us had introduced ourselves to each other.

A large easel by the front door held a sign that told us to take the path to the right of the building and come to the studio in the rear. We all walked around the gallery carrying the easels and supplies we'd each brought with us. Maybe some of the others had already owned theirs, but I bought mine after Char sent a list of needed supplies. Tomás, Char's assistant, joined our group at the back door, beaming with congeniality and making sunny observations about the gorgeous weather.

Inside the studio, Char, dressed in jeans, a black knit turtleneck, and a white smock, greeted us with a wide smile. She instructed us to set up in a circle, introduced herself; and Tomás then we went around the room and introduced ourselves, telling why we signed up for the workshop and what we hoped to get out of it.

When we'd finished and were standing awkwardly at our easels wondering what would come next, Char twirled in a circle. "My smock is new today, special for this occasion, but you can expect it to be a coat of many colors before the workshop is over." Everyone laughed and with that small remark, she had melded her workshop into a cohesive group.

"Not all of the paint makes it to the canvas," she said. "Protect your clothes, and then paint with wild abandon. I know not all of you are beginners, but today we're going to start from the beginning by talking about the ideal proportions of the human head then drawing them."

In no more than ten minutes, Char had the workshop moving. She drew us in to an amazing morning, teaching us that much of art is practice and technique. Talent helps. Desire is critical; study, desire, and practice enhance talent.

She instructed us to hold our hands against our sketchpads, mark top and bottom and each side. That was the size of the head we would start with. Char explained that eyes are midway between top and bottom. The face is five eye widths wide, with one eye width between the eyes. The underside of the nose is halfway between the eyes and the chin. The lower lip is halfway between the tip of the nose and the tip of the chin. The top of the eye lines up with the top of the ear and the underside of the nose lines up with the lower edge of the earlobe. And so, we engineered our human heads. Fascinating stuff. Who knew? Not me.

The aroma of coffee perking on a side table filled the room. While I was too absorbed in my sketch to notice, sometime during the morning someone brought in petite pastries. We took a break about ten, stretched, walked outside, talked to each other, had a caffeine and carbo fix, and then continued for the rest of the morning drawing faces with varying degrees of success.

Char made it look easy. With the proportion guidelines she'd given us, it was easier than I expected, but I could see that I would not become adept in a blink. I think the hardest part for me was letting go of my obsession with perfection and my tendency to overwork it.

Because she knew the workshop could be exhausting, Char had planned for long lunch hours, allowing plenty of time to gallery hop or shop or rest. After our break that first day, the afternoon was given to a study of drawing eyes. Char demonstrated the subtle contours of the brow, the lid, and the eye, with shadows and tones to add depth. Again, it was not as easy as it looked, but was easier once we knew the proportion guidelines to follow. The day sped by, and I felt tired at the end of it.

"Char, this is the best thing in the world to get me out of my rut. Thank you so much. What a rush. What can I ever do to repay you?"

"Oh, Maggie, I'm glad you're here to talk to and spend time with. It's pulling me up out of the pits, too. Thanks for going to lunch today with the group. I needed that time to regenerate until we get into a rhythm. In a couple of days, we'll have a routine, so let's plan to go to the spa during the noon break on Wednesday. Okay?"

Tuesday morning, Tiahna came in after the group got settled. I expected to see her in the colorful traditional clothes from that first day, but she wore street clothes.

Char introduced her to the class and while Tiahna positioned herself on a stool, she said, "Today we will practice what you learned yesterday. Use your sketch pads and charcoal to sketch Tiahna's eyes, her nose, and her facial structure. Her face is a classic oval. Faces don't get any better than this for artists. Tomorrow we'll start on an actual oil portrait. Don't worry about getting a perfect likeness. Use the proportions and you'll have a beautiful portrait, whether it looks like Tiahna or not."

We spent another day in total concentration. Tiahna, an excellent model, sat gazing into space for hours, with only occasional small movements and shifting of her pose.

After dinner, Char and I drove to the spa to participate in Randa's full moon drumming circle and labyrinth walk. A bigger crowd than I expected was gathered in the yard behind Randa's cabin, where a labyrinth based on the Chartres Cathedral model had been constructed.

When the full moon rose, Randa spoke to begin the evening event. "We built this labyrinth as a place of walking meditation, a way to connect body, mind, and spirit," she said. "You will each have an individual response to it. My own response is always silence. I don't want to talk about what I am feeling, I just want to meditate on it."

Saying nothing further, she began a measured beat on her drum. We joined in. I had experienced my own primal response to drumming before, but as always, I was surprised by the intensity of it. I was also surprised by how relaxed I felt afterward and how deeply I slept.

On Wednesday morning, day three, the double doors stood propped open. On a raised platform at one end of the studio, a circle of light caressed Tiahna. Her purple satin skirt shimmered; her bright pink velvet blouse gleamed. Heavy silver and turquoise jewelry hung around her slender neck and waist, dangled from her ears, and weighted her arms and hands. Her face, that perfect oval, wore an expression of calm dignity. Her straight black hair was twisted into a Navajo *chonga,* a yarn-wrapped bun. Such a beautiful girl! I couldn't take my eyes off the simple portrait setting Char had created for her students to paint.

I moved to the outer edge of the circle of students clustered around Char's easel. She began her demonstration.

"So . . . terra rosa here . . . a little yellow ochre, emerald, coral . . . not too much . . . Indian red . . . just so . . ."

I felt the old, familiar rush of awe as I watched the deft demonstration. Char painted people with a subtle, enhanced reality. With small touches, she made them younger, slimmer, and brighter. The morning passed more quickly than I could believe. Before I knew it, Char stood back wiping her brush, and then leaned forward to make a short glide through wet paint with her thumb. With that simple movement, the tilt of Tiahna's neck became more regal.

She wiped her thumb and called, "Okay, Tiahna, time for lunch break." She stood back to study the painting then turning to the class, she said, "I hope you won't mind taking an extra hour for lunch today. I am going to a small, private memorial service." She didn't mention that I was going as well. No one in the workshop knew, or needed to know, of our close relationship.

The model broke her pose, stretched, lifted her voluminous skirts and jumped off the platform. She walked past the easels, looking at each painting of herself with a noncommittal facial expression. Most of the student renderings were clumsy, some even ugly, but some had an unexpected grace or an arresting blend of color. When she reached Char's easel, she stopped. Lips parted, she seemed to inhale the painting as if searching for affirmation. Char had captured on canvas the quiet pride of Tiahna's pose and had given the painting a look of dewy freshness with highlights. Tiahna read the portrait with intense, smoldering eyes, and I wondered if her calm extended below the surface.

Char left her easel to circle the room and spend time with each of her students. I studied the portrait, comparing it to the live model standing in front of it. Her beauty was captivating. In contrast to her shining black hair and deep, dark eyes, her skin had a pale, tawny-golden cast. She was slender with unusually straight posture.

After a quick, sharp glance at me, Tiahna walked away toward a closed door in the back. In that brief glance was an edge in her eyes missing from Char's soft, sensuous, and, let's face it, commercial painting of her.

While we cleaned our brushes, the room buzzed with talk of lunch or shopping. Tomás turned off the floodlights around the model's platform then gathered Char's brushes from her and began cleaning them,

Char's voice came from behind me, "I don't know what I'd do without Tomás and Rita. They keep things flowing while I'm wrapped up in my work."

"You're lucky to have them. I'd love to have someone to keep things flowing for me."

Char shook her head with the rueful look of an old friend. "Everybody needs a housekeeper, don't you think?"

Tiahna came out of the back room wearing tight blue jeans, a white shirt, and a turquoise belt, her hair still in the traditional string-wrapped twist.

"Tiahna, remember my friend, Maggie McGinnis? You saw her in class this morning."

"Hello again, Tiahna."

Tiahna smiled shyly, without a trace of the sharpness I'd seen before. "Char told me you like to read mysteries. I finished a scary book last night. *The Screaming Wind*," Tiahna said. "Mysteries are my favorite late-night reading—after the coyotes start to howl."

"And the skinwalkers are on the prowl?" Tomás teased.

I'd lived near Native American Indian tribes all my life and knew the stories about Navajo skinwalkers, witches and ghosts. I took an anthropology class to study southwestern tribes, but that turned out to be dry historical facts with no cultural color.

I still felt a profound lack of spiritual understanding of my lifelong neighbors. To honor the sacred and secret nature of ceremonial culture, I never questioned my Navajo friends. Theirs was a closed society and they wouldn't have answered anyway. But Tiahna, and Tomás brought it up, not I.

I cleared my throat and took a chance. "Will you tell me about skinwalkers?"

Tiahna's face closed. "I don't know much about it, only what my grandfather says."

"Does your grandfather speak English?"

"No." She looked away, and our conversation ended with a thud.

Char stepped into the awkward silence. "Can you be back by two, Tiahna? We're going to a funeral, so you'll have a little extra time today."

"Sure. The extra hour will help me a lot. I have to stop to talk to my mother and see the baby. Victoria is going to the doctor for shots today." She glanced up at the clock on the wall. "Gotta run. See you later." And she was gone.

"I'm disappointed," I said. "I wanted to hear more about skinwalkers, or at least get to know Tiahna better."

"I can tell you what little I know on the way to the cemetery." Char removed her painting smock and picked up her bag while I waited beside the morning's still unfinished portrait. Under our paint-smeared smocks we'd worn black slacks and nice blouses. Our blazers were in the car.

"Char, your painting is alive with light. Tiahna seems to breathe."

Char paused by her canvas. "Thanks, but I'm uneasy about it. I haven't painted what I've seen. Tiahna's personal shadows are missing, and I can't deny I've glimpsed them. So it isn't honest art. It's technique. I've allowed Tiahna to do that to me."

"Even if it is just technique as you say, I'm amazed at how you achieve such an effect."

Char turned away from her beautiful painting. "Oh . . . contrast, harmony, light on dark. It's all surface impression, you know, forcing the flat canvas to appear three dimensional." She sighed, her expression grim.

There was pain in her voice and I didn't know what to say. She saved me from uttering something lame by heading for the door. I followed her outside. Tomás came out behind us, turned off the lights, and locked up.

Once we were in Char's car, I said, "Tell me about the skinwalkers, Char."

"Well, let's see . . . skinwalkers play a vital part in Navajo folklore. Ghosts, spirits, and mischief makers are part of the Navajos' everyday life." I murmured assent and she went on. "Their holy spirits are far from *holy* as we define the word. They are tricky instead. Ghosts are the spirits of the dead. In Navajo mythology, the dead do not go away to a mysterious heaven. They stick around and are not above taking spirited action to defend their space. They sometimes take the form of a coyote or an owl to warn of impending death.

"On the other hand, witches are living people who use secretive, psychological methods to get back at someone they hate or who they think did them harm. To be 'witched' is to know that someone close to you has a toxic hatred toward you. Witches manipulate through fear and sometimes they disguise themselves with coyote skins, so that makes them skinwalkers. Witches are the worst tricksters, and skinwalkers are witches. It sounds too blatant and obvious, but it's tied in with ancient rituals and the undeniable sense we all have of the unexplainable. It's complicated to our way of thinking, but it explains why the Navajo are so fearful in the presence of death and why they abandon living quarters where someone has died. The spirit of the dead one is still there and will remain there on guard."

"Every day must be scary," I said. "But Tiahna seems calm. Most of the Navajo people I've known seem serene. Sort of accepting, or in harmony with life."

"Yes, harmony defines the Navajo cultural aspirations," Char answered. "But all is not as unruffled as it appears. Witchcraft and tricks require elaborate ceremonial rituals to counteract the evil. And it is evil. It's black magic. Witchcraft is a crime, you know. The older generation of Navajos still believes they've been witched when they have a toothache, or a stomachache, or any kind of ache, and only a medicine man can cure them."

"It's very hard to uncover any of this because they are very protective of their ceremonies." I said. "I don't blame them for it, but because of it, an enormous gap exists in our knowledge of our fellow Americans."

"The Navajo are reluctant to talk about this because it is so critical to their belief system. Scoffs and skepticism would be too painful."

"Well, as long as we're speaking of cultural aspirations, and of scoffs and skepticism," I reflected, "Shirley MacLaine claimed she cruised through space on a silver thread in search of harmony and understanding."

"Silver threads, skinwalkers, the art spirit—we all search for ways to stay connected," Char mused.

"Yes." My thoughts were on Ron. "The search to find oneself goes on, doesn't it?" We soaked in a shared silence for a few moments, then I said, "A coyote's howl could have serious implications."

"Oh, yes. Within the context of Navajo lore, the howl of a coyote could be an advance notice of approaching death."

"So that's what Tiahna and Tomás were shuddering about. Tomás's Hispanic culture must have reverence for animal spirits. So they weren't joking?"

"No joke," Char said. "And you remember how lonesome and eerie a coyote sounds."

"I heard a coyote howl Saturday night when I stood out on the patio. The moon was shining, and the rain had stopped. It gave me goose bumps. I've always loved to hear that shivery cry in the night."

"I love it, too. It's exultant, isn't it?" Char mused. "It's not as if the coyote is lonely out there . . . and yet, the cry strikes a lonely chord in us."

"I still feel a tingle of satisfaction at the thought of coyotes laughing in the night," I said. "It's as if they chuckle at having found life's secret."

After a few minutes of contemplating murder, marriage, and coyote mysticism, I said, "Meanwhile, back at the ranch—do you think Tiahna is superstitious about the legends of her tribe? That the cry of a coyote is a warning of death? She looks so modern."

"Yes, she does look modern, and she's talented. She studies art. But I don't know how essential her Navajo background is to her."

We felt like interlopers at José's graveside service. We were strangers there. I picked out a young woman with two children I thought must be his wife, Maria. Everyone moved back to give us room, and most looked at us with wary eyes. We spoke to the priest, Father Quejada, and then walked to the outside edge of the group surrounding the plain casket by the open grave. Garcia, with Randa, stood there. He nodded and stepped to one side to make room for us. The service was in Spanish. Though I didn't understand the words, the emotions were universal, palpable, and moving. At the conclusion of the brief burial rites, Garcia took Char and me over to Maria to introduce us. She nodded shyly.

Before returning to the studio, we stopped at the spa to pick up a couple of sandwiches. While Char went to the restroom, I sat down in the foyer. Crazy Cat rubbed against my legs. I sniffed. He smelled like mayonnaise. Mayonnaise? He leaped up onto the bench beside me. I looked closely and saw a speck of red between his toes. It was the same shade we'd used in the studio that morning. Paint? He looked as if he'd just been washed, but the mayonnaise smell clung to him.

"Where is Randa?" I asked Joon Li.

"She and Victor are down in the massage rooms. They just brought Crazy in with red paint on his paws. She called the vet, who told her not to use turpentine 'cause it could harm the cat. She recommended mayonnaise or Vicks VapoRub, and then to bathe him. Poor cat. I don't think he liked it a bit. Randa took a jar of our mayonnaise down there to clean him up."

"Is it okay if I run down to see them?" I asked her.

"Sure."

In the massage room, I found the door to the bathroom open and Randa stuffing red-splotched rags into the wastebasket under the sink. She and Victor were laughing and making jokes about Crazy taking up painting in Char's studio.

"Are you ready to go, Maggie?" Char called down the staircase.

After a quick hello to Victor and Randa, I hurried back upstairs. The mayonnaise mystery was solved. I told Char about it on the drive to the gallery. Victor was right behind us on his motorcycle.

We ate our sandwiches in the car. At the gallery, I joined the other students walking to the classroom in back while Char went inside to get ready for the afternoon session. Tomás joined us at the back door, flirting with the woman walking beside him.

He unlocked the doors and swung the double panels wide, then exclaimed, "I did turn the floodlights off before we left, didn't it? I'm sure I did."

But they were on, highlighting the model's platform. Strange. We artists surged forward, curious. Those in the front gasped and exclaimed at what they saw. Char came up behind us, so we moved aside to let her through.

On the model's chair sprawled a pretty little Navajo doll. It had eyes that opened and closed, the kind of doll made for tourists. It was dressed in a native costume. Knotted around its neck with the ends tied to the chair top, a woven sash made a bright splash of color. No stretch required here to see Tiahna hung in effigy.

The doll's head twisted backward and down, so its shiny, half-shuttered eyes looked over its right shoulder. Arms and legs were twisted at grotesque and obscene angles. A tube of crimson oil paint had been squeezed in a clotted stream from the doll's mouth across its body, across the chair and into a heap on the floor. A cat's paw prints ran through the paint straight to the model's dressing room. *So this was how Crazy got paint on his paws, but who was with him when it happened? Victor and Randa wouldn't do this and then laugh about it, would they?*

Amid the hubbub, I followed the paw prints to the room at the back of the studio where I found traces of paint on the sill of an open window. Outside the window, the ground showed scuffmarks. The pit of my stomach churned with those unsubtle signals that come with fear of the unknown and with the queasy feeling of invasion of privacy. I returned to the studio. Char's eyes mirrored my own sinking sensation. She mouthed to me, "Get Victor."

My mind raced as I walked across the back yard to summon Victor.

All the horror of Saturday night's murder rushed back in and caught me unaware. That murder had seemed impersonal. Grotesque as it was, this attack smacked of a personal vendetta with Tiahna as the target. And Victor and Randa had cleaned the paint off Crazy's paws.

It looked like voodoo, or in Navajo culture, a witching. The gallery was an odd place for superstitions. Yet could this symbolic, ferocious act, which had slipped in through a back window during a sun-warmed noon hour, have been meant for the gallery, just as the body on Saturday had some unknown connection to the gallery?

Why would the targets of Garcia's drug investigation carry out this kind of intimidation on an art seminar? It seemed too complicated just to send him a message. Or could this vulgar display target only Tiahna, with a catch-her-where-you-find-her mentality?

Victor hurried back out to the studio with me. A frantic look came over his face and he was immobilized for a moment as he stood looking at the twisted doll.

Then one screeching voice rose above the clamor. "Look! They used my paint!"

Tomás spoke in a quiet voice to Char. She kept her cool. "If this is someone's idea of a joke, it isn't funny." She turned to the woman who had shrieked. "I'll replace your paint. Tomás has suggested that he take you to visit other galleries. Things will be back to normal in the morning. I assure you."

Uninvolved in the seminar arrangements, I stood near Victor and the brutalized doll, contemplating the queasy weirdness I felt. I remembered the trapped look I'd seen in Randa's eyes and the sadness in Victor's at the mere mention of Tiahna.

Just then, Tiahna sauntered in. "What's happening?" she asked. Everyone turned to look at her. "What?" she asked. "What have I done?"

When everyone's head swiveled toward the doll, she looked. She recoiled. She turned and ran nearly colliding with Randa at the door. The two young women stared at each other a moment then Tiahna brushed by and left.

"I've got to catch her," Victor said. "She'll think she's been witched."

"Crazy cat ran through this red paint," I said.

"Of course, it was Crazy. What difference does that make?" Char asked.

"He was cleaned up back at the spa."

"Randa and I cleaned him up," Victor said. "We didn't want him licking the paint. It's toxic. When he came into the gallery through his kitty door, we just assumed he'd been out here."

I wasn't sure why I kept after it. "After seeing this, I'm just surprised you didn't mention it."

"I hadn't seen this then, and I don't have time now." Victor started out, and then turned back. "What are you saying, Maggie? Do you think I did this? Or Randa?"

"No. I guess I'm just in shock. I just wanted to mention it right up front because this voodoo, or witching, might mean Tiahna is in danger."

"You're right," he said. "She might even think she's in danger from me. Maggie, why don't you go with me to find her?"

"Maybe we should all go," Char said.

I turned away from the still bright scene of the doll hanging and saw Char's morning portrait of Tiahna.

"Oh, no. Char, look at this!"

Her fresh painting leaned against its easel, ruined. Someone had scrubbed a brush through the wet paint. Anger suffused Char's face. "Go with Victor on the Harley, Maggie," she said. "I have too much to do here."

I followed after Victor and had a good look at Randa. The expression on her face and her rigid stance stopped me cold. Unaware of anyone else, she stared after her father as he ran to Tiahna.

"Come on," Victor shouted. His motorcycle roared to life.

FIVE

Victor stopped beside the Dairy Queen in Oak Creek Canyon. I got off first and then in one swift movement, he swung his leg over and put down the kickstand. We walked around to the Indian Market facing the busy road. Rugs, shawls, and strips of velvet or satin material against which turquoise and silver jewelry gleamed, were spread out along the sidewalk. Jewelry crafted from cedar berries and colorful glass beads, pueblo bread, pottery, baskets, and dolls made up the display. Some of the dolls were interchangeable with the one hung on Tiahna's modeling chair. The native vendors, some surrounded by children, sat on folding chairs behind their outspread merchandise.

Victor stopped. "There she is." He pointed at middle-aged Navajo woman. "Doria, Tiahna's mother."

I could not conceal my interest in her. Remnants of her early beauty remained, but she had lost the advantage of a youthful glow, doubtless from living with poverty and worry. Small-boned, she carried too much weight; her teeth were uncared for; and she looked worn and stoic. She wore, perhaps for the merchandising effect, traditional velvet and satin.

A plump and smiling baby sat in a jump swing beside her. She didn't smile when Victor said, "Hello, Doria," but looked at him with antagonism. She included me in the same scornful stare. Victor, who had to be damned miserable under her unforgiving gaze, knelt to talk to the baby. When he looked up, he said, "Have you seen Tiahna this afternoon?"

"You know she's modeling for your wife," Doria answered. "She left the baby here a few minutes after one."

"She came to work, but she left a few minutes later. We thought she might have come back here."

"Is something wrong?" Doria asked.

"I don't know. That's why I want to find her. You haven't seen her since she left the baby?"

Doria shook her head. Victor pulled out his cell phone and walked several steps away to make a call.

I turned back from watching him and said, "Victor forgot to introduce us. I'm Maggie McGinnis, an old friend of Char's, and I know you are Tiahna's mother."

"Are you a friend of Tiahna's?" her mother asked, still hostile.

"I'd like to be. We just met a few days ago."

I didn't see Victor walk away, but I heard the sound of his motorcycle as it came out of the alley. He slowed and called, "She's in her apartment," then roared away. I stood there staring after him. Annoyed, I wanted to race after him, screaming. He couldn't jerk me around like this. If I hadn't identified on a gut level with Char and Randa in their frustration with Victor, I did now. But he had disappeared from sight, so I turned back to Tiahna's mother.

I saw the worry and questions in her eyes, so I said, "Doria, someone tied a native doll, like these you sell, on Tiahna's modeling chair. They'd smeared red paint over it, so it looked horrible. Victor is afraid she thinks she's been witched."

Fear leaped into Doria's eyes, and I wanted to smack Victor upside the head for leaving me to convey this unwelcome news.

I didn't know much about witching, some from books, some from Char. From my viewpoint, it was comparable to voodoo: pain, disfigurement, or death inflicted on a doll or an image would materialize in the body of the person whom the doll represented if the victim believed it would. My first, and hopefully, my last personal encounter with witching had occurred not an hour ago. It was sickening. I understood why Tiahna ran. If such a thing happened to me, could I keep my cool? Maybe I wasn't as tough as I'd always thought. The air of evil intent surrounding the doll hanging chilled me. I saw that same effect in Doria's every movement.

She snatched up the four corners of her velvet display cloth and dumped everything into a suitcase, lifted the baby out of the jumper, and spoke briefly in Navajo to the woman seated next to her. Without a word to me, she hurried toward a faded yellow pickup truck.

I caught up with her. "Can I help? Let me carry the suitcase." She relinquished her hold on the suitcase without looking at me. With a crying baby and a loaded suitcase, we packed the pickup and Doria drove us back down the canyon. The front door to Tiahna's apartment stood open.

"Victor? Tiahna?" I called. No answer. The empty apartment echoed. We walked through the rooms. Drawers were open. Empty hangers hung in the closet. Doria showed no emotion. Her stoical expression unnerved me. In silence, we left the apartment and closed the door after us. Doria's face remained inscrutable.

"Where would Tiahna go?" I demanded with Anglo impatience.

Doria had no reason to trust me beyond the fact that I carried her suitcase. Maybe she never got any more help than that because she answered.

"She probably went to some of her friends at the art school."

"I see," I said. "Will you drive me to where my car is parked?"

"I can take you to your car, then I have to go back to the market. I'm driving my sister's pickup. I ride with her."

"When I get my car, I can follow you and take you anywhere you think we might find Tiahna."

"No." Her short answers wasted no time on charm. "Victor will find her. Maybe he already has."

My cell phone rang. It was Victor. Tiahna was with him. "Please tell Doria not to worry."

I climbed into the passenger side of Doria's pickup, and she drove me to my car at the gallery. With a helpless sense of empathy, I watched her drive away.

At the gallery, police car in the driveway announced an official presence. Hesitant to intrude, I stood in the courtyard thinking about the complicated tangle of events I'd stumbled into. Betrayal, infidelity, neglect, ancient witchcraft, and murder all in a tangled heap. They could be unrelated. Maybe.

After lingering for a few minutes, I went to the studio where a policeman examined the footprints outside the window. Inside, Char stood by her easel wiping her hands.

"Did you find Tiahna?"

"Victor found her. He called my cell to tell me she's with him so I could tell Doria not to worry."

Char looked at me questioningly. "Tell me later." She spread her hands to indicate the investigator and the cleaned canvas on her easel. "I've never had anything like this happen before. I'm afraid my students will think . . . ." She shrugged. "I don't know what they'll think. And I don't blame Tiahna for running. I'd run, too."

"She ran further than you think. Victor abandoned me at the Indian market and went to Tiahna's apartment. By the time Doria and I got there, Tiahna and Victor were already gone."

"Funny you should use the word 'abandoned.' That's what Randa feels her father has done to her. She's a grown woman, I know, but Victor has shown such extraordinary concern for Tiahna it hurts Randa."

"Of course it hurts. It's got to. This whole situation is so challenging, I am amazed at how calm you are, Char."

Char went on. "Jealousy is such a crummy emotion, so easy to see in others and so hard to admit to in oneself. What a mess!"

"Is Randa jealous you have Tiahna model for you? Have you ever had Randa model?"

"Once. She hated it." Char looked at her watch. "Oh, damn. I almost forgot I've got a last-minute committee meeting tonight for the reception Friday night."

"Has Tomás come back from the gallery tour?"

"Bless Tomás! He's such a gallant old flirt. Maybe he'll have everything all smoothed over with the ladies. But no, I haven't seen him."

"Char, who do you think pulled the doll trick?"

"I don't know, but it couldn't have been Victor. He's too protective of Tiahna." She picked up her bag and said, "Let's go home and see what we can plan for an evening of fun." Sarcasm if I ever heard it. "And let's hope Victor gets back in time to join us."

"Gets back from where?"

Char shook her head. "From wherever he's gone to slay dragons for Tiahna. Damn him. He just keeps on trying too hard."

"Wouldn't it be better if he would allow the Navajos to handle this exercise, or exorcism, or whatever it is? I feel like we've been caught up in something we know nothing about. With the best of intentions, he could make things even worse."

"I agree one hundred percent. Now if we could just convince Victor to back off."

Our evening of fun turned out to be pizza and wine, while watching the sunset without Victor.

The next day, Thursday, Tiahna did not show up to model for the workshop. Of course, everyone there had seen the doll hung in effigy, but still they asked curious questions.

Char handled it smoothly. "Tiahna was shaken by yesterday's incident. This morning we will work on body proportions, and then for the rest of this week, we will drive south to Oak Creek Village and paint Bell Rock. It's called 'plein air' painting."

I enjoyed the day, fascinated by the artful science of painting body proportions and then, after lunch, going outside to paint red rock monoliths. Char moved among us demonstrating the use and mix of very different colors from those we'd used to paint Tiahna. When we returned to the studio, Char excused herself, telling us she wanted to arrange for another model in case Tiahna didn't feel up to continuing. All of us taking the workshop agreed to meet for dinner. Under Char's skillful instruction, I was beginning to feel more confident about painting, and after an intense day, I enjoyed a quiet evening with some of the others. The feeling of going with the flow gave me a new concept of myself.

Friday morning, we gathered again at the studio and Tomás drove us to Oak Creek Village in the van. First, he took us on a guided tour of the Bell Rock vortex near the village. He was a unique guide, embarrassing and amusing in his flirtatious way as he told us that Bell Rock is called an upflow vortex, believed to spiral energy up into the surrounding air.

"Ladies, I'm sure you know as much or more than I do about upflowing energy." He went on in spite of gasps from his audience. "Upflow vortexes are known as electric vortexes. Bell Rock is supposed to release in you a feeling of personal power. Come to Bell Rock and, according to New Age wisdom, it will channel earth energy through you. You will climb to new pinnacles of success and achieve more than you ever dreamed possible. It's a perfect place for aspiring artists."

Immersion in all this art and cultural wisdom worked its magic on me. With so much going on around me, I could barely remember the Maggie who'd arrived in Sedona less than a week before.

Late in the afternoon back at Char's house, I showered and dressed for the reception Char was involved in. There were some Hollywood names tossed about. The cowboy artist, Joe Beeler, lived in Sedona, as well. What a kick! He was the one I wanted to meet. It was something to look forward to, and an excellent excuse to turn off all other distractions for the evening.

I dressed in an ankle-length off-white skirt, a cream silk shirt, a rust-colored fringed vest, and crushed leather boots. I piled my hair up in a French twist and fastened a single strand of turquoise nuggets with a hanging ornament in the center around my neck. I added matching earrings. I'd bought the set a couple of days ago at the Indian market.

I waited in the family room for Char. She swept in a few minutes later wearing a magnificent hand-painted silk caftan and a strikingly modern necklace of turquoise and gold. She graciously said, "Hey, hey, hey! You look terrific!"

"Thanks. But you know what? I've just discovered something about Indian jewelry. One piece is lonesome. I wish I had more—I want to load it on."

"Okay," Char said. "Let's bring out the family jewels."

In Char's bedroom, we added a concho belt, another gorgeous necklace, and multiple strands of liquid silver.

"This necklace is unique, Char." I fingered the necklace she'd just placed around my neck. "It's such a modern design, and yet it looks traditional."

"Tsosie Tsiniginnie made it. He's a very talented artist. Have you heard of him?"

"Victor told me about him this morning when I admired his ceramic and glassworks in your gallery. He commands a hefty price." I remembered her afternoon plans. "Did you find another model for next week?"

"Oh, yeah. I meant to tell you. The weekend is free so everyone can visit interesting places in the area, and one of my Hispanic friends will sit for us next week," Char adjusted my necklace. "She is older, with wrinkles and character in her face. She sat for us last year."

Victor rushed in, unbuttoning his shirt. I hadn't seen him for two days since he left me at the Dairy Queen with Doria. Char must have seen him in that time, but he evidently came in late and left early.

"How is Tiahna?" Char asked.

"Terrified. Sick."

"I don't doubt it. Sickening defines the occasion. Where is she? Is she going to be okay?" "She's safe for now, in a room at the inn," he answered. "I'd better get ready." His voice trailed off as he walked out of the room.

"We can't wait for you," Char called after him. "I'm on the committee and have to be there early."

"You go ahead. I'll meet you there," he called back over the sound of running water.

Victor had not mentioned the effect the witching might have had on Char. Granted, the target of the doll hanging appeared to be Tiahna, but it happened in Char's studio, her domain. It was obvious Victor's concern was not equal or balanced. Perhaps what Randa and Char felt was not so much jealousy as righteous indignation.

"Do you ever break loose and swear, or kick and scream?" I asked when we were in the car.

"Damn it and double damn it!"

"Now that's what I call breaking loose."

She shot me a look. "I guess some of it is my fault for trying to prove how bighearted and magnanimous I can be," Char said. "Maybe I'm trying to prove I'm above jealousy."

"Well, unselfishness has its limits. Even God has been accused of jealousy." I moralized without shame. "Remember the quote from the movie, *Network*? 'I'm mad as hell, and I'm not going to take it anymore.'"

"I'm mad as hell and I'm getting close to not taking any more!" Char bellowed at the top of her lungs in the closed car. "Oops! My discretion is slipping."

We laughed as Char drove away from the house.

The reception was held in one of Sedona's charming resorts, *Los Abrigados*. The discreet lights shining on the landscaping set the scene for an interesting experience. My spirits brightened after the dark doings of early in the week, and I reinforced my earlier decision to let it all go and enjoy the evening.

Randa, standing arm-in-arm with Garcia, grabbed my attention with her titian waterfall hairdo, sparkling now with glitter. I wondered if they realized what an extremely attractive couple they were.

"Hello, Maggie," Randa whispered into my ear as she hugged me. Garcia smiled and nodded.

"Have you heard any good crime stories lately?" he asked, teasing me.

"That's all I have heard since I got here. How about you?"

"A crime a minute. Sometimes easy to solve, but difficult to prove."

"The mystery stories I read always have a neat, tied-up finish. Your solutions are not so pat, are they?"

"You're not talking about us, are you?" Rita said as she and Tomás joined our group.

"Not unless you're a pat solution." Randa laughed. "Come to think of it, Rita, that's what the two of you are for Mom—brilliant solutions."

I looked around the room full of animated groups. "I've never seen so much gorgeous Native American jewelry at one party."

Randa wore a silver concho belt with turquoise nuggets slung low around the hips of soft buckskin gaucho pants, high-top buckskin moccasins with concho and turquoise closures, dangling earrings, several necklaces entwined around her neck over a fitted sweater, and assorted bracelets and rings. Garcia, with his tan, western cut suit, wore a discreet tiepin with a single turquoise nugget. Tomás, belted, buckled and arm-cuffed with massive coral and turquoise encrusted pieces, overdid it a bit. Rita wore earrings and a necklace of nuggets.

The room soon filled with Sedona's beautiful people, most with a distinctive Sedona look. Joe Beeler, the cowboy artist, with his wife, Sharon, added a genuine western touch to the reception.

Debbie Reynolds, with her familiar smile and her hair piled high, arrived amid a flurry of recognition, Char at her side. When introduced, she was gracious. So many people crowded around, it was impossible to chat.

Victor, resplendent in black, slipped into line next to Char.

Someone behind me broke in, "Ms. Reynolds, how lovely you look!" which forced me to move on.

Tomás popped up all at my elbow. "You are ravishing tonight, Morgan. May I call you Morgan?"

His hot brown eyes burned into mine. I've often thought brown eyes more soulful than blue, maybe because they're harder to read. *Do brown eyes ever look cold?* I laughed, not caring if he understood why. He didn't seem to care if his heavy and insincere dalliance offended me.

"No one has ever called me Morgan but my mother and my high school principal. Do you want to join that club?"

Victor stepped out of the reception line and moved around the room in a purposeful circuit, never taking his eyes off the door. He joined Tiahna standing in the shadows just outside then they disappeared down the hall.

I turned to Tomás. "I need a car. Do you want to go with me or let me take yours?"

"I'd go with you anytime, anywhere, Maggie. I mean Morgan." He winked.

"Come on then! Hurry!"

"Have I got time to tell Rita?"

"Not unless we pass her on the way to the door."

Watchful Rita saw us heading out and caught up with us. So we three rushed along the hall, through the foyer, and out the front door in time to see Victor and Tiahna turn the corner of the building heading for the parking lot.

"This way," said Tomás. I picked up my skirt hem, and we ran to Tomás's car. Victor's motorcycle roared out of the driveway. Tomás followed.

"Why are we following them?" Rita asked.

"Don't ask. I'm just following my instincts," I answered. "Tomás showed up just as I saw Tiahna and Victor leave together. I went into automatic and knew I needed a car. I'm glad you came along. I don't want you to think I'm trying to steal your man."

"That's good to know," Rita replied. "God help you if you try." We both laughed.

Tomás drove.

Victor's Harley turned into the driveway of *Galleria de Luz*. Tomás parked across the road. We shut the car doors with tiny clicks and crossed the street. We slithered and slunk our way to the back of the gallery where a light had just come on.

"Why are we doing this again?" Tomás whispered as we crouched outside the window looking in.

"Shhh."

Victor knelt on the floor, Tiahna behind him.

Tomás blew air through his teeth with an almost imperceptible hiss. "He's getting into the nest egg. No one knows that safe is there except family and Rita." I nudged him. "And me," he admitted.

"And now I know," I whispered back. "And Tiahna."

"That safe is nice and fat with fees from the workshop and the Texan's buys," Rita whispered. "Hmm. Maybe not."

Victor stood up empty-handed, looking puzzled and angry. It was apparent he hadn't found what he was looking for. He grabbed Tiahna's arm and rushed back out.

By the time the three of us got to the car, the Harley was gone, heading north from the sound of it.

"Do you think this is tied in with the doll hanging?" I asked.

"My guess is Tiahna needs money for a medicine man sing," Rita said. "It takes powerful medicine to overcome a witching."

"Who do you two think pulled that doll trick?" I asked.

Rita shrugged, and Tomás said, "I don't know, Maggie. Could have been anybody."

We returned to *Los Abrigados* where not a single person had missed us. The party continued, and everyone there seemed to be having a good time. But I didn't see Randa or Garcia anywhere in the room.

SIX

After the reception, Char and I returned to the house. My energy lagged for the first time that day and I knew I'd sleep well.

"What about you?" I asked Char. "Are you too keyed up to sleep?"

She said, "I'm upset about my workshop and about Victor disappearing in and out of things all day—"

Victor and Tiahna burst into the room.

"Char," Victor interrupted, "I have to talk to you. In private." He walked out of the room. I was startled at the astonishing rudeness, so unlike the Victor I had always known and loved.

Char followed him, an angry and determined look on her face.

He spoke before they were out of earshot. "Money . . . floor safe . . ." were the scattered words I overheard.

Char's voice was strident. ". . . give her my money . . . bother to ask . . ."

He shouted then. "I didn't have time to ask. You were too busy with your celebrities."

Char shouted back. "Of course you had time. As long as she's with you, she's safe."

I squirmed in embarrassment. Tiahna, too, looked mortified. We waited in silence.

Victor and Char must have moved away. Their voices were no longer audible.

Within minutes, Victor returned and said to Tiahna, "Wait here. I'll get money for you at the spa." He almost jumped through the front door and slammed it after him.

Char returned angry and hard-eyed. There was steel in her voice "It's not that I don't want to help you, Tiahna, but it was wrong to go behind my back and open my safe without my knowledge."

"Victor suggested it. I didn't know what else to do."

"Stealing should not be one of your options." Char turned in a swirl of colored silk. "I'm going to the spa. Randa will be more furious than I if her father takes money from her safe for you."

"We didn't take money from your safe, Char," Tiahna said. "No money was there."

"No money? That can't be true."

"But it—"

Tears glistened in Char's eyes and her voice trembled with suppressed rage. "But you would have taken everything if you could." She turned on her heel and left.

The front door crashed shut with a tinkle of glass. I ran to look. One of the brilliant stained glass inserts lay shattered on the floor. From the kitchen, I brought a dustpan, whiskbroom, and a pan in which to lay the biggest pieces.

I returned to the living room. Tiahna prowled restlessly, picking things up, putting them down. She examined Char's paintings and belongings, flipped through books. She didn't speak. In this strained atmosphere, I lit the wood stacked in the fireplace to warm the room against the chill coming through the broken door. Tiahna's caged nervousness stressed me out, and even as tired as I was, I didn't feel right about going to bed with her prowling like a restless bobcat.

At length, I said, "I'm going to the kitchen to make hot chocolate. Will you have some, or anything?"

"Um, uh, okay. Oh, no, I'll take a Coke if there is one. Thanks." Making even that simple decision seemed to task her.

Glad to get away even for a short while, I worked in the kitchen for maybe fifteen minutes tops loading a tray with my hot chocolate, her Coke and a glass of ice.

I pushed through the swinging kitchen door with my shoulder, jumped, gasped and dropped the tray. The mug shattered, splashing hot cocoa in every direction; the glass shattered, splashing ice and Coke the same way. The tall, muscular Native American standing in the hallway leapt backward. A flying shard of glass nicked his bare upper arm and his blood began to seep from the cut.

His abrupt appearance terrified me. The young man and I stared at each other across the cracked crockery on the once-shining Mexican Saltillo tile floor.

His long hair hung in shining strands over his shoulders, held at the forehead by a vivid band. From the neck down he looked like a heavy-metal rocker, except for the moccasins on his feet. He wore a black tee shirt imprinted with a grinning monster face, and the slashed-out sleeves let the armholes hang open to his waist, revealing glossy, coppery muscles.

We spoke at the same time.

"Who are you," I demanded, "and how did you get in the house?"

"Where's Tiahna?" he asked at the same moment.

Somewhere in my frazzled head I recorded the information that he knew Tiahna; therefore, his sudden appearance had a reason. I felt relieved, just a tad, but enough that my pounding heart began to decelerate.

"Where's Tiahna?" he repeated.

I picked my way across the glass and looked into the living room. "I left her here a few minutes ago. Maybe she went into one of the other rooms."

I thought he would wait in the hall while I searched for Tiahna. No way. On moccasin-encased feet, he padded behind me all the way, peering over my shoulder into each room. My flesh felt electrified, tingling, and cringing over my bones. My hair lifted in its follicles. My legs shook. As it became evident we were alone in the house, my heartbeat increased until I felt faint.

I accepted the fact Tiahna wasn't in the house. "How did you get in?" The quiver in my voice terrified me all over again.

"Through the open door."

The door wasn't open when I went into the kitchen. "Tiahna must have gone out."

He grinned at me and my tension faded somewhat. I started to call him "Geronimo" in my mind.

Without another word, he walked out, leaving the door open behind him just as he'd found it.

I went to the door, locked it, and sank to the floor feeling weak and sick. Somewhere I read about people dying of fright. It wasn't so hard to believe because I had just been scared almost to death myself.

I sat with my knees drawn up, arms crossed over them, and head down. I felt like I was being dragged into a cold, dark, menacing maelstrom of emotion against my will. I remembered the vortex at Bell Rock, where we'd gone to paint just yesterday, and the serenity I had felt there. Like the two sides of a coin, how easily one could be flipped and twisted, either toward emotional darkness or into an equally unreasoned rapture.

My humor returned when I phrased my thoughts. *It's so easy to get screwed up.* That helped me avoid being swirled away and led on by the beckoning blackness.

At length, even I began to feel overly dramatic, so I got up to clean away the mess in the hall. I had finished everything but the chocolate splotches on the ceiling when the doorbell chimed. Through the broken space in the door I saw Tiahna shivering on the doorstep.

I didn't know her well enough to understand her personal demons, but sudden fury at her engulfed me. I opened the door and demanded, "Where in God's name have you been?"

"My nerves . . . I couldn't sit still." She was meek as if I had a right to scold her. "I've been walking around the backyard trying to think."

"A young man just walked in here looking for you and scared the shit out of me. Who is he?"

"What did he look like?"

I had just started to describe him when the telephone rang. I looked at the wall clock as I moved to answer. Straight up midnight. *Hmmm, the witching hour.* But Tiahna's witching on Wednesday had occurred at high noon.

"Maggie . . . Maggie! Victor is dead!" Char's voice screamed over the wires. "He drowned in the cold plunge! Ohhh . . . My God!" The line continued to hum but Char had cut out, no longer on the other end of the line.

I shouted into the receiver. "Randa? Char? Anybody?" The line was dead. Swift shock confused me for a few seconds, then as gently as I could, I said, "Tiahna, we've got to go." Her back was to me. "Tiahna, listen to me." She jerked around. "They just found your father. Dead. In the cold plunge."

Her haunted brown eyes focused at last. "But he hated the cold plunge. He never went in." Her beautiful face sagged and she began to sway, wailing, her arms wrapped around her.

I wanted to wail and keen, too, but there was no time. I couldn't leave her there and Navajo superstition would preclude her going into a sudden-death scene.

"Come on." I grabbed her arm and headed for the door. She came without resistance, keening in a high chant.

My own tears threatened to blind me and I felt a closeness of spirit with her until she whispered, "*Chindi*," the laden-with-meaning Navajo word which, at its simplest, means evil spirits. The shared grief evaporated and left me with a chill of evil rattling my soul.

"How do I get to your mother's house?" I tried to talk to her as I drove. "Tiahna, the other day Victor said you had been 'witched.' Is that what you think?"

"I don't know." Her traditional reticence had taken over.

"Why would anyone want to witch you?"

"I don't know. It's a warning."

"Does it mean someone wants to do the same thing to you they did to the doll?"

Tiahna shivered. "Maybe they want to warn Char."

"But how can we interpret it?" I was asking too much, but might not get another chance. "How can we know who the witching was meant for?"

"Maybe somebody just wants me to think I'm witched," Tiahna said. "It's hard for me, you know. I'm caught between the Anglos and the Navajos, between Victor and Char, between Victor and Randa." She closed her eyes. "It's me. I'm *chindi*."

"Tiahna, don't. Why would you think that?"

"I have to talk to *Shamah*." I recognized the Navajo word for mother, and stopped asking questions.

We cried together while I drove. I drowned in grievous memories of Victor. It could have been the same for her, I suppose, or maybe she cried in fear of evil. Even in misery, we were separated by an enormous gulf of cultural differences. And yet, we seemed bonded together in the dark tension and fear that gripped us.

I remembered my swirling sensation earlier, that moment of tumultuous blackness. I felt sure Victor's death occurred in the moment I was swept up by that grim tornado.

Tiahna pointed out her mother's house and I pulled up to it. Doria opened the door and peered out at us.

Tiahna whispered. "*Shamah*, I have to . . . *Chindi.*" I understood only those few words.

They spoke in Navajo, then her mother pulled her into the house and shut the door, in her eyes a look of fear. Had her dark eyes begged me for understanding or was it my imagination?

I stood alone in the dark, the icy prickle of nerves coursing over me. I raced to the car and slammed the door to hell with sleeping neighbors.

The post-midnight streets were deserted. I turned on my flashers and drove beyond the speed limit. Luckily, no cops caught me, and I only had to stop for one red light.

It was barely fifteen minutes after Char's phone call when I pulled into the spa parking lot. Char's car and Victor's motorcycle were the only other vehicles there. The front door stood open. I ran through it. Lights were on, but no one was there. I ran past the open door of the office, down the hall, and out through the door leading to the hot tubs. All the exterior security lights were on.

I could hear Char and Randa, sobbing and straining. They were at the top of bloodstained steps, struggling to lift Victor out of the cold plunge. Without saying a word, I helped them get his head and shoulders out of the water.

There was deep gash on his forehead. "My God, somebody killed him. I thought he died of a heart attack." As soon as that realization hit me, I said, "We should leave him and not disturb the scene. Where's Garcia? Have you called the police yet?"

"Yes. Before I called you, but Maggie, we had to get him out of the water. I couldn't stand it." It was understandable neither of them wanted to leave him where he was, hanging over the edge of the cold plunge. "He was so heavy, we couldn't . . . ohhh . . ."

"Char, sweetie, come down and let's wait for the police. This is a crime scene."

For the first time, they stopped to grasp the implications of the words "crime scene," took their hands away from Victor and came down the steps with me. I reached the bottom of the stairs first and noticed a blue gleam off to one side. A turquoise nugget lay in the corner where the steps joined the tub. It could have fallen when Victor's attacker was at the top of the steps. The bright blue color stood out against the gold and tan gravel that lined the cold plunge enclosure. Someone would have seen it and picked it up if it had been there before that night. The grounds were kept raked and groomed at all times. I didn't touch it or mention it, but it had to be a clue.

As we came out of the plunge enclosure, Garcia ran up the path. "What's happened?"

He pulled out his mobile phone and hit the buttons.

I went back into the cold plunge with him while he looked at Victor's body and the bloody steps. Without saying anything aloud, I pointed out the turquoise to him. He nodded and pulled me back out onto the path. With one arm around Randa and the other around Char, he led them back inside the main building. I followed.

In his sweats and scuffs, Garcia looked like any ordinary citizen in the middle of the night. His hair, still damp from what was likely the hot tub and shower, curled boyishly over his forehead. At this moment, he lacked the dignity of his profession.

Randa, too, wore scuffs and a kimono, and her hair, though still in the glamorous style she had worn to the reception, fell in wilted strands and exposed the damaged side of her face through wispy tendrils.

Char, still in the silk caftan she'd worn to the reception, sat on one of the low benches looking dazed and depleted.

Two police officers arrived. Garcia led them out to the cold plunge where Victor's body still hung suspended, half in and half out of the water. When they returned, Garcia introduced each of us.

One of the officers said to Char, "Mrs. Cooper, are you able to answer a few questions?"

She nodded. He led her into the office and closed the door. The other officer began asking questions in the room where I sat.

"I am Sergeant Skidmore." He acknowledged Garcia's rank. "Lieutenant Lopez?"

Garcia nodded and said, "Go ahead, Sergeant."

"Can you give us any idea what happened here tonight?"

"I can," Garcia said. "Miss Cooper and I came here to relax after a reception in town. We sat in the hot tub first."

"No, first we drank some wine," Randa corrected him between sobs.

"Yes, you're right. In fact, we carried it to the hot tub with us in an ice bucket to keep it chilled. We stayed in the tub about fifteen minutes then went down to the massage room."

"You didn't go to the cold plunge?" The sergeant interrupted.

"No, we didn't even think of it," Garcia answered. "A massage is more relaxing if your body is warm."

"So you went to the massage room right after you got out of the hot tub?"

"Yes, Randa gave me a massage, starting with my feet. A full massage takes about an hour. She had worked up to my neck and shoulders when we heard Victor's Harley drive in."

"Please explain who you mean by 'Victor'?"

"He is Miss Cooper's father, and he's the man who has been found in the cold plunge, dead."

"What time did you hear this?"

"We weren't watching the clock, but it must have been close to midnight."

"Yes," Randa said. "Probably eleven forty-five. I heard the quarter-hour chime on the clock upstairs just about then. Garcia might have been too relaxed to notice."

"How did you know the sounds were made by Mr. Cooper?" Skidmore asked. "Did you go look?"

"Well . . . no," Garcia admitted.

"Did he come down to the massage room where you were?"

"No," Garcia said. "But . . ."

"Crazy, our cat, came down here with us," Randa said. "When we heard the Harley, Crazy went streaking upstairs. He doesn't react like that to the sound of any motorcycle but Dad's."

"You heard sounds in the night, and the cat went to check them out?"

"If you knew Dad and the cat, it might make sense to you." Even to me, Randa sounded like she was begging for understanding.

The sergeant nodded but looked unconvinced. "So the cat ran out. Then what?"

"We heard the front door open."

"You still didn't go look?"

"No, Randa went on with the massage." Now, it was Garcia who sounded defensive.

Randa said, "Then we heard the back door open and footsteps run up the gravel path to the tubs."

"And the sound of running didn't alert you?"

"No," Randa said. "Dad did everything on the run. We knew it was Dad. The way it turned out, it *was* Dad." The pleading note was still in her voice. "I just thought maybe he went to check the thermostats."

I was just an interested bystander there. It wasn't unreasonable to think Garcia, on his time off, would put his job on "hold" and relax into a romantic interlude. Even policemen have a glass of wine now and then. Understanding that, it still put Garcia, a trained homicide detective, in a decidedly weak position.

"Then my phone rang," Garcia said. "I'm not called on my night off unless it's urgent. I looked at it and found a text from my supervisor. He wanted me to look at a crime scene and give my opinion, so I had to leave. I pulled on my sweats and went out through the downstairs massage room door."

The officer turned to Randa. "So you were left here alone. Were you nervous?"

"No. I *knew* my dad was upstairs." Misery poured out in Randa's voice.

Skidmore continued, relentless in spite of Randa's obvious distress.

"When did you finally decide you had a problem here?" he asked.

"I heard running footsteps on the downhill side next to the massage room. Dad wouldn't have come that way under ordinary circumstances."

"What would be different?"

"He would have come in the way he went out, through the door upstairs." She drew a ragged breath. "Then I heard a car start somewhere out on the road. I waited, but I didn't hear the Harley start. The cat, Crazy, started to howl. That was when I got nervous."

"So what did you do?"

"I ran upstairs." Randa's voice trembled, her shock and stress obvious. Garcia put his arm around her to prop her up, offering physical and emotional support.

An ambulance arrived. Paramedics entered with a stretcher. Skidmore, after a piercing look at Randa, stopped his questioning to give them directions. As he stood at the backdoor pointing out the cold plunge to them, a photography crew came in. Skidmore talked with them and then they all went into the office for more photographs. While all the activity swirled around the room, Randa and Char cried in each other's arms.

Though it was after midnight and he must have been called out of bed, a man without a tie and wearing a sweater entered. Skidmore stopped speaking to look his way.

"I'm Mr. and Mrs. Cooper's attorney," he said. "John Faraday."

Skidmore walked with him to the office, tapped on the door, and let him in.

I heard Char's voice say, "John, thank you for coming in the middle of the night like this."

While this took place, Garcia spoke in a low voice. I wasn't trying to eavesdrop, but overhead. "Try to be calm, Randa. I know this is hard, but the officers have to find out what happened. They're just doing their job. My job."

"Don't tell me to be calm," Randa snapped. "It was all so cold and awful—"

"I made a stupid mistake leaving you without checking things out." As if he couldn't help himself, Garcia looked at the stains on the front of her kimono, her father's spilled lifeblood. Gory splotches dried on the cloth around her knees. Streaks on her sleeves showed where she had rubbed her hands. Dried blood streaked her face. Randa seemed unaware of her appearance or of what the police might read into it.

She reacted to his encompassing glance. "Garcia! I didn't do it. Do they think I killed my father? Do you think that?"

I'd noticed that Char's beautiful silk caftan was covered in blood splotches as well. I looked down at my own bloodied clothes and hoped my face didn't betray my fearful thoughts.

I came back to the moment when I heard Garcia say, "No, sweetheart. Of course not."

Randa stared at Garcia, seeming frozen, as though her mind had stalled.

Her tears finally stopped and Skidmore resumed his questioning. "Can you continue, Miss Cooper?" She nodded. "What did you do after you came upstairs?"

Randa breathed in deeply and released the breath with a small groan. "I looked in the office and saw the floor safe open the way it is now. Just then, Mother came in looking for Dad. She saw the open safe, too."

Garcia eyed Sergeant Skidmore whose face remained expressionless. "I know this makes me look like a careless fool."

Randa said, "The backdoor was wide open."

Char, her lawyer, and the officer who had questioned her came in from the office.

Skidmore looked up, but continued his questions. "What made you look in the cold plunge?"

A hysterical note tinged her voice. "I got the golf club we keep in the office, you know, just in case. I switched on the outside lights. I didn't know where to look first, but when Mother and I got out on the path, the cat jumped up from the inside of the cold plunge enclosure onto the fence. He just crouched there, yowling. The door was open, so we went in, but at first we couldn't see anything. Then we saw all the blood on the steps. We walked up the steps, and Dad floated there . . . just . . . suspended in the water. Under the surface, you know? Just the crown of his head showing, his hair spread out, and his hands curved as if he had clutched at the edge." Her words came out in strangled gasps.

"So that's how you got so much blood on your clothes?" Skidmore inquired.

I interrupted. "Wouldn't it be difficult to drown Victor or anyone who didn't want to be drowned without noise and struggle?"

"Oh, Mag," Char said, "whoever did it knocked him unconscious first. You saw that terrible wound on his forehead."

"Still, it would take a lot of strength to pull him up the steps and tip him over into the plunge," I said. "It took three of us to pull him out."

"Ma'am, will you please stay out of this?" Skidmore chastised me. "Please continue, Miss Cooper."

"I slipped in Dad's blood on the steps," Randa choked.

Skidmore turned to Garcia. "Uh, Sir," he said, "you know as well as I do what we're looking at here. I'm not accusing you or either of the Coopers of anything yet, but it sure does look suspicious."

"Yeah. It looks amateurish," Garcia admitted. "Hell of a time for that call. It couldn't have come at a worse time."

The other policeman came out of the office and huddled with Skidmore, speaking in a low voice.

"Was it awful?" I whispered to Char.

"Not too bad, yet. He was very considerate. I told him about the doll in the studio and the money taken from my safe." She paused. "And about the fight I had with Victor had over Tiahna before he left the house to come here."

Randa and Garcia came over to where I sat with Char and her lawyer. Char listened to him while her eyes scanned the room.

Randa said, "Are you all right, Mother? Do you need to stay with me tonight?"

Char looked up at Randa and shook her head. "Thanks, darling, but I'd rather be in my own room. Why don't you come home with me for a few days?"

Skidmore walked over and spoke to Randa. "What exactly is missing from your safe, Miss Cooper?"

"I don't know. I haven't looked. I just saw it was open."

"Nothing but some legal documents in there now," Skidmore said.

Randa gasped. "There was over five hundred dollars in cash and checks, and all my Navajo jewelry except the pieces I wore tonight. A couple of thousand dollars in jewelry."

He turned to Char. "And what about your safe, Mrs. Cooper?"

"Close to eighteen thousand dollars from the paintings we sold this week, and the workshop fees." Skidmore raised his eyebrows, but made no comment. He wrote in his notebook.

"You folks can go now, but don't leave town. Uhh—Lieutenant Lopez, you're wanted down at police headquarters."

Char, her face ashen, swayed when she stood. I slipped my arm through hers to keep her from falling. "Are you okay, Char? Do you need a drink of water?"

She nodded.

I looked at Skidmore. He glanced first at the office he seemed to be guarding. "I'll get her some water. No one goes in there while I'm gone."

I helped Char sit down again then whispered, "I'm going to just look inside the office before Skidmore comes back and stops me. It'll only take three seconds."

Char leaned back and studied me with pain-filled eyes, but didn't comment.

Randa rubbed her hands over her face. "Maggie, he said there's nothing left in the safe but papers, worthless uranium stock in that old Blue Lizard Mine up in Utah that Dad bought into years ago."

Nonetheless, both Char and Randa watched for Skidmore's return while I stood outside the door, stuck my head inside the office and looked around. I thought maybe there would be another turquoise nugget, but didn't see one.

The floor safe cover stood open. Bundles of envelopes were visible but no money or jewelry or anything that looked valuable. Everything else in the room looked the same as it had last time I'd been in it before all the strange events began. When Skidmore returned, I was standing outside the door keeping watch for him.

By the time we drove toward home, it was early morning. So much had happened in the past eighteen hours, so many mind-numbing details, I drove like a zombie. I could only imagine Char's state of mind. Even so, I was aware enough to realize we must have some rest from the relentless onslaught of hanging and running and drowning if we were to keep up this pace in the coming mournful days.

"Stop the car," Char said. I pulled off the road without question. She opened the door, leaned out and threw up, her body jerking, her breath coming in gasps.

"Migraine," she said when she pulled herself back up. "It hit without the usual warning signs. There's a pill in my bag." She slumped on the seat, vulnerable and defenseless.

"Hurry home, Maggie," Randa said. "I'll get the pill."

"Will the meds help after the migraine has started?" I asked.

"Not much, but it will make her drowsy, so it helps in that way," Randa said.

For a few moments after Char had swallowed her migraine meds, she remained silent then, "Maggie, let's go to St. John's. I want to pray, and light a candle for Victor."

Randa gave me directions to the Catholic Church. What a loving idea. Lighting prayer candles would have a soothing effect on us all, including me. I have always loved church buildings. Tired though we were, this would help us, Char and Randa most of all.

The priest stood in the open door, keys in hand, likely just unlocking it for the day. Early morning mass would start soon. I recognized Father Quejada, whom I'd met at José's funeral. He raised his eyebrows and his shoulders with a questioning look as Char and Randa went inside. I stayed by his side and filled him in on the tragedy they had just suffered. He crossed himself, his sympathy instantaneous.

"Anything I can do to help, please let me know," he murmured. "Rita, Char's manager, is my cousin."

The few moments we spent in the church brought me a small measure of peace. I had faith that the curling smoke of the burning candles carried our whispered prayers toward heaven. I hoped Char and Randa felt some peace as well.

Char's empty house offered solid refuge. It was still lighted as I had left it. Randa and I helped Char into bed. Randa looked ready to collapse, and I felt like the floor of a birdcage.

Before I closed her door, Char said, "Maggie, can you handle things for me for a few days if anyone comes?"

"Of course," I answered. "Don't worry about greeting people. I'll take care of it."

Six o'clock in the morning found them in their own rooms with their own thoughts and their own pain. I went back out to my car.

Here I am, taking over for Char already.

I worried about Tiahna. I didn't want her to feel left out of the family mourning or Victor's funeral, but neither did I want to upset Randa. I thought that someone should talk to Tiahna and Doria before any more time elapsed.

Doria's house looked deserted. I knocked once with no answer. Knocked a second time. Still no answer. I decided to try one more time and then leave. I had just raised my hand when the door opened, and sour whisky breath smote me in the face. A drunken Navajo man stood swaying in the doorway.

"Is Doria here? Or Tiahna?" I asked.

He answered with unintelligible mutterings. Maybe another Navajo would have understood him, but I couldn't. Still mumbling, he stepped back and fell over, then rolled up in a fetal position and began snoring.

I hesitated then pushed the door open wider, and called out, "Tiahna? Doria?" Except for the snoring, there were no sounds of movement or human presence.

Though I've lived near the Navajo Reservation for years, hired a few Navajos, and dealt with some of their alcoholism problems, I hesitated briefly about what to do. I'd heard of several cases of drunken Navajos freezing to death. Temperatures had plummeted with the recent rain, and a morning chill was in the air. Just inside on the couch there was a Pendleton shawl. In a rushed moment, I stepped over him, picked up the shawl, and covered him. I stuck a pillow under his head, pushed his legs inside a few inches with my foot and shut the door, holding my breath the entire time. It was what any human being would do for another though I didn't kid myself. Most likely he would wake up and continue his destructive agenda, never knowing what I had done for him.

Back at Char's house, I climbed into bed, tired to the bone.

Leave town, Skidmore? Not me. Not until I see what I can do for Char.

SEVEN

I shifted in bed, exhausted but sleepless. Not accustomed to sleeping in the daytime, the sun shining outside the pulled draperies kept me awake. At some point I dozed, but my recurrent nightmare of my soon-to-be ex-husband Ron's back receding in the distance jerked me awake.

Ron worked for the Bureau of Land Management stationed in the Arizona Strip District, and we lived in Page, Arizona. He was often away from home for several days at a time. When he set off for work after he kissed me goodbye, he whispered in my ear, "Don't shoot till you see the whites of my eyes."

We both loved Lake Powell. In the unpopulated desert area on the border between northern Arizona and southern Utah, we could disappear into the wilderness and go for days without seeing anyone else. We were one with the desert like lizards and cactus. I worked, but saved up all my vacation days and sick leave so we could spend warm and wondrous days together on the lake.

I thought we would go on forever. I thought we both loved our way of life. But he didn't leave our way of life, he left me. He loaded up and drove away last February. I hadn't seen him since. I was still mad as hell, also horny as hell. He left me high and dry in more ways than one. The black nightmare of his car disappearing around the curve of Navajo Drive in Page has never left me.

A friend, who is a dream consultant, has talked with me at length about this nightmare. When I asked for her interpretation, she said, "My interpretation isn't necessary. What's essential is what you think about it." In my dream he was never coming toward me, always going away. She said it was my subconscious telling me to give him up.

"I am *not* a quitter," I said.

"Sometimes you have to lick your wounds, let them heal, and move on.

I never got a grip on Ron's true reasons for leaving and that embarrassed me, left me with damaged self-esteem, torn emotions, and an angry, wounded heart. Whew, madder than hell just barely began to describe my anger. I had been consumed with it for too long.

Still staring into the shadowy gloom, my libido spoke up, *Shit, shit, shit! Screw the whites of his eyes; I want to shoot him where it will hurt the most.*

Sometime during those early hours, I faced up to the fact that this trip could no longer be about me. Time to let go. *So long, Ron, have a good life. I'm staying here to help Char, at least until after the funeral.*

Char's problems were so much bigger than mine. Both Char and Randa had been struggling with Victor's obsession over Tiahna for too long. Plus they faced the grief of his sudden death while their emotions were tangled with jealousy and resentment.

Energized by my decision, I faced the morning with renewed zest. Questions began to pop into my head one after another as the events of the previous three days began instant replay.

Tiahna was Victor's lovechild from twenty-some years back; Randa was jealous and upset about it; Char was in denial, tried to hide her anger and to rise above it at the same time. Native witches haunted Tiahna. An intense stress level manifested in all three of them.

Could any one of those three have killed Victor? Char and Randa were modern, gentle, and refined women whom I'd known forever. They both had some deep anger issues—but no, Char couldn't kill Victor. Randa couldn't kill her father. Char and Randa together couldn't do it. *Could they?*

Tiahna was in the backyard when Victor was killed. At least that's what she told me. And she was only out of my sight for maybe thirty minutes, not enough time to make it over to the spa, commit a cold and bloody crime, and return to act as if nothing had happened. I knew little about her but she had definitely not remained calm in the dicey situation at the studio. She panicked and ran from the doll hanging. Also, there was no available transportation to take her from the house to the spa.

These were all small women, none with the strength to whack Victor on the head, pull his limp body up the steep steps and tip him over into the cold plunge.

What about Geronimo, the handsome young man who popped in looking for Tiahna? He couldn't have done it either, simply because he couldn't be in two places at the same time.

All my questions were just academic. Who was I to get involved in a murder investigation? I'd read so many mysteries, my second nature kicked in to see if I could solve it from the meager clues I had.

The clock on the bedside table showed ten forty-five Saturday morning. Thank God Char had arranged for the weekend to be free or this Saturday morning would have been unimaginable. I'd promised Char I'd talk to people who came, so thought I'd better get up and see what needed to be done.

I'd worn myself out going over everything that had happened in the week that I'd been in Sedona. Nothing made sense to me, but the most illogical happening of all was the paint-smeared doll. Well, actually nothing about Victor's murder made sense, but the doll simply didn't fit into any scenario I could imagine. Either I didn't know enough to find the key to it or else I was in complete confusion about Navajo folklore. Should I have given more weight to the witching, or less? Afraid of starting back on the treadmill of my thoughts, I swung my legs out of bed. *Let's see what's going on in the house.*

The house was quiet and I didn't want to disturb anyone behind closed doors. I decided to jog. While jogging, I'd occasionally found it wasn't easy to go the distance. I was too good at talking myself into cutting the time short. To avoid shortchanging myself, I adopted Nike's motto: Just Do It. So I jogged away from the house for about thirty minutes and then jogged back. When I returned, Randa was leaning against the kitchen counter drinking coffee, tears rolling down her cheeks. She looked weighted, perhaps haunted, by memories.

"Do you remember the summer I turned five?" she asked, apropos of nothing. "Mother and I were in Page visiting you and Ron, and Jen and

Alex. I always loved Page and the lake. When Dad came to pick us up, we spent a week camping on the shores of the lake. Remember?"

I poured coffee for myself and listened as Randa rushed to release a flood of recollections, which in any other context but Victor's death would have been delightful and soothing. My memories responded to her vivid word pictures.

In one of the canyons, we discovered an ancient cliff dwelling with water lapping at the doorstep. Under an overhang two hundred feet down from the rim of sheer cliff walls, the dwelling crouched on the cliff face several hundred feet above the water when first built, ages ago. How in the world had they reached it? That summer, with the closing of the dam to fill the lake, the water rose fast and, at the moment we discovered the dwelling, rippled just inches away from the entrance, almost ready to spill in onto the hard-packed dirt floor. We stepped off the bow of the boat into the ancient home and, in awe, climbed through apertures into the several rooms. No one spoke, afraid of shattering the fragile sense of time standing still. The spirit of the rooms surrounded us with an almost palpable resonance as if the occupants had just stepped out for a few moments. When we returned to the entrance, water had begun to spill in over the doorstep.

In a side canyon of the Escalante River, we hiked in to the Cathedral in the Desert, a watercarved amphitheater in the center of a cliff, bathed in an ethereal light. We could look up at the holes in the top where the water had swirled through for eons and eroded the sandstone. Cool and majestic, the cathedral walls sheltered little green growing things. We stood shadowed in the bottom and looked up at the massive yet delicate forms above us. Char said she felt as if she stood in a seashell looking out.

Randa reminded me that Victor said, "Remember this. The water will fill this cathedral in a few years, and it will be gone." That magnificent cathedral, even though it is now under hundreds of feet of water, stood there as another example of an erosion-created vortex. Why do vortexes seem to be everywhere? It must be that spirals formed much of the universe.

On the last day of our camping trip, Ron had stopped the boat on a sandy beach in Padre Bay, The Crossing of the Fathers, to play in the water and have lunch one last time before going home. Randa hopped from one rock to another in the shallow water calling, "Look, Daddy! Look!"

He called back, "Be careful!" just as she slipped and fell, hitting her chin, biting her tongue, and getting a mouthful of blood and sand and water. She thought she would drown. Victor, in three long steps, picked her up. He soothed her, helped her rinse out her mouth, and washed the blood from the cut just under her chin. When we got into Page and the doctor's office, she had to have four stitches.

That night when Char tucked her into bed, Randa said, "Daddy saved my life, didn't he, Mommy?"

And then, last summer, she'd learned that while she and her mother had been visiting us in Page, Tiahna had been conceived. She'd been tied in knots over it ever since. Although I did not want to hear it, Randa continued to relate the details of the day her father told her about Tiahna.

He had been awkward and embarrassed. Her mother had refused to come and help him. "It's your story, not mine," she'd said.

He had psyched himself up, and it showed. He came across as too loud, too strong, heartless.

"Randa," he had blurted out. "You have a sister."

"What?" she'd said. Her eyes distant, Randa related in painful detail how she stood fixing sandwiches for the spa snack bar, a serrated knife in one hand, and a loaf of whole wheat bread in the other.

"She's twenty-one years old. Half Navajo."

"You've got to be kidding," Randa had said.

"No," he replied. "But I didn't know, I didn't know, Randa, until last night."

"How could you not know?" she had demanded. She realized later how naive and obtuse she must have sounded. The conversation was extremely uncomfortable for them both, and she had done nothing to make it any easier for him.

He told her that while she and her mother were visiting in Page, he traveled on the reservation buying Navajo rugs and jewelry. He stopped at the Navajo Tribal Ceremonial in Gallup, New Mexico. As he'd stood watching the parade, he'd seen the princess of the ceremonial riding on a float, dressed in beaded, white buckskin.

The romance of the exotic, plus his own erotic energy, blew him away. Almost unaware of what he was doing, he began to walk along the parade route, keeping pace with the princess float. The princess soon became aware of the strange man staring at her. She smiled and waved. At the end of the parade, he approached her. Though shy, she told him her name, Doria, and he swept her away with him. She impressed him with her drama and beauty and eagerness, but he never saw her again until she brought Tiahna to ask for help. He couldn't deny her story. He knew that he had betrayed his wife and daughter for a momentary obsession. As soon as he saw Tiahna, he knew. She had his mother's high forehead and cowlick.

"I was getting so angry," Randa looked at me, with sad eyes. "I could feel myself getting colder. My face felt like granite."

And then he had said, "Come off it, Randa. You're not a child."

She had tried to understand and perhaps did a bit because of her erotic nature. That is, until she saw Tiahna. Even then, in time, she thought she could have handled it if her father had kept his perspective. But he had tried to make up for the past twenty plus years all at once. And Randa, with a cold burn, felt that Tiahna exploited his guilty eagerness to atone.

A few days after Victor told her about Tiahna, Randa was driving back to Sedona after shopping in Flagstaff. As she drove through Oak Creek Canyon, her mind bitterly focused on the new sister, a deer suddenly appeared in her high beams. It froze in the road, looking at her with wide, startled eyes. She jerked the wheel. The car rolled over. That was all Randa could remember.

Later, her mother told her how Victor fought with the doctors to keep them from shaving off her hair because he knew how much it meant to her. She appreciated that as she recovered, but not enough to make up for Tiahna. It was as if Victor assumed Randa had her share of his attention and didn't need him anymore. She questioned how he could be so insensitive when she needed his love and support to recover from the accident that had disfigured her face.

Now, Randa wept for herself, for her mother, and for her dead father.

"Oh, Maggie, you saw how the wound on his forehead had dented his skull. It was like a sharp heel print in wet sand. His hair spread out on the water like a gray cloud . . . and his fingers were clutching . . . oh, God!"

I reached for her and held her, not saying anything.

"Why didn't Garcia and I go straight upstairs to check out the night noises?" she sobbed. "We were there to be alone. If only . . ."

"Randa, please don't."

"Garcia wanted to leave the reception last night by ten thirty." She went on as if she couldn't stop. "He'd had it with crowds, and with people who come at him all the time. We decided to go to the spa, sit in the hot tub and then give each other a massage." Her voice faltered and the sobbing took over.

"It has been a terrible week." I wanted to head off any more intimate revelations, but she needed comforting. I held her and let her cry.

After a while, she calmed down and excused herself to wash her face. I found some tomato soup and heated it up. When she came back, we shared the soup and two iced Cokes. Food is so normalizing.

As we ate, I ventured a question that had been on my mind for a few days. "How is Garcia's investigation coming?"

She sighed. "Slow. Careful. One step at a time. It's a tangled mess of illegal immigrants, huge bales of marijuana, smuggled cocaine, a bunch of local kids mixed up with more than they can handle. It's codenamed 'Skylark,' a pretty name for a dirty business."

The shift in conversation eased my mind but not Randa's. She spoke again, almost in reverie. "We needed to forget all that and wanted to spend time by ourselves. Gar loves me to caress his neck while we're driving." She returned to telling me the intimate details of the night before. My imagination responded to her words. An image of the sensual massage room leapt to my mind: the candles, the music, and the scented oils. I thought of their moonlit walk on the paths to the hot tubs, holding hands, carrying wine and glasses.

I imagined an abundance of lovers' details, from their reluctance to be interrupted by Victor's arrival, to their passionate culmination rudely suspended by the insistent beeping of Garcia's cell phone. I did not want Randa to give me a description, but I did want to give her my warm and close attention.

"Garcia had to respond to his call, so after he left, I stayed there on the massage table and thought about Dad and Tiahna and the voodoo doll, damn mad about everything. When I heard the footsteps run past, I listened for the Harley, but a car engine started up instead. I've been so mad at Dad, and I thought he had just run off and left the back door unlocked in the middle of the night, so I put on a kimono and went upstairs. Then the cat started his horrendous yowling, and Mother came in. I looked in the office for the golf club and grabbed it, saw my floor safe open then found the back door open, too. We ran out . . . Oh, Maggie," Randa began to cry again. "Mother's scream when she saw Dad keeps coming back to me. That and Dad's clutching fingers."

Garcia called out from the front of the house, walked into the kitchen just then and immediately took in Randa's state. I moved back and he took my place at her side. As I tiptoed away, he began murmuring softly.

I went to my room to shower and think. Even I could see that Randa had to be a top suspect. The golf club she kept in her office may have been used to hit Victor. Ironically, it was Victor who advised her to keep it there, perhaps had even given it to her to be used in case of a break-in. Nevertheless, with no one having seen this mysterious assailant, her story could be impossible to prove. Her state of shock and grief could just as well be judged hysterical guilt as much as normal sorrow for her father's death.

If I, who loved Randa as a daughter, could see signs pointing to her guilt, what would the police be thinking? I went back to the kitchen and there was Char, standing at the counter drinking coffee, reading the newspaper.

My heart went out to her. "How are you feeling this morning, dear friend?"

I needn't have asked. She looked up at me, her face white, dark circles under her haunted eyes. Tears spilled down her cheeks.

"Oh, Maggie, listen to this: 'Love Nest at Health Spa. Sedona Policeman Implicated in Murder. Drug Investigation Halted.' This is going to be a nightmare."

"Do you want me to stay a few more days, Char?"

"Could you, Maggie? Be my proxy for a while? So many questions need answers, and you've always been so adept at that."

I took her left-handed compliment, knowing she intended it with sincerity. "I'd be glad to if you don't mind me fielding questions and prying into your life. You're correct in saying that's right up my alley."

"I've already told you about the skeletons in our closets. If more are found . . ." Her voice trailed off as if she realized the incongruity of what she said.

The body in her gallery garden, the mutilated doll in her studio, infidelity, jealousy, Randa's accident, and finally Victor—her eyes mirrored the horrible improbabilities that had already marred her perfect life. I could see the morbid thought of skeletons jarred both of us. What more could happen?

"Randa is not a killer, Maggie," she said. "She's like you in some ways. When she's riled up, she says so to Tiahna or Victor or anyone.

And Victor . . ." She paused to consider her husband of so many years. "Victor didn't deserve to be murdered just because he rushed around like a crazed bull. And now Garcia is caught in the middle. His career could be ruined."

The telephone rang. I answered. A man asked for Garcia. I went to find him and met him and Randa coming toward the kitchen.

His side of the conversation consisted of, "yes, no," and "soon." After he had disconnected, he turned to Randa. "They want us to come to the station. They have a few more questions and we have to sign off on last night's reports. I'm being put on leave until this investigation is over."

"Will they arrest you?" Char asked. "Or Randa?"

"Not yet," he replied. The implication of that distinct possibility was unnerving.

"Do you have any idea who it might have been?"

"I have ideas, but they are not yet concrete."

Garcia and Randa left the house. Char sat down at the table. I picked up the paper and scanned the article under the headlines. As is often the case, the newspaper had created this tantalizing article out of bits and pieces, making it sound as if the crime busters had already busted the crime.

Minutes after Randa and Garcia left, Tomás arrived looking as if he, too, had been sleepless.

I whispered to him, "Char's suffering is terrible to watch."

Tomás nodded without comment. We went into the kitchen. Char looked up. When she saw Tomás she stood and hugged him, "Oh, Tomás, thank you for coming. I don't know what I'd do without you." From the distressed look on his face, the hug surprised him.

Char stepped back and saw his discomfort. Always quick to perceive feelings, she reverted to business mode. She said, "I'm so glad you're here. What can we do about my workshop?"

"Rita called Esteban. He agreed to take over for the last week. Under the tragic circumstances, he'll do it for fifty percent plus space for two of his paintings in your gallery."

"Who is Esteban?" I asked.

"He's my competition. He started having workshops the year after I did, just to prove that anything I could do, he could do better. I don't think he proved that, but I just hate the idea of turning my class over to him. He's such a promoter. I'd do it for him for nothing." She paused. "Okay, give him the space, but not forever, just a few months."

"He's way ahead of you. He said he'd take six months, beginning next month and ending in April."

"The parasite," Char said.

Tomás went on, "And, with Tiahna gone, the class won't be able to finish their portraits of her. Rita has arranged for Esteban to take the class outside again this week, to paint more of Sedona's towering rocks on location."

"Hey, that's a smart idea. I asked Carmen Alvarez to pose, but the Sedona Plein Air Festival is in a couple of weeks. We can cancel Carmen, she won't mind." With a thoughtful expression, she considered the plans. "Our artists will learn how crucial the light is, and how fast it changes." Char, even with exhaustion tingeing her voice, spoke with conviction. "What do you think, Maggie? You're one of our artists."

"Sounds great to me," I said, appreciating an artist of Char's caliber calling me one, too.

"Well, then, will you go down Monday morning and explain to my class?"

The next morning, the Sunday edition of "The Arizona Republic" from Phoenix gave Victor's death a prominent place on the bottom of the front page. Speculation about José's gruesome murder and *Galeria de Luz* figured largely in the article.

I read it all, feeling frustrated by the negative publicity and sense of helplessness. It's such aggravation to read the papers and think that they've got it all wrong.

All day Sunday, I answered the door and talked to friends and neighbors of Victor and Char. Many of them brought food. The newspaper wanted an interview with Char or Randa, but they remained secluded.

Monday, I planned to involve myself in searching for Tiahna, but first went straight to Char's studio to explain to the class what had happened. Of course, most of them had heard it all on television or read it in the paper, but a personal response from Char through me helped smooth out disappointments over the tragic turn of events.

". . . so please accept Char's regrets." I finished making my sorrowful comments to the workshop students. "Char has offered to refund your money for the second week if you would rather not continue with Esteban."

Shocked, sympathetic, and curious, the students broke into a babble of questions. Every one of them was generous and understanding, and no one wanted to cancel. Tomás asked them to check with Rita in the gallery about where to send flowers or cards, and then he and I left the studio together.

Esteban, wearing a beret and dressed in a painting smock over jeans, was on his way to the studio. Tomás introduced us. He greeted us both with a big smile and seemed to be enjoying to the hilt his chance to influence Char's workshop students. I waited in the back garden while Tomás escorted him to the studio.

When Tomás returned, I said to him, "Someone ran just a few steps ahead of Victor all Friday evening. Who do you think it could have been?"

He shook his head. "I don't know. Whoever it was couldn't have known Victor would look in the floor safes that night."

"In that case, they must not have known about the attack on Tiahna. Or, they must not have known how far Victor would go to help her. Or maybe they were so desperate for money they were willing to take any risk."

"They almost got away with it," Tomás said.

"Maybe the attack on Tiahna is not related to Victor's murder at all, or maybe it is in some subtle, clever way. So many possibilities."

"Are you aware of how much Randa hates Tiahna, and how angry she was at Victor?" Tomás asked.

"I wouldn't call it a murderous anger or hatred. I have never seen violence in Randa."

"How about calling it jealousy? Or intolerance? Or getting even?" Tomás's tone rose. "Or racist?"

"Racist? Give me a break, Tomás. Randa is not angry about race. She felt betrayed." I stared at him. "What are you saying, Tomás? That Randa hung Tiahna in effigy?" He'd voiced some of the same questions I had been asking myself. But what right did he have to question Char or her family? "You are not implying she killed her father, are you?"

He shrugged. "Who knows?"

We entered the gallery through the back door and walked down the long hallway into the main display room, stopping before one of Char's brilliant landscapes

"Who knows?" I repeated after him. "Well, I don't know, but I intend to find out. Will you help me?"

A fleeting expression of reservation crossed his face. "In what way could I help?"

"I don't know my way around this town very well. What if I wanted to look at something or other without enlisting the entire police force to help me? Could I call on you?"

"Of course," he said. "I'll do anything I can to help." He couldn't resist adding, "Especially you," in his suggestive voice.

Rita walked in from the adjoining room where, if she'd been there all along, she would have overheard. *Oh, well, so be it.* I had nothing to hide from her.

But I knew now that Tomás had suspicions about Randa or at the very least some cultural hostility he kept hidden most of the time. Maybe both.

I left them at the gallery.

Aside from the two murders, two smaller questions nagged at me: *Where were Tiahna and Doria? And who was the guy I nicknamed Geronimo?*

The police would handle both Jose's and Victor's murders, and I had been specifically told to butt out. That left me with Char's request to cover for her. To do that, I thought the best action I could take would be to find Tiahna.

Tiahna was an art student. A logical place to inquire would be the Sedona Arts Center and the Nassan Gobran School of the Arts on Art Barn Road right at the edge of the tourist-oriented center of Uptown Sedona.

The Sedona Arts Center welcomed visitors with a blooming garden and sculptural art pieces in front as well as artistic benches in the shade of the portico. The gallery's assistant greeted me. "Welcome. Can I help you find anything in particular?"

"Thank you. I would like to talk to the school director or manager if he or she is available."

"That would be Jan Carruthers." She pointed out the back windows. "The school and the administrative offices are over there. Do you have an appointment?"

"No, sorry." I still didn't know if the director were a he or a she. Jan could be either.

"Can I ask what your visit pertains to?"

"A young woman named Tiahna goes to school here. Do you know her?"

"You'd need to talk to the school personnel about a student. I can call the office and ask if you can speak to someone over there." When she hung up the phone, she said, "Jan is in her office. You can ask her what you need to know."

"Thank you," I answered, reassured by her friendly helpfulness. "I appreciate your help." I went down a flight of stairs and out through the back entrance. A woman whom I took to be the director came toward me. I realized I had seen her at the reception Fri night. We met under the portico of the art barn.

After I'd introduced myself and told her why I was there and what I needed, we spoke for a few minutes about the murder. "Victor's death was such a shock," she said.

"We're all in shock," I replied.

"About Tiahna," she said. "One of our most successful former students, Tsosie Tsiniginnie, teaches here. He and Tiahna have become friends. I think they've been going out some." She looked past my shoulder and said, "Here's Tsosie, now. Maybe he knows where Tiahna is."

I turned and found myself face-to-face with the midnight visitor, the one I'd been calling Geronimo, the one who'd terrified me as he followed me through Char's house looking for Tiahna. I did a double take. For a moment I just stared at him, seeing again in memory his sudden, startling appearance the night of Victor's murder. He stared right back at me, surprised to see me as well. This time he wore a paint-spattered artist's smock over blue jeans and had tied his hair back into a ponytail. He still wore moccasins.

"Tsosie is an artist of the highest caliber," Jan said. "He's gaining international fame for his unique silver and turquoise jewelry designs."

"I've seen some of your work." I offered my hand and he took it. "Char Cooper let me wear a necklace of yours to a reception Friday night, the same night you scared me so much when you came to her house. I actually felt the hair rise on the back of my neck."

"Sorry about that," he said. "Are *you* looking for Tiahna this time?" He must have overheard some of my conversation with Jan.

"Yes, I am. You knew about her father?" I asked. He nodded. "Do you know where she is?"

"She's gone with her mother to her grandfather's place in Navajo Canyon. He's a medicine man, you know. She needs some powerful medicine after everything that's happened the last few days."

"Could you get away sometime today?" I asked. "Could I take you to lunch? I'd like to talk to you some more about this."

He glanced at his watch. "It's just twelve o'clock. My next class isn't until one. I could go now if you have time."

"I've got time," I answered. "Where would you like to go?"

"Hey, I'm easy. We could walk to a half dozen restaurants. A hamburger would suit me just fine, but with all the tourists, it might take longer to get served than I have time for. There's a Burger King just past the junction."

Where should I begin? I wondered after we picked up Whoppers, fries, and Cokes at the Burger King counter. We sat at an outside table and Tsosie saved me from wondering by digging into his lunch with relish, then asking, "What can I help you with?"

"I'm worried that Tiahna will feel left out of Victor's funeral."

"Humph." It was a combination huh, chuckle, and snort. "You don't need to worry about any Navajo feeling left out of a funeral. We even try not to speak the name of the dead. The kindest thing you could do is to leave Tiahna out of it. Besides, you couldn't include her in a funeral now because she's in Navajo Canyon getting ready for ceremonies of her own."

"It's not just because of the funeral that I'm concerned, but because of the strain between her and Randa and Char."

He snorted again, but before he could answer, his cell phone rang. He rose and walked away from the table. I overheard him speaking in Navajo for several minutes. When he came back, he said, "That was my cousin, Tony, in Willow Water. Snow fell on Navajo Mountain last week, so Tiahna's *Yeibichai Dance* has started. Man, she's lucky it snowed. That dance can only be held after the snakes are asleep and there's no longer any danger of lightning. I'm going up there to be a *Yei* during the last two days of the ceremony."

"You're a *Yei*?" I asked.

"Sure. All Navajos are *Yeis*. It's at the end of a *Yeibichai* ceremony that the young Navajo boys and girls are introduced to the secret of the *Yeis*."

"Can you tell me the secret?"

"Yeah, why not? You can read it in just about any book on Southwestern Indian ceremonies. The masked *Yei* dancers represent supernatural beings who possess enormous powers."

"I've got several *Yeibechai* masked dolls," I told him. "Don't they frighten the young children?"

"No. The kids are taken to the dances from the time they're on the cradleboard. Their mothers prepare them by washing their hair to purify them. By the time the dance reaches the end, everybody is jolly and happy. The fun spreads to the kids; they look forward to it. I remember rubbing my body with the white clay that is part of revealing the secret."

I listened to every word with rapt attention.

"The boys are blessed with sacred meal and then ceremonially whipped with yucca leaves by the masked figures. The girls are marked on the feet, hands, shoulders, and head with sacred meal and touched with ears of white and yellow corn wrapped in spruce twigs."

"It sounds like sort of a game."

"Oh, yeah. And then, soon after the corn meal blessings, the *Yeis* take off their masks so the children can see they're just ordinary humans playing the part of supernatural beings. One of the male dancers places his mask on each of the boys in turn, while the female *Yei* places hers on the girls so that each child gets a view of the world through the eyes of the *Yeibichais*."

"And that comes at the end of the ceremony?"

"Yeah. The first days are a healing ceremony, and that is what is happening for Tiahna right now. On the last two days, we initiate our young people. Throughout our lifetime, each of us is expected to participate in this initiation ceremony four times."

"Thank you, Tsosie, for sharing that with me. I'm—I can't think how to express this—I'm—I'm just amazed at the hugeness of this ceremony and that it can be arranged so quickly."

"Yeah. The biggest problems these days are paying for food to feed everybody for nine or ten days, and for people to get off work so they can go."

His cell phone rang again. Once again, he walked away from the table to converse in Navajo. This time it was, "Another cousin, a desert tracker."

"A desert tracker? I know what that sounds like, but I'm not sure I know what it is."

"*The Smithsonian Magazine* published an excellent article about them a couple of years ago. You can look it up on the Internet. Key in *Smithsonian Magazine* and then 'Shadow Wolves.'"

Ancient rituals, *Yeibichais*, desert trackers, Shadow Wolves, cell phones and the Internet—my mind reeled.

"I admire your traditions, Tsosie, what little I know of them. And I admire your creativity."

He fingered the pouch hanging around his neck. "I make drums and flutes too," he said.

"You do?"

"I sure do."

"That's fascinating. I go to a women's drumming circle in Page, and I went to one with Randa at the spa a few nights ago. So much has changed since then." That grim reminder interrupted the flow of our conversation, so I picked it up again. "The beat of the drums stirs me right to my soul."

"Yeah," he agreed. "Powerful medicine."

Hmmm. This guy's focus on his native heritage impressed me, but I didn't want to stray too far from my focus on finding out more about Tiahna's witching and Victor's murder. I wanted to know so much more about coyote skins, and other powerful stuff. The only way I'd find out was to ask. Even though I had just met him, this was my best opportunity.

"Did you read about the body found at Char's gallery last week?" I asked him.

"Yeah. I read in the newspaper the ideas about Native American ritual, and it just isn't so, at least not with Navajos or Apaches. I'm half of each. My mother is Navajo, my dad Apache. We don't take our cultural traditions to the outside world. Our beliefs and traditions are for our own protection and well-being. Native Americans are not terrorists; we don't smuggle people over borders, and our peyote is only used for spiritual purposes. If you want to know something about us, look up the Shadow Wolves, and read more about the Code Talkers."

I wasn't too far off when I called him Geronimo. He was an achiever.

He kept touching the pouch around his neck. "I wear my talisman for protection, and I've built a few rock shrines at vortexes I visit often. Tiahna doesn't practice her native protection rituals any more. I want to help her get back to that. That Mexican kid she lived with has got her too far off the Navajo Way."

With his every word, my admiration increased. He didn't ask me anything, so I just listened to him. In this way, while he talked and ate, I listened and ate. Tsosie and I became friends. I drove him back to the art school, and when we parted, he said, "Thanks for the Whopper."

I drove away convinced he had nothing to do with Tiahna's so-called *witching* or with Victor's murder at the spa. I seriously doubted he had anything to do with the body at the gallery.

I returned to Char's house where all was quiet. Char was probably sleeping. So as not to disturb her, I went straight to my room, booted up my laptop, and looked up Shadow Wolves.

Anyone who's read *The Last of the Mohicans* would be familiar with Indian tracking, or "cutting sign." Physical evidence, like footprints, dangling threads caught on mesquite thorns, broken twigs, discarded clothing, or dropped bits of paper, tells a story to an experienced tracker.

EIGHT

I leaned against the cushions of the couch saying to myself, *I won't get in the way of the police, but I can't stop thinking about it.*

In my head, I detailed the specifics of all the improbable happenings since my arrival in Sedona. I tried to connect the dead illegal immigrant, the paint-smeared doll, the robbery of the safes, and my newly-identified friend, Tsosie, to the attack on Victor. Maybe no relationship existed between each incident, but wasn't it too much a coincidence for it all to have happened at once? According to some "new thought," there is no such thing as coincidence. Everything is related. I agreed. In this case, it was, indeed, too much of a coincidence.

Since I couldn't accept coincidence in those happenings, then what about the fact that Randa lived and worked on the murder scene? That she was engaged in massaging life and love into her relationship with Garcia at the moment of Victor's death? What about the fact that Garcia left that scene at precisely the right moment? Could the text he received have been pre-arranged?

I didn't want to think that. Maybe the call could have been coincidental. Such thoughts leading back to Randa made me feel disloyal and guilty. How could I help Char and where should I begin? But hadn't I already begun with my contemplation of Randa's involvement? If I were to feel disloyal at every thought, I might as well have gone home.

I will not meddle, but I will stay alert.

Victor's murder might not have been premeditated. Given the fact of the open safe, plus Randa's mysterious intruder, someone with whom Victor had no previous connection could have attacked him. On the other hand, perhaps Victor had known the intruder, who was forced to kill to protect his or her identity. That was true only if one accepted Randa's story of an intruder.

Char, pale-faced and dark-eyed, came in and sat on the other end of the couch.

"Hi, Char," I said. "Neighbors have been bringing food. Can I make you a sandwich or something?"

She came to the kitchen with me and while I put her sandwich together, I asked, "How long have Rita and Tomás worked for you?"

"Let me think. Tomás has helped me with the last two workshops, and Rita has worked in the gallery—oh—it must be six years now."

"They were on vacation the last time I visited you, two years ago, so I didn't meet them then."

Char bit into her sandwich, chewed for a moment, and then put it back on the plate. "I told you, didn't I, that they have a son, Rubio? They call him Ruby. He worked for me during summer vacations. Then he got into drugs and left me stranded. I think I've told you that Tomás offered to fill in for him."

"Yes, you did. And Tomás seems to have made himself almost indispensable," I said.

"He is. Almost. He takes care of all sorts of details for me, and my art students like him. He flirts with them, you know."

"Yeah, I know," I said with cheerful sarcasm.

"Tomás is fun, and helpful, and harmless. He's always up front—what you see is what you get," Char said. "He swaggers a bit, but Rita has him under control."

"But Char, he seems to be particularly familiar, almost intimate, with your private concerns."

"That's my fault," she said. "I have a weakness for turning business associates into intimate friends. Victor warned me about it. He felt as an employer, I should be friendly but not familiar." She picked up her sandwich. "But you must have noticed that Tomás puts himself on familiar footing with women, all women, almost as soon as he meets them. And that includes me."

"Yes, I noticed that. But Victor gave you sound advice, Char. Tomás has given me information about your floor safes, your money arrangements, and Victor's relationship with Tiahna. And he claims that Randa hates Tiahna."

Char shook her head. "Sounds like he's been talking out of school. Randa doesn't hate her. I mean she doesn't wish her harm. Tiahna arrived unannounced into our lives. We had no warning, so we didn't have a chance for a gradual acceptance of the idea of her. By the way, where is Tiahna?"

"Oh, Tiahna," I answered. "She reacted in such a disturbed way Friday night that it scared me. All her Navajo cultural background surfaced. She whispered 'chindi' over and over." I couldn't force her to go to the spa with me to see Victor's body, so I took her to her mother. I've never seen anyone more terrified than she was when I told her what had happened. I guess she thought his spirit would still be there at the spa."

"Yes. And even more in the case of a violent death." Char choked up with emotion. "Thanks for not bringing her to the spa. Ghosts and witches and Tiahna whispering 'chindi' and looking haunted were more than I could have taken right then . . . or now."

"I hope my not bringing her there won't make the police think I was obstructing justice, but I was afraid she'd freak out." I looked at Char and stopped. She looked back at me with deep pain etched in her face. Emotion flooded over me. I put my arms around her, and we cried together.

Char said, "I'm so glad you're here, Maggie." She wiped her eyes. "I've got to go lie down. I didn't sleep at all last night."

She got up slowly and started from the room.

"Char, to answer your question, Tiahna and her mother have gone to the reservation for a healing ceremony that will last for days."

"Hmm," Char said. "I hope it helps her. I wouldn't know what else to suggest."

"What about Tomás's son? Is he still around?"

"I haven't seen him all summer. I know Rita worries about him all the time. I can't say I blame her."

"I might have seen him the other day," I said. "When I got to the gallery, Rita and a young man were standing closer together than strangers stand. And I accidentally overheard a few words."

"What did you hear?"

"Rita said, '*Ruby, you know we don't have that much money.*' They both looked serious, and she looked worried."

"Ruby is a big worry, and I'm not surprised he has money problems." Char sighed. "Well, mothers everywhere worry. I'm worried about Randa right now. I don't know if she's strong enough to withstand an accusation of murder."

"We'll help her. Three of us together can withstand it."

"Thanks, Maggie, you're a rock."

"Char, do you worry that Rubio might be privy to your affairs?"

"No, of course not. I trust Rita with no doubts at all, and Rubio always liked me. I gave him a job when he needed one. He just got off on the wrong track. He'll wake up when he gets older."

She looked so wrung out I just nodded and let her go.

Char's so trusting, not like me, trying to solve a paradox with logic. She just feels her way through.

I thought as well of my own tactlessness and, as usual, excused myself. In some situations, it was impossible to say the right thing, unless all you wanted was to be charming, and never cut through to the core.

The kitchen door swung in with Randa and Garcia. Randa looked stressed. "How is Mother?"

"She just ate a little, and has gone to lie down. Can you eat something? The neighbors have brought a lot of food." I rinsed and dried the cups and set them on the table. "Have you heard anything new this morning?"

"We've just come from the police station. They have an interagency agreement with the Department of Public Safety to send a detective to replace Garcia during the investigation. Their man is coming today. Garcia had to move out of his office." Randa poured coffee into the two cups I had just set down.

"I'm at the top of their list of suspects." Randa's young and fragile face looked crumpled.

Still aware of my internal dialogue about tact, I said nothing for a moment and then decided to hell with tact.

"Who tops your list of suspects?" I asked.

"Gar has a theory," Randa answered, turning toward him. But Garcia did not respond. After a short silence, Randa said, "I'm going to look in on Mother."

She started from the room then turned back. "Where did they take Dad?"

Again touched by sympathy, I put my arms around Randa. "They had to do an autopsy. I don't know when his body will be released to the mortuary."

"Poor Mother. This is all so awful for her." Randa seemed to drift away, moving without dynamic force or energy, unlike her usual briskness.

I turned to Garcia. Vibrations of fierce but controlled energy emanated from him.

"What a bitch of a day," he said. "And it's still got hours to go."

"We read in the paper you've had to abandon your Skylark investigation."

"Media hype," he said. "It won't be abandoned, just exposed, slowed down. Skylark is still my baby."

"Randa said you have a theory?"

He turned questioning eyes on me. "What are you up to?"

"I promised Char I'd be her official question asker." It sounded defensive even to my ears. "Besides, I'm a counselor, so I am compelled to know what happened here. I'm sure to make a nuisance of myself."

Garcia laughed. "More power to you, Maggie. Go for it. We need all the answers we can get." He shrugged. "I guess I've always seen myself as part of the solution, but now I'm on the other end of the problem."

"But you do have a theory?" I questioned again. "Do you still think someone left the body at the gallery as a signal to you?"

"Maybe it's being egotistical to think Victor died because of me, but I gotta believe the same person followed and trapped me at the spa in incriminating circumstances to stop Skylark. One thing went wrong though. Whoever set the trap didn't know I'd get called away at the crucial moment."

"So you think Victor just happened to stumble into it?"

"Yes."

"And it was Victor who opened the safe before he heard sounds and ran outside?"

"No, I think he found the safe open when he got there. Whoever opened it counted on me to come upstairs to investigate, which I would have done if we hadn't heard Victor drive up on his Harley. I think the bike covered up the sounds of the intruder upstairs."

"So if that's true, when Victor came in the intruder ran, and Victor ran after him. Or her. And how did they get a key to get in?" I pondered that question a moment. "Hmmm. The police closed the spa, didn't they?"

"That's right." Garcia yawned. "Will you tell Randa I've gone to my apartment to sleep? I'll call her later."

I sat alone at the kitchen table, deep in thought about Tiahna's visit to her grandfather, the medicine man.

Randa must have taken a nap. The house was quiet and for the next couple of hours, I was able to research Navajo medicine rituals on my laptop without interruption. When Char and Randa came out again, they worked on the details for Victor's funeral after the police released his body.

Early the next morning, I stepped outside the front door just as Tomás and Rita headed from their car to the house. Garcia drove in right behind them. Randa had come earlier and was already inside having coffee with her mother.

I stooped to pick up the *Red Rock News* and uncovered a folded sheet of paper. My name was on it. Surprised, I picked it up. A crude but vivid painting of a doll dressed in red, its neck twisted and tied, leaped out at me. Crude printing beneath said, "GO HOME, BITCH!"

I glanced down to see my own red robe. Startled, I thought—another coincidence? *No such thing—I wear this same red robe every morning.* All of our friends have seen it.

What have I done that could be called bitchy? I asked myself. The only person I questioned outside Char's house was Tomás, and all I asked him was who he thought had done it. Oh, yes, I did speak to him in a sharp tone when he called Randa "racist." Well, screw them. Nobody could make me go home until Char told me to.

I looked up. Three of Char's intimate friends walked up, three of my newfound friends. And Randa had also come into the house through this door just moments ago.

"Did you see someone leaving here as you came in? Anyone on the sidewalk?" I asked.

"People going to work," Tomás said. "Nobody special."

"I saw a guy on a skateboard. Why?" Rita asked.

"I just picked up an anonymous, threatening letter."

"Let me see it," Garcia demanded. He took out his handkerchief to hold it while he looked it over carefully. Rita and Tomás looked over his shoulder.

"Detective Richardson arrived today," Garcia said. "Show this to him."

"He'll just tell me to mind my own business," I said.

"Maggie, have you been minding anybody's business but your own?" Garcia asked.

"Would I do that?" I looked at Rita. "How are you two this morning?"

"We're okay. We just came by to see what we could do for Char. Is she up?" Rita asked. "Has Victor's body been released yet?" When I shook my head no, she and Tomás went into the house. Tomás had a strange, unreadable look on his face. *What's that about?* I wondered.

Garcia and I stood on the doorstep talking. "Do the police have any suspects?" I asked.

"Just Randa and me. They are investigating that turquoise nugget you spotted, but turquoise nuggets are plentiful around here. They fall out of jewelry sometimes and have to be replaced."

"This is a crazy, mixed-up case, isn't it? Did that paint-smeared doll have anything to do with Victor? It wasn't he who placed it at the gallery. I'm sure of that. He wouldn't do that to Tiahna, or to Char's workshop. I promise I won't meddle in the case, but you can't stop me from thinking about it. Will you at least let me do my thinking and ask you about where my thoughts lead me?"

"Well, you noticed that nugget by the cold plunge, so I know you're observant, and I believe you might be a clear thinker. Have at it, Maggie. I can't talk to you about it, but you can ask me questions and if I can answer them for you, I will."

"The doll smeared with red paint just doesn't make sense. No one close to Char would mess up her workshop like that, or rub a brush through one of her fresh paintings." I stood there wondering whether to share my latest thoughts with him. He'd just told me to go for it, so I blurted them out. "I don't want to believe that Tiahna pulled that doll trick on herself, but nobody else I can think of would have done it either. I want to talk to Tiahna in the worst way. Maybe Rubio could tell me something about her."

Garcia shook his head. "Randa doesn't like Tiahna, we all know that, but I can't see her hanging a doll, or smearing red paint, or any of this voodoo symbolism. It just doesn't fit. She's tuned in to peace and love and healing. And health food."

"Yes, I know. I can't picture it, either—or you, in a kimono, hitting Victor on the head with a golf club."

He gave me a skeptical look. "This has got to be cleared up, Maggie. Officially, I'm hogtied, but unofficially, I've got to know what's happening."

"Could you, unofficially, have that note analyzed for fingerprints?"

"Yes. I plan to, but I'll be surprised if we find any prints on it."

I thought for a few more seconds. "You know what they say. Follow the money. It's always the bottom line. If it's okay with you, I want to talk to Rubio. I think he was desperate for money, and so was Tiahna." I told Garcia that Tomás, Rita, and I had seen Victor and Tiahna open the safe at the gallery and found it empty. That had to tie in with the empty safe at the spa. I told him of seeing Rita and her son having a serious talk that sounded to me like it was about money, and then I said, "Rubio is heavier than Victor and just as tall. He could have clubbed him, pulled him up the steps, and then tipped him over into the water. Can you arrange for me to meet him? I'll just ask him about Tiahna and try to get a handle on the kind of person he is."

"Yes, I can do that, but please don't go without me. He's bad news."

"Okay. But let's wait until after Victor's funeral."

We went back into the house.

NINE

Perhaps because of the bizarre circumstances of his death, and all the media coverage, Victor's funeral evolved into a somber circus; a collection of colorful characters dressed in black.

Char, Randa, Garcia, and I stood together at the graveside. I knew each of us was sad in our own way, each trying to behave with dignity. Beside me were my son, Alex, and daughter, Jen, who'd driven up from Tucson and Phoenix. They had to go back late in the afternoon, but Victor had been like a favorite uncle to them since they were born, so they wanted to come. Randa, wrapped in a dark paisley shawl, stood in our midst weeping.

Tiahna's absence brought her to my mind, though maybe no one except me even thought of her.

Tomás and Rita stood near Char while their son, Rubio, who looked uncomfortable in pressed slacks and a shirt, hovered behind them. Rita probably made him dress that way for the services.

Photographed, reported, and recorded for the evening news on television, we were all unsettled by the notoriety.

Char and Victor, as well as Randa and Garcia, had many friends and associates in Arizona. It looked like most of them attended the funeral. A large number of them came to the house afterward. It seemed that they all wanted to talk to Char. She looked pale and drawn but insisted on speaking to everyone. Since most people are diffident in the presence of death and grief, no one demanded more than a few seconds. So many people passed through the house, though, that Char stayed standing far too long. Randa stood at her side. Garcia and Tomás were roving ambassadors, and both came in and out of the kitchen often.

I had volunteered to be in charge of the buffet for family and friends. Alex and Jen stayed to help me in the kitchen, so we were able to catch up on family affairs. They wanted to hear all about the happenings here in Sedona. They listened in as Garcia told me Rubio had agreed to meet us the next day near the Pink Jeep Tours office.

"That's a very public place," I objected.

"He chose it. Maybe he feels safer with lots of people around."

"Mom," Jen said. "What more are you getting yourself involved in?"

I'd told them the backstory about Victor, Doria, and Tiahna. "I'm just trying to find out more about Tiahna. She went to the reservation for a ceremonial medicine sing with her grandfather."

"Be careful, Mom. You're involved in some deep shit here," Alex said.

"Tell me about it." My two kids and I have always had a straight shootin' relationship, thank goodness.

Most of the guests came and left without eating, and so much food had been brought in, I didn't know what to do with it all. I asked Garcia on one of his passes through the kitchen, and he suggested we talk to Father Quejada, who arrived late after almost everyone else was gone.

When I walked into the living room to speak with him, I saw Randa and the priest taking Char down the hall toward her bedroom and the back patio. I thought they might be going for private prayers.

It was almost an half hour later before Father Quejada came back to the kitchen. I asked him if the church could use some of our excess food. He was delighted with the offer. Tomás came in as we were packing it in large baggies.

With my head down, I said, "Tomás, what time is it?"

"I don't have my watch today, Maggie. Rita took it in for a new crystal."

Father Quejada said, "It's three thirty."

"Thanks," I continued packing food, leaving some in the casseroles they arrived in. "I'll pick them up in a couple of days to return to their owners," I told him.

Randa came in. "Mother went to sleep at last. I don't think she has slept for over a week. And neither have I." She and Garcia left. Garcia said he'd pick me up tomorrow for our meeting with Rubio. Jennifer and Alex had a long drive back to Phoenix and Tucson, so they left a few minutes later. A couple of Char's neighbors and I cleaned up the kitchen, and then I collapsed, too.

The next day, when Garcia and I reached the Uptown Sedona shopping street where the jeep tours originated, we didn't see Rubio. We waited almost twenty minutes before he showed up. He ambled toward us. He seemed to be trying to play it real cool.

"Hey, man, you're grounded, right?" he said to Garcia. "So you can't have any business with me."

"This is just a private conversation between us," Garcia said. "Mrs. McGinnis is a friend of Mrs. Cooper's and of your parents. We want to know who you think is behind that voodoo attack on Tiahna."

"Oh, hell, that coulda been anybody."

"Come on, Rubio, just 'anybody' would have no reason to mess up Mrs. Cooper's workshop or to attack and intimidate Tiahna. Who'd want to frighten her like that?"

"I don't suppose you've thought of Randa? No love lost between them two." He seemed distracted and I turned to see what he was so interested in. Nothing special. A large black car cruised by much slower than the other traffic. His eyes followed it. "Or how about Mrs. Cooper? Tiahna upset her play-party for sure."

"But why would Char give Tiahna a job modeling if she intended to frighten her?" I asked.

"Why not? Painting her is a convenient way to frame her, right?" Rubio laughed unpleasantly at his own joke. "Or what better way to scare the hell out of her and still look innocent?"

"You mean you think she planned to ruin her own workshop in advance?"

"Hell, I don't think nothin', ma'am. I'm just tryin' to answer you guys' questions."

I looked up to see that same black sedan making another slow pass by us. Rubio, downright jittery, kept his eyes on it and wouldn't make eye contact with either Garcia or me.

"Do you know anything about Victor's death?" Garcia asked.

"I know it hit one hell of a blow to Tiahna. He's been supporting the baby since I'm out of work right now."

"What do you mean?" I asked.

"I guess you don't know Victoria is my baby, too." The black car stopped. A jeans-clad Hispanic man got out and started toward us. Rubio watched him cross the busy street and start down the sidewalk toward us. "Hey, you guys, I gotta go." He turned, jogged off in the opposite direction and disappeared into an alley.

The approaching man turned around, dodged through the crowd and stood at the curb gesturing to the black sedan, which had to make a U-turn and was held up by traffic.

Spurred by Rubio's sudden dash, Garcia and I hurried back to Garcia's car. Garcia pulled into the line of traffic a few cars behind the black sedan just as the light turned green. A block away, Rubio appeared from a side street on a motorcycle and sped away.

Garcia settled in to follow the car ahead.

I said, "Rubio gives the same answer everyone has given about the doll hanging: *anybody could have done it.* Same with Victor's murder. Everyone points out motives for everyone else and they all sound plausible."

Garcia nodded. "And what do you think, Maggie? Do you suspect anybody in particular?"

"No. But I'm pretty sure Tiahna didn't do it. She stayed with me for all but a few minutes from the time Victor left the house until Char called to say he was dead."

"How can I be sure you and Tiahna didn't do it together?"

"I guess you can't, unless you want to take my word for it."

I looked at him and saw by the smug smile and gleam in his eye he was pulling my chain. In the tourist-packed streets of Sedona, Garcia was able to keep the black car in sight. Rubio on his motorcycle had the advantage of size, weaving in and out without going into the approaching line of traffic. Nevertheless, the black car seemed to keep track of him.

"Maybe they've got a tracer on his bike," Garcia said. We followed Rubio and the black car all the way down through Oak Creek Village and beyond. The clogged traffic in and out of Sedona was bumper to bumper with tourists. Consequently, Garcia didn't need to hide the fact we were following. He moved up until he was behind the black sedan.

"Get the license number, Maggie," he directed.

I wrote the number on a clipboard he had on the seat between us.

In an unexpected move just ahead of us, a car pulled out to make a left turn and collided with a speeding little convertible. That brought us to a standstill. The black car pulled away beyond the fender bender. Garcia stopped, jumped out, and ran over to the side of the road to see which way the motorcycle and the car turned at the southern end of Oak Creek Village. The T-shaped intersection allowed traffic to go left toward Interstate 10 or right on Beavertail Flats Road toward Cornville and then to Cottonwood and Jerome. Garcia got back in the car.

"They went right."

Fifteen minutes passed before a detour unsnarled the backed-up traffic, allowing us to bypass the minor accident. By the time we reached the intersection and turned right, the black car passed us on the opposite side of the median, going back the way we had come. Garcia called an APB on his radio for traffic patrolmen to watch for the car.

"They're probably headed for Phoenix," he said to the dispatcher, "but, just in case, check on the way to Flagstaff, through Camp Verde to Payson, or back through Oak Creek Village and Sedona."

We continued on toward Cornville to look for Rubio on the motorcycle, but there was little hope of catching him. We had not gone far when we saw a motorcycle skiwampus by the side of the road and Rubio slumped against a mesquite tree. His face was bruised and swollen, and he was semiconscious. We picked him up, loaded him with as much care as possible into the backseat and headed back to Oak Creek Village. Garcia arranged for the motorcycle to be picked up and asked me to drive before we continued on to Sedona. The traffic was still bumper-to-bumper in both directions.

"Where are we going to take him?" I asked.

"To a clinic. I'm going to call a deputy meet us there," Garcia answered.

"Take me to Tiahna," Rubio mumbled.

"Tiahna has enough to handle without having you show up bloody at her door," Garcia growled, turning in his seat to watch Rubio.

"Of course she has. The first person you need is a doctor," I said.

"Take me to Tiahna."

"I guess we could stop by her mother's house," Garcia conceded.

"She has disappeared," I said. "I last saw her at her mother's house, last Friday night."

Garcia raised his eyebrows with a questioning look. "Hmm," he said. That was even more proof that nobody had been as concerned about Tiahna as I had been.

"Rubio," Garcia said. "You know José was killed?"

"Yeah."

"Did you know he was helping us track smugglers? Drugs and people?"

"He was? No shit? Well, I'll be damned," Rubio's swollen lips garbled his words. "Is that what got him killed?"

"If you didn't know, he kept it hidden pretty well, but somebody knew something, that's for sure," Garcia's terse words betrayed his anger. "Before he was killed, he gave us information about smuggling that included you."

Garcia indicated a medical clinic. I pulled the car into the parking lot. We helped Rubio out of the back seat and through the entrance. A deputy got out of a police car and followed us in. Garcia gave him a heads-up on the situation, telling him that Rubio could be a material witness for Skylark and could identify his attackers, if he would talk.

We then drove to the police station where Sergeant Slejak looked up and said, "Hello, Lieutenant. Good to see you." She nodded to me in recognition.

"Thanks, Sergeant. Good to see you, too. Can we see the lead detective? Richardson?"

"Let me call him and find out."

Moments later, Richardson came out of Garcia's office. Big, craggy, ruddy and hard-edged as a desert butte in appearance, Richardson fit the southwestern landscape. He exuded tough confidence, even arrogance, and he looked pissed. Damn! My treacherous libido kicked in.

He gave me a noncommittal inspection, and then said, "What's up, Garcia?"

"I just picked up an assault victim who's relevant to the Skylark investigation and took him to see a doctor. A deputy is there with him now. I'd like to put him into protective custody."

"Garcia, you're not on duty, you know. What did you do, make a citizen's arrest?"

"I might have lost my status, but not my mind, sir. I have been here on the scene, and I might have background information that could be helpful."

"Come in the office. Tell me about it." He turned away.

"Inspector, I'd like you to meet Maggie McGinnis. She's a friend and a colleague."

I looked at him. *Colleague?*

Detective Richardson nodded curtly. All business. "How do you do, Ms. McGinnis? You'll excuse us?"

"But Mrs. McGinnis is—" Garcia began.

"It's okay, Garcia," I said. "You go right ahead. I have other things to do." I turned to leave, but Garcia stopped me at the door.

"Maggie," he whispered. "I forgot to tell you. The only fingerprints on your threatening note were yours and Rita's. Mull that one over for a while." He turned to go inside for his meeting with Richardson.

Rita? Why would she want me to go home? I'd just have to ask her. Maybe she had a reasonable explanation. *Yeah, right, what's reasonable about an anonymous, threatening note?*

So there I was, afoot again. Lucky for me, Char's house was just a short distance away. I walked there; at least I'd be close to my car in case I had another inspiration.

The sun, a gigantic orange ball of fire, sank rapidly into the jagged red rock monoliths of Sedona's horizon. What a relief. Another day, which had offered so little positive reinforcement, flamed out in splendor.

Thinking a change in surroundings would do Char some good, I made a plan that would get her out of the house and appease my need for a Mexican food fix. When I let myself into the house, she wasn't there but had left a note saying she and Randa had gone to Flagstaff and would be back late.

An evening at Oaxaca restaurant in Uptown Sedona was the treat I chose for myself. I climbed the stairs in the restaurant designed to look like an old Spanish hacienda, with many arches, much Mexican tile, and walls painted to resemble old stone. My window table looked down on Highway 89A and the sparse "city lights" of the uptown businesses. Rejecting the luscious-looking margaritas in favor of a safe drive back, I ordered freshly made guacamole as appetizer and a combination plate of which I planned to eat half and take home the rest in a doggie bag. The tortilla chips were warm, the salsa warmer, and while nibbling, I couldn't help but think about the latest developments in this sad and twisted mystery.

My clues were meager: a turquoise nugget found at Victor's death scene, rags covered with smears of red paint used to clean Crazy Cat after the doll hanging, the doll itself hanging Tiahna in effigy, and the warning note from that morning with Rita's fingerprints. No clue tied anything to anybody except for the note, which was so random it wasn't necessarily even connected to the other events.

Garcia was at the scene with Randa before the crime but apparently away from her at the time of the actual killing. Could the phone call have been prearranged? He owned at least one piece of turquoise nugget jewelry and wore it to the reception the night of the crime, but at the time of Victor's murder, he wore the spa kimono and no jewelry, or so he said. He claimed both Victor's murder as well as Jose's were warnings aimed at him, to stop his investigations into human smuggling. Yet Garcia knew of Randa's jealous and bitter feelings toward Tiahna and of her anger toward Victor. Would it be too farfetched to think he saw Jose's murder as a diversionary tactic he could use to get rid of his future father-in-law?

Randa was on the scene before, during, and after the crime, but she only had those few minutes of Garcia's absence as murderous opportunity. She and Garcia either gave each other an alibi or they were both guilty. She also wore jewelry with nuggets that Saturday night, but she, too, wore only a kimono at the spa. Her apparent state of shock could have been caused by the discovery of her father's body and the horrible violence of his death or, if she were guilty, the discovery of her own capacity to kill.

My dinner arrived, piled high with a taco, an enchilada, a tostada, and rice and beans, all covered with melted cheese. "Could I have more salsa?" I asked the handsome young waiter with the flashing eyes. He brought it. I inhaled the aroma of my hot dinner while continuing my cold calculations.

Char, my dear Char, was next on the list. She had substantial reasons to dislike Tiahna but had gone to great lengths to conceal any outward evidence of it, going out of her way to help Tiahna. She was first to return to the studio after lunch Saturday and could have set up the doll trick then. I hadn't forgotten the anger she concealed over a decades old betrayal, and I also hadn't forgotten her outrage and hurt when she learned Victor and Tiahna had planned to take money from the gallery safe. Still livid with anger, Char had followed Victor to the spa Friday night.

Putting aside my prejudice in favor of Char and Randa whom I'd known and loved for so long, these murderous scenarios still seemed implausible. They just didn't fit.

I took another bite and had a gasping attack over an extra hot jalapeno pepper, bringing Tomás to mind. Oh, no, not Tomás, way too chicken. *Come on, Maggie, somebody you know killed Victor. Why not Tomás?* The only time I'd spent with either Tomás or Rita was when we'd followed Victor and Tiahna. I knew them the least well of anyone. Tomás knew where the Coopers kept cash. He and Rita stayed Saturday noon to lock up the studio. No one saw them go back in, but they could have waited until we were out of sight to set up that macabre thing with the doll. His turquoise-studded watch was at the jewelers for repairs. A new crystal, he'd said. Did he and Rita go straight home Friday night after the reception? The three of us saw Victor and Tiahna at the open safe in the gallery. If they went home, did they stay there? The chance I'd find the truth about their movements was remote. They provided alibis for each other.

So what about Rita? Char trusted her without reservation, and Rita knew the combination to the gallery safe. Did she know the combination to the spa safe as well? Although Rita was Victoria's grandmother, she disliked Tiahna. Rita also wore turquoise jewelry to the reception. Her fingerprints were on the note to me. She must know by now that her youngest son, Rubio, her baby, had been beaten up by strange men in a black car. She had to know he was in deep trouble, but how much she knew about Garcia connecting him to the investigation into human smuggling was beyond me at this point.

I knew almost nothing about Rubio, but he seemed to be a connecting link between Garcia's theory about illegal people, drug smugglers, and Victor's self-created tangle of infidelity and jealousy. I speculated that he was beaten up as a warning from men to whom he owed money. I had no proof of this, but it made sense. That's what happens in the movies. Did he know how to get into the safes? Maybe he tried to force Tiahna to get money for him on the strength of their mutual parenthood. If he ever had jewelry, he probably would have sold or pawned it for cash. Maybe Garcia knew or could find out more about Rubio. Unless, of course, Garcia was implicated in the nether world of crime, but Garcia gave the impression of being clean and trustworthy. Rubio didn't. Appearances could be deceiving.

Tiahna was the first, and only, person Rubio wanted to see when we brought him back to town. She posed, highlighted, at the center of the entire conflict. Victor went after Char's money, and Randa's, as well, on

Tiahna's behalf. But she *had* been terrorized. *Is it a crime to hang a doll in effigy? Is it a crime to 'witch' someone?* Property damage was a crime as was breaking and entering. What some mysterious assailant had done to the doll and to the workshop had to be taken as malicious.

As with Rubio, I knew nothing of Tiahna's depths but wanted to think she couldn't have carried out bloody sacrifice on a doll that represented her. Too, she was with me, more or less, during the murder of Victor. To me, Tiahna was one of the innocent victims here, but something about the doll effigy nagged at me still.

What about Tsosie? No. I was of the opinion he had nothing to do with any of this Anglo intrigue.

Doria's was the last name on my list. She acted with open hostility toward Victor, but she didn't fit as a killer of strong men. I found it difficult to imagine her racing around in the dark of night. And she'd been at home when I delivered Tiahna to her within such a short time after Victor's murder.

So I had a swarm of suspects, but no evidence, and only one clue had even a shred of identification. The most damaging information I had was the news about Rita's fingerprints on my note.

I looked down at my plate and realized I ate it all, every bite—so much for my plan of self-control and a doggie bag. I gave silent thanks for the expandable waistline of my Chico's jeans.

I looked up and saw Detective Richardson sitting alone at a nearby table. He watched me as I became aware of him then he dipped his head in greeting. Flustered, I smiled and gave him a small wave.

The waiter brought my bill in a leatherette folder. After I had paid it, I gathered my thoughts and my bag and stood. Richardson stood as well and said, "Ms. McGinnis, will you join me for a moment?"

"Sorry, Detective, I have to be going. No one knows where I am."

"Sit," he said.

So I sat, with a palpable feeling of being drawn into another vortex of energy, an energy that felt different from the peacefulness of nature. This energy crackled with male hormones; it crackled with my own female hormones. I had started to call my raging libido "Libby." *Down, Libby. Good Girl. Wow.* I sneaked a quick glance at his left hand. No ring there. I couldn't believe I cared, but hormones would tell.

"So in what way are you a 'colleague' to Lieutenant Lopez, Ms. McGinnis?"

Oh, Lordy! Here's a guy I could like. He cuts right to the chase.

"Garcia, you mean?" I had forgotten Garcia's last name was Lopez. "I've only known him for a week, but we both have an intense, personal interest in Victor Cooper's death."

"And that makes you a 'colleague'?" He looked doubtful then, "Just what is your connection to this case?"

"I have been friends with the Coopers all my life. And Garcia is engaged to Randa, the Cooper's daughter."

"I see, but 'colleague' usually refers to a professional relationship between people, doesn't it?"

"You're right. Garcia and I don't have a professional association at all. Maybe he used the term loosely."

"But he intended for you to come into his meeting with me this afternoon."

This guy had zapped me in our first conversation.

So I told him the truth. "Mrs. Cooper is in deep mourning and asked me to be her eyes and ears for a few days. So what can I say? I have an inquiring mind and inquiring minds want to know? Garcia and I've been kicking around our ideas trying to help the family any way we can, and it was a coincidence I was with him today when he picked up Rubio. It wasn't official business at all. We just happened onto him after he'd been injured."

He looked at me with speculative eyes but remained silent. I began to squirm in the silence. "Is that all?" I finally asked. "Can I go now?"

"Ms. McGinnis. Don't even think about getting involved in this investigation."

"I am involved in it," I said. "Do you think I could just walk away from my best friends and pretend nothing happened?"

"I'm not kidding, Ms. McGinnis. Be extremely careful you don't overstep the boundaries."

"Okay. Boundaries. You got it," I stood up, and answered him in my tarty voice, the one I saved for occasions such as this. "But it would be all right if I kept my eyes and ears open, wouldn't it, and if I maintained my friendly relationship with Lieutenant Lopez?"

"You're a sassy old gal. You know that?"

"Be careful who you call old," I flung back over my shoulder as I walked away.

It was still only eight o'clock, plenty of time left to follow up on my one solid piece of evidence. I could cut right to the chase, too. Rita locked the gallery earlier than this, so I called her at home. No answer. *Dang. How does one cut to the chase if no one answers the phone?*

If anyone observed me as I drove away from Oaxaca, they would have seen my mouth going a mile a minute as I replayed my conversation with Richardson. *Pompous ass! Okay, okay, so he annoyed me while he did his job. Did he follow me to the restaurant? No, that's gotta be coincidence— at least he likes Mexican food—sharp though, he picked up on Garcia's intro of me as his 'colleague.' Admit it, Mag, he's a hunk. Wow! And no wedding ring!*

I drove to Char's feeling as if I had done a lot that day without accomplishing anything. Char's bedroom door was closed, so I went straight to my room.

The next morning after my run and shower, I found a note from Char in the kitchen. She had appointments with her lawyer, doctor, and others, and she wouldn't see me until evening.

I left the house shortly after I read the note, stopping first at the gallery to talk to Rita. On my way, I rehearsed how to pussyfoot around the question of her fingerprints without accusing her of anything. My every approach came off lame and amateurish, so I decided to ask straight out.

After "hello" and "how-are-you" at the gallery, I said, "Rita, you know that voodoo note telling me to go home?"

She nodded, a guarded look in her eyes.

"Do you know anything about it?"

"I'd rather not say," she answered.

I shrugged. "Garcia had it tested for fingerprints. Mine and yours were the only ones on it."

"Oh, damn. I guess I'll have to tell you or look guilty myself."

"So you do know something about it?"

"Yes, I do." She drew a deep breath. "When Tomás and I drove up to the house, Randa was kneeling on the front step. She got up, waved to us, and went in. The corner of the note was sticking out, so I picked it up and read it."

"But you were standing by the car when I came out."

"Yes, when I realized Randa must have put it there, it blew me away. I don't want to know that kind of stuff. I couldn't think what to do so I just put it down and went back to the car. I wanted to leave but then you came out and Garcia drove up. I know I shouldn't have picked it up." Rita clenched her hands in agitation.

I knew Randa's fingerprints weren't on it. "Was Randa wearing gloves? She didn't have gloves on when she was in the kitchen."

"I don't know," Rita said. Her eyes dropped from mine. I was certain she was lying, but I had no clout here, not with her or anybody or anything. I consoled myself that Garcia knew about the fingerprints.

I felt shaken to my boots. The emotional malignancy encroaching into my life and into the lives of my friends sickened me. Rita and I stared silently at each other. Her eyes reflected some awful knowledge that sent me reeling. Could Randa, my Randa, who was like my own child, have devised the voodoo note? A large part of me refused to believe it, but with shame, I recognized a tiny kernel of doubt in my mind. Deep in Rita's eyes, I read flickers of doubt and suspicion.

After sitting stunned for several moments, I rose. "I'm like you, Rita. I would rather not know any of this. But anyway, thanks for talking to me."

Back in the car, I checked my cell phone. I'd missed a call from Randa. Dreading it, I called. She answered, saying she would like to talk to me. Could I come out to her house at the spa? I drove there. *What am I doing here? Why punish myself and tarnish my trust in my friends? Why not just go home like the note said?*

I read somewhere that everyone, in some small secret sanctuary of the self, is nuts. I believed it. Not only did I ask myself questions, I listened to my own answers. *Don't think that I'll go home just because I've been told to. I won't be manipulated by invisible evil.* Randa and Char needed me there.

Crime tape still surrounded the spa. Randa lived in a small, rustic cabin on the premises. An officer waved me to a stop and walked to the car window to inform me I could not enter the scene of a crime.

"I'm looking for Randa Cooper," I told him. "She lives right up there. You can watch me all the way to the door."

"What is your name?" He looked at his watch, recorded the time and my name in his police report then waved me through.

I parked the car and walked up a short driveway of the same ornamental gravel used inside the cold plunge. I crossed a shady flagstone patio and knocked on the front door.

"Oh, Maggie, come in."

The cabin and the spa were built of cedar logs against the side of a typical Sedona foothill of jutting red rocks that rose toward higher mountains. The sun shone from behind a ridge, which threw long shadows over the house. Even in broad daylight, it was dim inside.

Sleek art lights illuminated oil paintings, some of them by Char. Baskets, jugs, and a bronze cowboy sculpture were displayed in lighted niches along the walls. A concho belt lay draped over the back of a chair. A turquoise nugget filled the center of each concho. I lifted one end for a closer look. One empty-gem concho caught my eye. I looked away, not wanting Randa to see my reaction to the missing stone.

"Would you like something to drink? Iced tea, hot tea, coffee? Or diet soda?" Randa looked tired.

Despite Randa's weary appearance, I said, "Hot tea sounds good," knowing it would take time for her to heat water. I needed a couple of minutes.

"No problem," she said and went to the kitchen.

I removed a small writing tablet and a pen from my bag, measured a couple of the stones in the belt, and marked corresponding lines on the paper. In my mind's eye, I compared it to the size of the nugget from the cold plunge. I finished making notes and sat innocently turning pages of a scrapbook on the coffee table when Randa returned with the tea.

"Your scrapbook caught my eye, Randa. I see you keep it up-to-the-minute."

"It's one of my hobbies."

"You already have clippings of the reception the other night."

Tears sprang to her eyes and she seemed unable to speak, only nod. She set my teacup on the table and began to nervously twist a simple child's ring of tiny turquoise stones she wore on her little finger.

I drew a deep breath. "Randa, I know you and Garcia are at the center of the police investigation. They may even suspect the two of you killed your father accidentally while searching for a prowler and were so horrified you tried to cover it up."

"But that's not true! A prowler entered the spa. I *did* hear running feet." Her voice cracked.

"Who could it have been? Tomás? Rubio? Char?"

"Oh, Maggie, how can you even think Mother had anything to do with it?"

"She's under suspicion, too. She followed Victor to the spa to try to stop him from taking your money for Tiahna."

"But she didn't arrive in time. We found him together."

"So it seems."

"Damn you, Maggie." Randa screamed at me, close to hysteria. "I thought we could count on you. How can you stay at Mother's house and say these things behind her back?"

"Your mother and I have discussed this, Randa. A murder investigation is a dirty, nasty job. Everybody who knew the victim is suspect. The more intimate they were with your father, the more suspect they will be."

"Well, Mother didn't do it, and Garcia didn't do it, and I didn't do it!" Her voice rose higher and tighter with each word. "Why don't they look at Tiahna and some of her mysterious connections?"

"They will, but prepare yourself, Randa. The police will probe your soul if they haven't already."

"They have," Randa said.

I dreaded the next question, but I had to ask it. "Randa, Rita said she saw you kneeling on the porch just before I found that horrible note yesterday. She said she saw the note, picked it up and read it." Her wounded look stabbed me to the heart. "I *know* you didn't put it there, but did you see it? I'm trying to work out who really left it and when."

She pulled herself up with rigid dignity. "I was expecting Garcia. I heard cars and went out to have a private moment with Garcia. It had been a really hard week and Garcia's strength sustains me. I saw Rita and Tomás were there, too. I knelt down to tie my shoe and went back inside. That's what she saw."

"So you don't know who put it there, either."

Randa's shoulders sagged in despair. She looked crushed and defeated.

I waited a moment, feeling as miserable as Randa looked. Hoping to break the tension, I asked, "Have you found Crazy Cat since the night . . . since Friday?"

"Yes. Crazy came home . . . came here, I mean, because Dad's motorcycle has been here, in my garage, ever since . . . ever since that night. They say animals go away to mourn alone. Crazy has lived—eating, sleeping, and sitting—in his basket on Dad's motorcycle. When he came home, he jumped up to that basket and just spread-eagled in it."

A sharp rap on the door made us both jump. I hadn't heard anyone outside. I followed Randa to the door. Detective Richardson and a uniformed officer stood on the doorstep.

"Miss Cooper," Richardson said. "Will you go to the station with this officer, now? Garcia is there waiting for you. We have more questions for you both." He paused. "And we have a search warrant for the spa and your house."

Randa, fear in her eyes but a defiant tilt to her chin, picked up her bag.

"Just a minute. We need to search your bag, too."

She handed over her bag with an exasperated roll of her eyes. After he had thumbed through it, he handed it back and Randa walked out the door without another word.

I followed.

Richardson turned to me. "Do you have a minute, Ms. McGinnis?"

"Call me Maggie. Yes, I do. May I come inside the spa with you? I want to show you something."

His look said, *My God, you've got gall.* Aloud, he said, "No."

"But I think it is evidence, sir."

"How did you get evidence?"

"The day of the doll hanging, I was in a massage room with Randa. I saw it then."

"If you've fouled up my case, you're in serious trouble, lady." His eyes were hard, unrelenting. "Okay. Come in and show me what you're talking about."

In the massage room, I opened the cupboard under the sink. The paint-smeared cleaning rags were gone.

Richardson said, "The rags found in this cabinet were already taken into evidence. You seem to think we're incapable of handling an investigation."

"I'm glad you found them. I think they will prove Randa's innocence."

"That's where we differ," he growled. "We think they prove her guilt."

"But those rags were used to clean the cat after the doll hanging at the studio. What connection do you think the doll has with Victor's murder two days later?"

He ignored my question, sighed and crossed his arms over his chest. "Okay, Maggie. Why don't you tell me how you've got this all figured."

I did just that, told him everything about everybody I'd outlined in my head at the restaurant.

When I finished he looked at me with annoyance and spoke to me as if he were talking to a child. "Here's the way I see it. Miss Cooper burned with jealousy of her half-sister. When jealousy grows to huge proportions as I think Miss Cooper's had, it feeds off the puniest incidents. Miss Cooper's envy of her Navajo sister's good looks, of her dad's concern, even of her mother's painting her half-sister tore at her soul. Frustration ate at her, so she savaged the doll to scare her sister away. But it backfired on her. Her dad started robbing the family till to help her hated sister. So when Miss Cooper discovered her dad in *her* office safe about to take her hard-earned money to give to this interloper, she lost all control. I think she murdered her own father in a jealous rage. And it all started with the petty detail of her cat running in the paint when she hung the doll."

His complacent summation gave me goose bumps. My own suspicions had led me along the same trail. However, I had no intention of revealing any doubt whatsoever to Detective Richardson. Instead I leapt to Randa's defense.

"You're taking the easy way out," I accused. "Blame Randa and the case would be closed. No sweat."

I could see I had not succeeded in putting him on the defensive. He laughed, thus keeping me defensive. Damn.

"It's so simple," I said. "Victor and the cat arrived at the spa with the cat's paws covered with wet, red paint. They assumed the cat had been to art class. I came on them while they were laughing about it and cleaning him up so the paint wouldn't be tracked around the spa. No big deal."

I still didn't shake him. "Tell it to the judge." He dismissed my thoughts and me as unimportant. "In the meantime, I've got to tell you, I love to see a woman enjoy her food."

It was not easy being me at that moment, but I did manage to get out of the spa, into my car, start it up and drive away without screaming and kicking him in the shin. After I got away, my mouth started going a mile-a-minute while I discussed the situation with myself. And while I was so angry with him, my alter ego Libby, who kept trying to remind me how damn attractive he was, had to be restrained.

TEN

Char, Rita, and Tomás sat around a small table on the patio, going over figures in a ledger. Randa and I parked ourselves in a wooden garden swing, and Garcia leaned back against the low wall surrounding the patio.

"Where the hell is Tiahna?" Garcia asked.

"First time we ever needed her, we can't find her." Randa's tone was bitter.

"Her mother took her to Willow Water," I said.

"How did you know that?" Garcia asked.

"Tsosie Tsiniginnie told me."

"Well. You do get around, Maggie. I'll call Richardson, and he can ask the Navajo Police if they'll pick her up, and her mother, too, for questioning."

"Garcia, I've been thinking," I said. "I need to go to Page to pick up some clothes. If I could get there before the police, maybe I could talk to Tiahna and Doria. I know the area, and I know the trader at Willow Water."

Garcia stood away from the wall. "That's a nifty idea, Maggie, as long we go together. Richardson won't let me near his investigation, but if you can get me to Tiahna and her mother, I'd like to talk to them, too. Besides, if Richardson or the department ever found out I let you go up there alone . . . well . . . it wouldn't be pretty. So I go with you, or you don't go."

Hmmph, like you could stop me, I thought, but I said, "We can leave early in the morning and come back the next day."

"Is five in the morning early enough?"

The scenic route from Sedona to Page winds up through Oak Creek Canyon around the east side and out the north side of Flagstaff. It heads down off the mountain into the pink and blue desert and along the Vermilion Cliffs. Running up through the big cut, through sage and cedar flats until beautiful Lake Powell in the distance guides one into Page, Arizona. The breathtaking landscape appears to be mile after mile of uninhabited scenery. In fact, Navajo people do live there, but away from the highway where the tourists fly by. The highway is dotted with Native American market shacks, filled with rugs and cedar berry jewelry, much like the one where Doria works near Sedona.

"Lots of empty space out here," Garcia commented.

"Yes, and I love it—hot and wide and empty. The clouds and the rocks and the silence remind me of the Navajo."

Garcia pulled out to pass a slow-moving motor home. As he turned, we heard a thwack, and the steering wheel spun in his hands.

"What the hell!" he exploded. "The steering is gone!"

We were halfway out into the oncoming lane. A fast-moving truck topped the hill coming toward us. The truck horn blared. Garcia, instantly grasping our only chance, stepped hard on the gas and we shot across the lane.

My mind leaped into a detached dimension. I watched disaster race toward us, like watching a movie play out in slow motion.

Garcia's small, fast sports car responded with ease. The front wheels grabbed the dirt on the soft shoulder and spun the back end toward the truck. The rear end of the truck, almost past, popped a glancing blow to the rear bumper of Garcia's car and whirled us in a crazy circle. The car skidded across the rough desert floor doing mega_miles per hour backward, scratched over sage brush, bounced off rocks and slammed into a scrub cedar tree, which it climbed to the top, still backward, before it slammed back down on its nose. The hood popped open as the air bag knocked me back, then just as quickly it was gone, leaving me in a haze of smoke—no, wait. Not smoke. It smelled like, what? Powder. Really?

I hung face down at a goofy tilt. The seat belt cut across my chest into my left hip.

In my detached state, I noticed small, specific details like Garcia's hand reaching to turn off the motor. It struck me as funny and I think I laughed. It occurred to me I should unbuckle my seatbelt, but I didn't. I heard Garcia's voice, but he sounded far away and I wasn't in the mood to put up with his cop machismo just then. I didn't answer him.

After what seemed like hours, someone reached across my body to disengage the seatbelt, lifted me to the ground, and covered me. A few minutes later, Garcia lay beside me, protesting.

"Look in my wallet. I'm a policeman, dammit . . . I want to look under the hood."

I opened my eyes. Blue sky above us. The sun's rays still slanted from low in the east. I wasn't out very long at all.

I began to move my arms and legs. Everything worked.

Navajo Police, Arizona Highway Patrol, and a few curious onlookers crowded the scene. I struggled to sit up.

"You'd better lie still, Ma'am," a patrolman said.

I heard a gruff voice say, "The crazy son of a bitch pulled out right in front of me." Must have been the truck driver.

"The steering went," Garcia said. "Look under the hood."

I opened my eyes again to look at Garcia. His nose, swollen and bleeding, dominated his face. His eyes were turning black and blue.

"Thanks, Garcia," I said. "You did good." I tried to lift my right hand toward him and saw it, too, was swollen and bleeding. For the first time since the impact, I felt pain.

Another voice said, "The tie rod has been cut at least half way through."

Garcia exhaled a gust of air.

He reached over with his left hand to grasp my hand, and I winced in pain. He jerked his hand back and turned his head to meet my eyes. In that brief moment of suspended time and shared pain, we bonded.

And then he whispered, "Somebody tried to kill us, Maggie."

Stunned, shaken, grateful to be alive and unhurt in comparison to how awful it could have been, Garcia and I spent the night in the Page hospital under observation. The doctor who attended us, a friend I'd known for many years, said neither of us had serious injuries. The highway patrolman said it was Garcia's skillful driving that saved us. A claims adjuster from Garcia's insurance company said his car was totaled and that the accident didn't look like an accident at all, more like foul play.

The truck driver said, "Omigod, you guys scared me."

The motor home people never saw the wreck and had continued on their way.

Garcia's nose was broken by the airbag. Apparently, my right hand was thrown back against the window or the frame. My wrist was sprained and my little finger broken, plus multiple contusions on my face from the force of the air bag. Who knew they deployed with such power? And thank God, they did.

About noon, we were released from the hospital. Garcia had arranged for a rental car to be delivered to the hospital, so we drove to my house a few blocks away. Just as we walked in, the landline began to ring.

Randa, almost hysterical, shouted in my ear. I handed the telephone to Garcia and listened to his side of the conversation.

"We've been in the hospital. Our cell phones had to be turned off. We just walked in the house, and I haven't turned mine on yet."

He took the time right then and there to turn it on and read messages while he continued to listen to Randa. He mouthed to me, "Sixteen missed calls." All I heard on his end were hells and damns, from which I concluded that things were not going well in Sedona.

After he hung up, he turned to me. "I've got to get back to Sedona. Randa and I are officially the prime suspects, and she's just about to flip out." He sat quietly in the chair by the desk for a few minutes, and then said, "Maggie, I don't want to leave you here alone. Who knows what will happen next?"

"I'm not alone in Page. It's my home. I know everybody here, and nobody in Page will try to kill me." I tried to reassure him. "You're in more danger than I am."

He looked up at me with blackened eyes that made him look like a masked cat burglar, or Zorro. "Let's call the Navajo Police to find Tiahna. You're not safe wandering around alone looking for her. Something genuinely screwy is goin' down here."

"I know. And it just keeps getting screwier, but Garcia, Tiahna is Navajo, and the Navajo nation is a sovereign state. Whatever we say, they'll do it their way."

I tried not to offend him but I disagreed about a couple of things he said. "I think whoever cut the tie rod in your car wanted to get you, not me. I'll be safer on the reservation than you will be in Sedona. And I won't be 'wandering around' as you put it. I'll know where I am just about all the time. Let's wait before we call any police departments. Give me a chance first."

So Garcia left Page driving a rented car.

Soon after, I went downtown for a sandwich in the four-wheel drive Ford Bronco that Ron had kept for desert treks. He left it behind when he took off. I had not yet sold it. When I walked in the Glen Canyon Steak House who should I see but Ron, my ex, sitting in "our" booth with his back toward me. Snuggled against him, a thin, suntanned blonde threw back her head and laughed, her mouth open and all her beautiful teeth showing. It was Casey, the girl whose job I had salvaged. My stomach seized up as if a giant hand had squeezed it. I turned mid-stride and rushed out, walked around the corner of the building into the shade and gasped for air. It only took a minute for my anger to kick in. I sucked in a deep breath, marched right back inside and over to their booth.

"Well, fancy meeting you here."

They looked at me in astonishment. Casey's mouth dropped open and her face flushed deep red. She put her face in her hands and hid from me.

Ron stared at me, speechless for once in his life.

"What's the matter, Ron? Did the mountains get too rugged for you?"

"Maggie, I can explain."

I put both hands up, palms outward. "Don't start. The last explanation you gave me was pure bullshit. Who needs it?" I raised my brace-enclosed right arm in what I hoped looked like a nonchalant salute and left the restaurant.

Having said my piece, I got back in the car and headed for the Willow Water Trading Post to ask about Tiahna. By the time I reached Willow Water, I'd controlled my breathing. That was the first time I'd seen Ron since he left. He didn't appear to be losing any sleep over our failed marriage, so why in hell had I continued to have nightmares over it?

At the trading post, the trader confirmed Tiahna was at her grandfather's hogan in Navajo Canyon.

"Tiahna came home 'chindi.'" He shook his head. "She arrived in such a storm, she suffered in body as well as spirit. When the early snow arrived last week, her grandfather began the dance. The *Yeibichai* will go on a few more days."

Unwelcome at the ceremony, I went back home. It was six forty-five when I arrived. Too tired to think, I took one of the pain pills the doctor gave me and fell into bed, my broken bones throbbing. Somebody wanted one or both of us maimed or killed. The thought gave me goose bumps. Only Randa, Char, Rita, and Tomás knew of our trip unless Garcia mentioned it to someone else because I hadn't. I had to admit I was scared. Plus, after the restaurant, I had to come to terms with Ron and Casey. Before I fell asleep, Tsosie entered into my consciousness. *Thank goodness for my Geronimo.* If necessary, I knew he would help me unravel the Navajo side of things.

The pill kicked in and I drifted off to sleep. Don't think I even moved until the land line by the bed awakened me. I looked at the clock. It was only one fifteen in the morning. I'd been asleep about five hours.

"Hello?" I was still groggy.

Garcia said, "Rita's dead." No time wasted with preliminaries.

I was instantly wide-awake. My throat closed up and the words I spoke sounded strangled even to me. "Rita? How? When?"

"Someone killed her last night about around ten or ten thirty. A blow to the back of the head just as she arrived at St. John's for confession."

"Poor Tomás. What will he do without her? She anchored him." My thoughts scattered. "Who did it?"

"Don't know yet. Richardson thinks it could have been me and Randa. From the shape of the wound, they used a blunt, heavy object but no weapon was found at the scene."

"My God. I can't believe this."

"They're also looking for Tiahna now. They think maybe she's still here somewhere."

"No, she's definitely in Navajo Canyon at her grandfather's place, sick in body and soul. I'm going there in the morning after I stop at my office."

"Sorry to wake you up, but I wanted you to know. Also, Char wants to talk to you, asked you to call her."

"You sure, Garcia? It's the middle of the night."

I called her.

Her voice was tight. She was obviously distraught. "Tomás is numb with grief."

"How are you?" I asked. "Randa?"

"Richardson has been busy trying to build a case against her, but there is no evidence except her presence at the spa. Now he seems to think she killed Rita, too. She's on the edge. Garcia and I are trying to persuade her to see a therapist."

We talked a few more minutes, and then Char said, "Oh, Maggie, please hurry back. We're falling apart."

I couldn't go back to sleep. After eight-thirty, I went to the office and learned Casey had called in sick. She was safe from me. I'd accepted Ron's right to do as he pleased and had no intention of bringing personal issues into my workplace. I filled my boss in on why I'd have to be out longer, not least of which was my sprained wrist and broken finger. Everyone said they missed me. I enjoyed seeing them all and my spirit rebounded.

I returned to Willow Water in what I now considered my Bronco. In the back was my sleeping bag, a Coleman stove, and camping gear. All Ron had taken was his sleeping bag. I could only guess that he was trying not to be a complete horse's ass, and would replace what he needed with newer stuff. I put in what food I would need for an overnight, just in case. Ron had trained me well. I asked directions at the trading post.

"Are you sure you can drive with one arm?" the trader asked. "You will be going over some pretty rough roads. You probably can't get into the *Yeibichai*. It's sacred and the dancing goes on all night. The whole thing is a private, insider's dream." He looked at me hard and seemed to be thinking. "You should take gifts anyway. Just in case. A ceremony is an extremely expensive undertaking, especially for people on welfare. The family giving the sing feeds everyone who comes, no matter how long they stay."

Under his direction, I bought lengths of brightly-patterned sing cloth, flour, a twenty-five pound bag of pinto beans, sugar, and coffee. I added baking powder and shortening when Bob told me fry bread is the staple for the dozen or more people who would be there for several more days and nights. He didn't know how many days they had sung, only that it started the week before after the snow.

After he had helped me load the supplies, the trader said, "Stay on the most traveled road. You can't miss it."

First time around, I did miss it because I was talking to myself about the trader, yet another guy who turned me on just by being friendly, and he had a cute butt to boot. Too bad the ring on his left hand made him off limits.

Yeah. I chose the left track at the fork in the road, which took me in a wide loop back to the highway by way of *Tsai Skizzi*. An hour and a half wasted, all because of Libby's libido. Alter ego or not, she was getting out of hand.

I drove back to the starting point: a dirt road leading away from the highway toward Navajo Mountain. It was hardpacked at the turnoff, worn smooth with ruts, but the road graders had not been out since the storm.

A couple of miles in I saw a Navajo hogan on a rocky rise above a valley. Navajo Mountain, capped with fresh snow, rose behind it. Pink cliffs overlooked Navajo Canyon on one side. Square Butte and White Mesa edged the other side, and with the long valley dotted with scrub cedar and browsing cattle in front, the hogan sat surrounded by wide-open space. A quarter mile further along, a scruffy white trailer shared the scenic beauty.

Between the hogan and the trailer, I chose the opposite fork in the road. With confidence, I turned to the right. Up the hill, around and down I whizzed in the Bronco, and saw that I was once again in sight of the same hogan and white trailer.

When I came out of a blind curve, a pickup trailed by a great cloud of dust raced toward me at breakneck speed. Still nervous after the incident two days before, I pulled off onto the sandy verge. The pickup zipped by a young Navajo in a hardhat behind the wheel.

When I turned my steering wheel with my undamaged left hand, the tires dug into the sand. I had neglected to put my old SUV into four-wheel drive.

I got out to look the situation over. The tires were not too deep in the sand yet, but I didn't dare try again in my one-armed condition. I looked around. On the left, the valley rose to a rocky ridge. Atop the ridge, a Navajo couple, he in a red shirt and she in a flowered blouse, sat watching me without expression. I looked back at them for a moment, but they gave no sign I could ask them for help even though they looked straight at me. I waved. As soon as I made the first gesture, they arose and started down the rock-strewn hillside. The man's left wrist and hand were wrapped in an ace bandage.

"*Yah-te-hey,*" I said, meaning hello, how are you, greetings. I stuck out my left hand. "I'm Maggie McGinnis from Page. Maybe you knew my husband, Ron McGinnis?"

We shook hands all around, smiling and nodding. The woman had pink and blue plastic curlers in her hair.

"Well, I heard that name," the man said. "I'm Husky Begay, and she's Ruth." He lifted his chin to indicate his wife with his lips pushed out in the Navajo way. "What're you doin' way out here?"

"Trying to get down into Navajo Canyon to where they're having a ceremony. Am I on the right road?"

"Well, you've been going in circles. We watched you. Turn right over there and go past that trailer," again with the pursed lips. "That's Helen Betony's place, and that's my place right over there. We sit out here almost every day when I'm not working construction."

I turned to look. It was the place I admired. "*Nizhoni,*" I said, meaning beautiful. "Are those your cows?"

"Yes. One of the calves kicked me in the arm the other day." He laughed and held up his bandaged left hand.

"Frisky calves just gotta kick," I said.

"Yeah, but she took care of me." He stuck out his lips toward his wife.

Ruth laughed and said, "Yes, I chased that calf away good."

"What happened to you?" Husky pursed his lips toward right arm.

I described the car wreck and Husky said, "We heard about that. *Ni'itso hoteni . . .* you were lucky."

News travels fast on the reservation.

"I hoped you could help me put the Bronco into four-wheel drive, but I wouldn't ask you to risk rehurting your sore arm."

"Three of us can do it. It's easy."

Husky and Ruth helped me switch the wheels. He was right—with three of us, it was no problem. I got in and drove out of the sand onto the roadway. I stopped to say thanks and Husky said, "They're having a *Yeibichai* down there at Hatathlii's."

"I know," I answered. "I'm looking for Tiahna and Doria."

"Hatathlii is singing for Tiahna. She came back sick. *Doh haly ahndi . . .* not thinking right. She's down there. That's where you'll find her."

"Thanks." I turned my face toward the road.

Husky said, "Well, now you know where we are, you come back and see us again. We sit out here every day."

I nodded and started to drive away. Husky called, "Are you going to stay down there at that sing?"

"They don't know I'm coming," I said. "Maybe they won't want me to stay."

Husky shrugged. "They sing all night, you know."

I looked at my watch. One o'clock. I couldn't seem to break away from this powwow here with my newfound friends, not without being rude.

"I'd like to stay if they'll let me. Nothing I can do but go there and ask." I lifted my hand in farewell and took my foot off the brake. I had the Bronco in gear, so it moved forward before Husky could say another word. He asked as many questions as I do.

The road coming down off the mesa lived up to the trader's description, steep and rocky all the way. It was all I could do to keep my vehicle on track. Winding down the road on the side of the cliff, I could see several pickups parked around a hogan at the bottom. What a relief it was when I pulled in beside them.

Doria stepped outside the hogan but didn't speak. "How is Tiahna?" I asked. "Bob Redd at the store said you're holding a ceremony for her."

"Yes. After my father saw Tiahna, he could feel the sorrow that made her sick. He knew no one else could help her. The ceremony will make her better." Doria's dark eyes seemed to defy me to understand.

I felt humble. Perhaps it was impossible for me to understand ancient, esoteric tribal ritual. Nonetheless, I didn't forget why I had made this difficult trip. "Can I talk to Tiahna?" I asked.

"No. She can't talk to anybody during a sing or for four days after."

"The police in Sedona want to talk to her. They have contacted the Navajo Police to come and get her, and you, too. I wanted to get here before they did."

"The ceremony is dangerous. If Tiahna or my father makes even one mistake, she could be blinded or crippled for the rest of her life. The spirits direct the ceremony, and it must always be the same." Doria's eyes remained impassive, her voice implacable. "The Navajo Police know this. They know how to avoid the danger of angry spirits. They know she can't come out until the ceremony is complete. We have ways of working around the white man's commands."

Her news made me feel better. The Navajo Police would do things their way, according to their understanding of tribal culture. I thought Tiahna would definitely benefit from her ceremony if she had faith in it. I sincerely hoped for her recovery, whether I was able to talk to her or not.

"Tiahna stayed with me from the time Victor left the house until we got the telephone call saying he was dead." I tried to explain my thinking to Doria. In her patient way, she listened. "I'm sure something more than Victor's death is bothering her. Is this ceremony because she felt *witched* by the doll hanging?"

I received no answer. Doria remained remote and steely.

"I want to help her, and you." I heard the pleading in my own voice.

"If one of your people suffered in the hospital, the police wouldn't force them out," Doria said.

"You're right, they wouldn't," I answered. I could tell Doria thought me both presumptuous and wrong to intrude, even if with good intentions. I backed off. I remembered the gift. "Doria, I've brought food from the trading post and some sing cloth. The trader told me what you might need."

She walked with me to the back of the Bronco. Together we managed to get the tailgate open. My injury kept me from helping much, so Doria called to some of the men in the encampment to carry the boxes of supplies.

Scattered all around the hogan and along the floor of the canyon were temporary camps of people there for the sing. People sat around campfires or were sacked out in sleeping bags. Those who participated in sings slept all day to prepare for long nights of intense spiritual activity heightened by the peyote used in their religious sacraments.

I climbed back into the driver's seat, my right wrist throbbing, my head aching, and my zeal for discovery shot. I would have stayed in spite of my pain. I wanted to be a part of, or at least witness, the curing ceremony for Tiahna, but a vast gulf of cultural differences precluded my participation. Unable to get a grip on the inscrutable without help and most of all, not invited or welcome, I knew I had to leave. The ceremony belonged to the Navajo people.

I started to drive out of the yard. Doria, hand raised, called, "Wait."

I stopped. Doria came to the car and got in the passenger side. Her eyes were filled with tears. Her face crumpled, she spoke in a hesitant, stumbling voice.

"My father got so mad at me when I had a baby with a white man who had no heart for *Dineh*. He said I would destroy the harmony of my family but his warning came too late. By then, I was pregnant. I didn't know Tiahna would be the one without harmony. I didn't know."

Doria stared at the cliffs in unbroken silence for several minutes. At length, she said, "Tiahna is important to my father. After her birth when he stopped being angry at me, he told me harmony is born out of disharmony because only when we feel at war will we feel the need for peace. He said Tiahna brought us a gift of beauty, but that disharmony would come to her as it came to me as it comes to everyone who needs to learn to walk in beauty.

"I didn't want her to be the one who suffers, so now I have to spend all I've got to bring her peace. For her to have peace, my father must drive away the spirits who haunt her. Each of these people here takes part in the ceremony. It costs a lot to feed so many people."

She sighed and then gave a little self-deprecating laugh. "I stopped carrying my little bag of cornmeal years ago, but now that this trouble has come to Tiahna, the ceremonies were the first thing I thought of. The ceremonies give me the power to live in the white man's world and still be glad I'm Navajo."

She stopped speaking and got out of the Bronco.

I, not having had a chance to speak and now unable to because of being all choked up, waved and once again started to drive away.

"Wait," Doria called again.

My spirit jumped up in hope until Doria said, "I think Tiahna will talk to you when we return to Sedona."

"Is Tsosie here? He told me he would be a dancer at the end of the ceremony."

"Yes. Today is the last night of the sing. He's sleeping now, but he'll probably leave here early in the morning."

"I don't suppose I could stay for the ceremony tonight?" I asked, already knowing the answer.

"No. If anyone who doesn't understand or who doesn't accept what is happening is in the hogan, the spirit of harmony will be blocked. Harmony must be free to flow around the circle or everyone there will be in danger of violent spirit anger, and the ceremony will be wasted."

I turned away. For the third time, Doria stopped me. "Do you want to come back and talk to Tiahna?"

"Yes."

"I'll ask my father."

I waited while Doria went into the hogan. When she returned she said, "My father said you should come back on the third day from today."

I went home to Page encouraged, hungry, and sleepy. Over the course of the next two days, my life took on new meaning, not vital, just different. My imminent return to the hogan in Navajo Canyon upended my logic. My imagination bewitched me with ideas of mystical attraction and gave me a sense of plunging into unknown depths. During the evening of the second day, the trader at Willow Water called with a message from Doria. She had sent word she would catch a ride to the trading post for supplies, would meet me there, and ride back down with me. I said I'd be there early the next morning.

ELEVEN

I was told Doria would stay the night in Willow Water with some of her family. The morning I drove there, I came upon her, supplies stacked around her, waiting for me at the turnoff. We loaded her boxes and bags and were on our way in the lightening sky just before sunrise. As we rode, Doria talked to me about going on the placement program of the LDS Church when she was eight years old. She went to San Bernardino to live during the school year with a Mormon family whom she called her foster parents. She came home to Navajo Canyon each summer for three months and spent her days herding sheep or helping her father gather wild plants to dry for ceremonies.

"Plants?" I asked.

"My father has always used a lot of sagebrush," she said. "It works for headaches or colds or burns or just about everything. He uses it to clear away disharmony. It smells good." She talked eagerly. I hoped it was because she decided I was a friend instead of a foe.

"One summer, when I was sixteen, my foster family took me with them on their vacation. We drove across the country and camped in National Parks. We saw the Statue of Liberty and the White House. I didn't get home until the middle of July and my mother wouldn't let me go back to California that year. She was afraid I would never come home again."

"Did you want to go back?" I asked.

"Oh, yes. My foster mother called the trading post and cried. The next summer they came to see us at my father's hogan. My father doesn't speak English. They tried to talk to him about my education, but he's a medicine man and he knows the best ways for the Navajo people."

We turned off on the dirt road as the sun came up and soon saw Husky and Ruth's homestead. Cattle still browsed in the long meadow of pale gold grass dotted with patches of old snow. I looked toward the ridge and saw a solitary figure in silhouette. I touched Doria's arm and pointed.

She looked and then said, "Yes. There's Ruth." I stopped the Bronco to wait as Ruth started down the rocky path to meet us.

"Hello!" I called out in my Anglo way. Doria remained silent. Ruth and Doria shook hands and said *"Yah te hey."* Ruth, solemn and unsmiling, then shook hands with me. I felt I had been too exuberant in the dignified presence of these quiet Navajo women.

Oh, well. "Where's Husky?" I asked.

"He's in Massachusetts."

"Massachusetts?"

"The union called him on a construction job last week. He'll be back for Christmas."

Hmmm, I thought. *No wonder he liked to sit on his hill and watch cows eat grass.*

The sun illuminated the mesa when we finally drove into Navajo Canyon. Light slanted across the eastern sky, but the depths of the canyon were still deep in shadow. Smoke curled up from the top of the hogan. Dogs barked, and the Bronco motor hummed. I turned off the ignition and heard a keening Navajo song that blended with the sky and the canyon and the mountain.

"They came outside early to prepare for your coming," Doria said. "My father is singing the "Blessing Way" for you and for what will be spoken of today."

The old medicine man stood, arms upraised on a woven Navajo rug by the hogan, facing east, chanting. Another smaller figure knelt at his feet. Their breath steamed in the frosty air. A small fire burned before them.

He wore a plaid fleece-lined coat, a red and black plaid hat with fleece earflaps, and a bright Pendleton blanket around his shoulders. She knelt with her head lifted to the sky, wrapped in a colorful, fringed Pendleton blanket. The trader had told me the men wrap themselves in warm woolen Pendleton blankets without fringe; the fringed blankets are worn by women.

At first, I felt I intruded upon sacred and private prayers, but I couldn't turn away. I succumbed to the drama of the moment. I had just spent impatient days drawn by the compelling spirit of primal ritual and I found it here, wrapped in warm winter blankets, right before my eyes.

In spite of being caught up in my own imagery of native ceremony, awareness of why I had come here never left my mind. I had come to try to take Tiahna away. What kind of horrendous effect would this have on the beliefs of this frail old man?

Richardson would scoff. I could almost hear him. "Come off it, lady. What makes you think you'd have any effect at all?"

Throughout the day, diffidence and a sense of the sacred stirred within me.

Doria got out of the Bronco and carried a box into the hogan. The two figures remained as they were, with the singer standing and Tiahna seated, their faces turned east. The old man's voice never faltered in song.

I sat very still, listening to the repetitious ululations until the sun's rays streamed over the canyon rim. Tiahna arose and stood with her grandfather still looking to the east, faces and arms lifted to greet the sun. In a slow, rhythmic counterclockwise rotation, they offered salutations to the north, west, and south. He concluded his ritual facing south, then in a clockwise motion, turned west then north. Within minutes, they were bathed in sunlight. His song ended when the sun touched the canyon floor, where I sat watching. I got out of the Bronco. He offered his hand. As I clasped it with my good left hand, I noticed the protective bandana knotted around his forehead under his fleecy hat. He nodded, genial but wordless, then turned and walked into the hogan. Tiahna saw me, but she moved without speaking as if in a trance. I followed her inside remembering Doria's warning that Tiahna could not speak for four days after her ceremony. That time had now elapsed, but I waited for Tiahna to speak first.

The interior of the hogan surprised me: big and round and warm, colorful with hanging rugs and baskets, aromatic with hanging herbs, burning cedar, frying bread, and coffee. An onrush of sensory perceptions came at me. A weaving loom of stripped cedar posts stood on one side bearing a half-finished rug. Sunlight streaming through the hole in the top of the hogan lit the bright weaving. Piles of fluffy carded wool spilled out of a cardboard carton nearby.

The old medicine man sat in an overstuffed chair near the fire. His eyes had a faraway look. His wife brought him a steaming mug of a greenish tea. Tiahna sank down by the fire at his feet. Her grandmother gave her a mug of the same hot brew.

Doria brought a mug of coffee for me, and fry bread with honey on a paper towel. She offered canned milk and sugar.

Victoria gurgled in her baby carrier. The old man picked her up and held her on his lap while he drank the steaming tea in great gulps. When he finished, he put his empty cup down on the hard-packed dirt floor, tucked Victoria back into her carrier, and then disappeared behind a hanging piece of flowered oilcloth. In just minutes, snoring came from behind the curtain.

Tiahna, too, disappeared behind a curtain on the opposite side of the room. Her grandmother, chanting either to herself or to her gods, worked at the weaving loom. Doria cleaned cast-iron frying pans with salt and paper towels.

I knew the differences between Navajo and Anglo social customs. Where an Anglo hostess tries to put guests at ease by sitting with them and exchanging small talk, the Navajo custom is to leave others alone in peace to make their own choices. They left me free to stay or go, without question. I felt a bit adrift, but I sipped my coffee, gazed at the fire and thought my hesitant feelings must be somewhat akin to the feelings of Navajos in the Anglo world.

When Doria finished her work, she sat beside me and said, "My father and Tiahna will sleep for several hours. When they wake up, we'll talk."

"Is it all right if I go out and walk in the canyon? When I come back, I'll rest in the Bronco. Don't worry about me. Just call me when everyone is ready."

"Okay, Maggie. Enjoy your walk."

I turned back to look at her. She smiled and waved.

For the first time, Doria had called me by my name.

All bundled up in my down-filled jacket, knit cap and gloves, I walked west in the canyon toward Lake Powell. Murder and intrigue seemed impossible to contemplate in this serenity of nature, so I let my mind wander through timeless corridors, meditating upon my own notions of transcendence in this lonely canyon deep in the heart of the desert.

I had walked several miles before I sat on a flat rock with my back to the sun, soaking up warmth and solitude. I thought about the medicine man's singing and reflected that the words of the old songs must be an appealing way to clear one's mind of ugliness, perhaps like New Age visualization and self-talk. To participate in the beauty of the sunrise, to keep oneself in harmony with earth and sky, to be surrounded by family, to feel the warmth of a good fire in the crisp chill of the changing seasons can't help but calm one's soul. But life is so fluid, so changing, not everyone can live in a remote canyon untouched by modern life. Not many want to. I thought about the ambiguity of the peacefulness surrounding me, reflecting that life for the Navajo is not always as tranquil as it seemed that morning. In all our tribes, it took enormous strength of purpose to stay in tune. I wondered about Tiahna and what she wanted for herself, and I thought of her life as it was in the here and now: Tiahna was an art student; she posed for artists who found her beautiful; art and beauty, as defined by the world, were heady things, hard to give up. Tiahna walked two divergent paths, the path of the Navajo and the path of the Anglo, but her sense of balance between the two worlds had been shaken. The medicine man sang of walking in the way of beauty, but the beauty he sang of was an interior abstraction, about which everyone wanted to voice an opinion, but which was, in fact, determined in private by the person who dwelt in that interior. Tiahna's grandfather must have possessed a vast reservoir of wisdom to help calm her soul as well as the restless souls of his people poised on the edge of so much attractive technology.

The medicine man had me in the palm of his hand from the first moment I heard of him, but if I got too caught up in the mystical beauty of the unknown, I might have forgotten why I was there. If I felt the need to hold on to my own center, the medicine man must have felt he was losing his hold on his people. It seemed to me the main thing, for him, as well as for me, was to keep trying.

I relaxed against my sun-warmed rock. The air moved against my face. The earth was solid beneath me. I looked at the twisted cedars on the rim of the canyon. New Age people claimed some sort of supernatural power in the vortex and that cedar trees were twisted by the mystical energy of it, a theory to which I did not subscribe. In my view, the cedar trees most vulnerable to twisting grew on the edge of ridges where the wind funneled upward. The nature of wind is to swirl. And, of course, the swirl is a vortex, completely natural. Not all cedar trees grew twisted. The limbs of inland trees, those not on the edge, grew straight, and many of the cedar trees grew more like bushes when they weren't battered by the prevailing winds. Made sense to me.

I let go of all my jangled perceptions. In solitude and silence, I regained my sense of balance. If only I could retain it when I was back in the presence of that powerful old man.

When I returned to the hogan, Doria served fresh mutton stew and fry bread in blue-speckled enamel bowls. The old man had awakened from his sleep and watched me with curious, bright eyes. Tiahna, too, was awake and seemed relaxed.

After lunch, the baby went to sleep. *Shamah*, Doria's mother, weaved at her loom. The grandfather, Doria, Tiahna and I sat in chairs pulled up to the fire, where a pot of beans bubbled.

Silence. We all waited for the old man to begin. When he did, he spoke at length. His singsong intonation sounded eloquent and weighty. Doria interpreted. I knew she oversimplified for my benefit. "Welcome to my hogan. What is it that you want?"

I told him about the doll and the fruitless search for money in the safes, money which had already been stolen by someone else. I told of Tiahna's disappearances from the studio, her apartment, Char's house, and finally from Sedona, and about Victor's murder. I didn't mention the first killing at the gallery because it seemed unrelated to Tiahna's situation.

"It started with the doll," I said. "Tiahna must know who did that, and why."

After Doria translated, Hatathlii spoke. "It started long, long ago . . ."

Almost four hours of song and legend followed, translated by Doria. Hatathlii began with the emergence myth, and then sang "Changing Woman," "Sun and Water," "White Shell Woman," and the "Twin War Gods." He made broad, sweeping gestures with his arms indicating the four directions, the overarching sky, the path of the sun, all sung with eyes closed, in major triad intervals, rhythmic and repetitive.

After the first couple of hours in the warm hogan, filled with the savory scent of beans and the hypnotic chanting, I found myself slumped lower in the chair, relaxed as a mote in the sunlight, drifting on currents of sound.

Doria's voice took on the same singsong quality. I was sure her translation, while splendid in its rendition, left much unspoken. "The land is for our good. The land is our strength. The sky surrounds us¾east, north, west, and south. The Spirit of the East gives us light to look outward. The Spirit of the West gives us courage to look within. From the north, we learn the wisdom of age and from the south, the wisdom of the child. Each of us must learn lessons from the circle of life to find the way of beauty."

The old man's voice changed and Doria's with it. More harsh, more strident, they sang of ghosts and witches and disasters beyond the ability of ordinary people to predict or to control, of magical events manipulated by supernatural beings, and of men's footprints in the snow, dotted with scattered drops of blood, turned into the paw prints of a coyote found wounded at the end of the trail.

"Keep to the way of wisdom," Doria intoned. "Stay away from witches who steal from their people, and who bring sickness and death."

Alert once more, I glanced at Tiahna. She sat with eyes down, tears dripping in a silent, steady stream onto her cheeks and from her chin. Her nose ran with her tears. I took several tissues from my handbag to offer her. *Shamah* reached out and grasped my wrist with a firm hand, took the tissues, and tucked them into her own velvet-covered bosom. Tiahna's eyes and nose streamed unchecked.

The old man seemed to be saying Tiahna had been the witch, the evil woman who brought sickness and death, that it was she who failed to guard her good spirit against the capricious evil of the myths.

His voice changed again, softened. Doria whispered. "It is not easy to be *Dineh*. The spirits wait for us, they watch for a chance to trick us. We can't always see them. They tricked Tiahna. They tricked me. The spirits witched my father, when he was a young man. He knows how hard it is to be strong, to find strong medicine to fool the witches. Hatathlii has given Tiahna protection in the ceremony, but only she can find the way to her own spirit beauty. When she finds it, she will be a woman of *Dineh*. The witch who tricked her will find evil at her own fire."

The chanting stopped. The grandmother brought a mug of water and gave it to me. I took it questioningly. The old man indicated I should drink. After I had sipped, he took the cup and each one in turn drank of the cold water.

Hatathlii spoke again, this time in just a few short sentences.

After a moment, Tiahna began to speak in English. Now Doria translated into Navajo for Hatathlii and *Shamah*.

"Always, I had two pathways to find. What is beautiful in one is not always beautiful in the other. Among my mother's people, everyone loves the children. A child always has a home. If the parents can't take care of it, grandparents, or aunts, or brother, or sister, or cousins, or clan take care of it. Many children in the same family have different fathers, different mothers, and different names. It makes no difference. My father's family did not welcome me. My sister made me feel ugly and hated. My father's wife made me feel . . . unreal. When she painted me on canvas, everyone said, 'How beautiful' and 'You've captured her' but it wasn't truly me. The pictures are of *Navajo Princess* or *Indian Maiden*. She captured and used me. She got compliments on her paintings of me, she sold them for thousands of dollars, but she didn't like me. She didn't treat me like a real person.

"I met Rubio when I first started to model for Char. I didn't know anybody else in Sedona, and he was kind to me. He went to school there, so he knew all the young people. He asked me to go places with him. And then he asked me to move in with him, so I did. Then I got pregnant, and he started to be mean to me. He got into drugs, and that got him into big trouble. I haven't seen much of him since Victoria was born, but he always needed money. He kept asking me for money. He's the first one who told me about the floor safes. But I didn't know how to get money, and I didn't want to come right out and ask Victor for it."

Tiahna drew a deep breath. "Rubio hung the doll, and I squeezed out the whole tube of red paint over the doll and the floor. After I did that, I got carried away by the evil spirit. I smeared Char's painting of me with red paint."

I listened, horrified, to Tiahna's calm voice. She didn't seem to realize that in killing the Navajo doll, in symbol if not in fact, she had killed herself. Or maybe she did know. Maybe she wanted to extinguish the unreal concept of herself that Char's artists take such delight in painting. Perhaps she was wiser than I gave her credit for. Then, as Tiahna continued her story, I began to understand the great gulf between my thinking and that of the old spiritual leader, Tiahna's grandfather.

"I don't know what made me think of it. Grandfather says evil spirits witched me. During my sing, he went out from here with the hand trembler. When they came back, he had old cans and bottles, faded and covered with dirt because they'd been buried. Pushed down inside an old Twister wine bottle, he found a stick doll with bits of cloth, woman cloth, tied around with long hairs from my head and red yarn tied around her neck. And one of the old pop cans had been turned inside out, and on the inside he saw a scratched figure of a hanging woman. My grandfather said these things jumped into his hand from out of the ground where they had been buried.

"He said witches caused it all. They made me do it, and it worked. Victor thought danger surrounded me. He suggested giving me money to go away to some other place. He treated me with kindness, but I don't think he liked me. I made him feel uncomfortable. He would have been glad for me go away. My mother's people, *Dineh*, make room for children. They make a place for each new child without becoming uncomfortable or unbalanced the way Victor did.

"I didn't want to destroy the harmony of their lives. I just thought everyone who is born has a place. I fill my place and you fill your place, and we try not to push each other. But the witch made me push.

"I wanted to help Rubio, but I should not have tried to take money from my father's family. "Changing Woman" helped me though, against the witches because I didn't get a chance to take any money. Somebody else had taken it before we got there. I acted like a witch, but I don't want to *be* a witch!" she cried.

My feminist instincts were aroused. *Tiahna is taking all the blame here, and it's Rubio who instigated the entire scene. All this talk of witches . . .*

My anger at the way Tiahna had been manipulated smothered me. It seemed the Navajo way of looking at it was to see Rubio as having been influenced by evil spirits, thus passing the influence on to Tiahna. If Hatathlii and I could only converse, perhaps we could find common ground.

I wanted to put my arms around Tiahna and comfort her. I wanted to say, "You have been misled, Tiahna, We know you're not a witch." Seated at the fire of Hatathlii, I said nothing so as to avoid interfering with the flow of his medicine. He began to sing again. In Doria's voice, his strong words of advice struck Tiahna's tear-dampened form.

"Little daughter, put your hand in the fire."

Tiahna stared at him. With little faith, I also stared at him, worried I would have to interfere and disrupt his flow if she obeyed. Slow as time, she raised her hand. Slow as ice, she inched it toward the fire, never taking her eyes from his. Then with swift intent, she placed her hand straight into the flames then snatched it back.

Hatathlii nodded with grim satisfaction. With the same slow movement, he moved his hand toward the fire never taking his eyes from hers. Then, with steady deliberation, he placed his hand into the flames and, with equal slowness, drew it back.

"The spirit of the fire is your friend, and it is your enemy. You must study to balance the fire of your life." Doria translated as he began to sing:

Sun shines before me. Sun shines behind me.
Sun shines all around me.
Rain falls before me. Rain falls behind me. Rain falls all around me.
I walk in the sun. I walk in the rain.
I plant the corn. I sing the songs.
The corn grows.

The powerful spiritual presence of the old medicine man dominated the room. From a pouch hanging on a buckskin thong around his neck, he took a pinch of corn meal and sprinkled it over and around Tiahna. He bent his old knees to kneel in front of her and placed the pouch around her neck. He said, "You are real to your own people."

Tiahna sat wordless, in a hush that stretched out almost to a silent scream. Doria shifted her weight. I eased a cramped muscle. Victoria wailed. The old man, grown stiff from long hours of sitting, stood up.

At last Tiahna spoke. He stopped and turned to listen to her.

"Maybe what I did led to my father's death, and brought sorrow to his family, but I didn't kill him. And it wasn't witches who killed him, either." She paused and then raised her eyes to look with a strong and gentle spirit at her grandfather.

"My father's people are my people, too. I hope they can forgive me."

Doria, Tiahna, and Victoria made plans to return to Sedona the following day. I told them I would meet them there. We walked out of the hogan and stood talking in the fading afternoon light. Along the steep canyon road, headlights approached. Within a minute or two, music from a boom box thumped as a pickup stopped a few feet from where we stood.

Two men were in the pickup. The passenger door swung open, and the drunken man I had talked with at Doria's house got out. His gait was unsteady, but he was not falling-down drunk. He walked straight to Doria and, without warning, punched her in the face. She fell to the ground. I pushed him away. He pushed me back and kicked Doria, muttering what sounded like Navajo obscenities.

He turned and walked away, cursing. I helped Doria to her feet. *Shamah*, Tiahna, and Hatathlii came out just as the man came back around the hogan carrying a stick of firewood. He rushed forward, lifted the firewood with both hands and swung it at Doria, striking her shoulder. *Shamah*, Navajo Mother, leaped on his back and wrapped her arms around his neck. He staggered back and dropped the wood. *Shamah* jumped off, grabbed one of his fingers and bent it back until it cracked.

The power of the medicine man did not emerge in the viciousness of the sudden attack. The power of *Shamah*, weaver, corn-grower, giver of life, turned the force of the assault, with swift mother instinct, back upon the aggressor.

The stress level accelerated. The sound level increased. The screamed language was Navajo, except for my garbled exclamations, all accompanied by stereophonic rock from the still-idling pickup.

Doria bled from the nose and mouth and held her shoulder. I heard the man's name—Tully. Although he continued to mutter, with his little finger sticking out at a right angle from his hand, *Shamah* had him under control.

Doria spoke to Tiahna. Tiahna went into the hogan and came out with keys, which she started to hand to Tully until *Shamah* said, "No!"

Speaking swiftly in Navajo, she pointed to the pickup Tully arrived in. He hurried to the still open door of the pickup, climbed in, and he and his buddy sprayed gravel in a whirling exit from the canyon. Another maelstrom, another vortex.

Shamah was the only one who exerted much effort, but we were all breathing hard.

"Doria," I said between gasps. "Let me take you to the hospital in Page."

"No hospital." Stoic. "I will see you again in Sedona."

She and her parents went back into the hogan.

"Tully is my mother's husband." Tiahna said. "He is angry because Doria brought me here in the pickup and she has stayed two weeks.

"Is it his pickup?"

"No. My mother bought it."

"Does he need it to get to work?"

"No. He worked last year, but he got laid off for coming to work drunk, so he hasn't worked for a long time."

"Has he done this to her before?"

"Yes."

I was enraged, and said I would go straight to the police.

Tiahna said, "No."

"But Tiahna, he hurt her."

She shook her head, "It isn't our way," and turned away.

It was cold and dark when I drove back to Page, all the intricate relationships, all the obscure cultural decisions, all the complex mysteries, just all the damn knotty problems running through my tired mind. The Navajo matriarchal society in operation had been something to behold. It seemed they neither wanted nor needed my help. I let it all go, relinquishing control to the purpose of the greater intelligence at work.

I was standing at the kitchen counter going through my mail when my cell phone rang.

I picked it up and heard Garcia's voice. "When will you be back? It's time we compared notes."

Aha, I thought, *maybe I was a trusted colleague.*

"I'll be there tomorrow afternoon. And so will Tiahna and Doria."

"Well, I'll be damned. You got them, huh?"

"Or they got me," It was a feeble attempt at humor. "If you don't see me tomorrow, you'll know who's got whom."

TWELVE

T he next afternoon, unrested, antsy, and itching under my brace, I pulled up in the driveway of Char's house.

Char flew out the door, looking as if she had lost ten pounds. Her dark blue sweat suit hung on her.

She threw her arms around me and breathed, "Thank goodness you're here."

Arm-in-arm we walked into the house.

I asked my first question as she shut the front door behind us. "Who mugged Rita?"

"I wish it had been a mugging," She shook her head. "No, I don't mean that like it sounds. I don't want it to be connected to Victor, but the police are treating it as if it were. Richardson is convinced Randa and Garcia killed her. He's keeping pressure on them, hoping they'll crack."

"What makes him think they did it? What motive would they have?"

"I don't know what he thinks about motive. I don't know what he thinks about anything. When Garcia got back from Page, he and Randa went out to dinner. There were people at the restaurant who knew them, so there are plenty of witnesses. They left the restaurant between eight and eight thirty but don't have anyone to back them up on their whereabouts after that. Garcia was exhausted and his broken nose hurt, so he took Randa home and went to his apartment to crash. Rita had an appointment at ten with Father Quejada over at St. John's. Father is her cousin. He waited on the steps for her, but another parishioner came just before ten and he went inside with him. They were only there for ten minutes or so. When Rita didn't arrive, Father Quejada waited inside until about ten thirty. He went back outside and found her in a pool of blood. Someone had," she was having a hard time keeping it together, "bashed her head in. Oh, Maggie."

"Oh, no." It was just too much; the tears came. "The viciousness of these murders of just ordinary people terrorizes me and breaks my heart. I can only imagine how you and Randa must feel."

"That's why we need you so much, Maggie. Can you stay longer?"

"I'll stay as long as I can. I talked to my boss. I have accrued vacation and sick leave I can tap into. He said they could cover for me for a while longer."

Together we carried my bags to the guest room.

"What does Richardson say about the car wreck Garcia and I had? Doesn't that prove Garcia is innocent?"

"Garcia doesn't think Richardson has anything substantial to go on. He says Richardson thinks Randa killed Victor, and is just bluffing and taking shots in the dark where Rita's death is concerned."

"The man is like a bulldog," I exploded. "He gets an idea into his head, and nothing will change it. I want to find some real answers just to show him. Damn him anyway. Why am I letting him put me on the defensive?"

While I unpacked, Char called Garcia to tell him I had arrived. He asked to speak to me.

"Maggie, I have something to investigate. If you want to go with me, I suggest you eat now then sleep four or five hours. What do you say?"

I looked at my watch, six o'clock. These telephone calls from Garcia were guaranteed to destroy my sleep. Every time he'd called me, he'd reported chaos, but I felt such satisfaction at being included that I said the only thing I could say. "You're on."

Contrary to my dire predictions, I slept deeply until my alarm rang at eleven thirty. Garcia picked me up in front of Char's house at midnight.

"Are you sure you want me with you?"

"You're a fast thinker, Maggie, and I need an extra observer."

"Where are we going?" I asked.

"We're going to break into Tomás Avila's garage," he answered. "But first, let's talk. I'll fill you in on what's been happening while you were gone."

After I had been told to butt out more than once, his words soothed my insulted soul. Garcia wanted to talk to me about the case. Yahoo! I leaned back against the seat and listened, trying to absorb it all, as he drove and talked.

"They've determined Victor was struck on the forehead with the solid steel water-hydrant key used in the spa and gardens, then he was dragged up the cold plunge steps and held under the water until he drowned."

I blew out a whoosh of air. "Just think of the grim intensity of it . . ."

Garcia ignored my interruption. "The police found the weapon in the cedar trees on the hillside behind the cold plunge enclosure. It looked like it had been flung there and no attempt had been made to hide it. That might be significant. Or not. The only fingerprints on the key were Randa's, Victor's and the Mexican gardener's, all of whom turned the water on and off regularly."

"So do you think the Mexican gardener could have done it?" It was bad timing for the feeble joke, but I couldn't help myself.

Garcia shrugged and shook his head, but didn't deign to answer that question. Some people just don't have a sense of humor, but it really was bad timing.

He went on. "Failure to conceal the weapon seems to indicate Victor's murderer did not premeditate, that the killer panicked and ran. But the lack of prints leads to the conclusion the murderer was wearing gloves, which does indicate prior planning."

"Maybe the person was wearing gloves to rob the safe, and then had to kill Victor after being recognized," I interjected.

He looked at me, "Maybe," then, "Vanloads of illegal immigrants arrive here on a regular schedule and there's a group that defies the law to provide sanctuary to those newly arrived. Father Raphael Quejada, Rita's cousin, has been instrumental in that movement. Drivers, including Rubio, have been followed to a shop in town where they pick up their payoffs—payoffs presumed to be for drug smuggling, not immigrant smuggling."

"Wouldn't it be for both drugs and immigrants? I've read that the immigrants pay to be smuggled in."

"Right. And we've followed Rubio among others. We've watched him steal cocaine for himself, a baggie or two at a time, from a suitcase secreted in the engine of a pickup he uses to drive in illegals. That's why he's in such trouble now."

He continued. "According to an official report, the immigrants are picked up in ones or twos or small family groups. The process is easy to watch because no one is trying real hard to hide. The narcos are more concerned with concealing drugs from the Shadow Wolves than hiding the human smuggling. The illegals are driven to towns and cities where they assimilate almost without effort, given the increasing population of Mexican nationals all across the country We just do not have the psychological makeup to be a walled-in country. Yet. But maybe it's coming to that."

"All this has been part of your Skylark investigation?" I asked.

"Yes," he answered, "but the primary objective of the investigation is still, and always has been, the cocaine smuggling. Our discoveries led to intriguing questions: did Father Quejada know his sanctuary movement was the means to an end for the drug traffickers? Was the people running financed by the drug running—or the other way around? Did Rita know about Rubio's illegal activities? Did Victor? What was the connection, if any, between those two killings and the first one at the gallery?"

"Well, you know more about it than I do. I don't have any answers," I said. "But it seems to me Rubio is the cord that ties the murders together."

When Garcia spoke again, it seemed as if he agreed, but also disagreed. "Rubio is such an insignificant little twerp to have opened the gates on this flood of destruction and death. He has no focus, no direction, and no reliability." He shook his head in exasperation.

"Perhaps there is more to Rubio than meets the eye," I suggested.

"Maybe. He has superior mechanical ability. I've heard he can make an engine sing."

"Let's think about Rubio in relation to Rita and Victor's deaths." I began counting off facts on my fingers. "Both of the murders were spineless, in a sense. Not gutsy. Not coordinated. They both appear to have been committed in sudden fear rather than passion. Victor's death seemed spur-of-the-moment and unpremeditated, while Rita's murder had to have been planned. Of course, the same person could have done both, but could Rubio have done both? Is he really capable of killing Rita in cold blood?"

"In spite of his lack of character," Garcia said, "I find it hard to believe he could or would kill his own mother."

"Me, too," I agreed. "But, on the other hand, I can see him sneaking around, stealing, and killing Victor when he got caught."

"Me, too," Garcia echoed. "So let's go take a look in his dad's garage."

We drove to Tomás's house, parked several houses away, and walked back using the utility right-of-way behind the house.

"What made you think of looking here?" I whispered.

"Tomás and Rita were on the patio with us at Char's house when you and I planned our drive to Page. Somebody who knows engines messed with the insides of mine."

Garcia picked the lock on the garage in the dark of midnight— interesting skill for a policeman. He carried a small flashlight and a small camera. The streetlights glowed through a window. Garcia draped his jacket over the window. I stumbled over some immovable object before he got his penlight turned on.

Wow. Impressive. Ordinary and unremarkable on the outside, the inside of Tomás's garage revealed a showcase. A well-stocked tool bench stood against one wall, replete with hammers and saws and every sort of wrench from Allen to monkey to socket, all cared for, wiped clean with oiled rags, and neatly hung on pegs. Wrenches were arranged by size. Toward the larger end, one empty peg jumped out, indicating a heavy steel wrench that usually hung there was missing. Garcia took a picture of the conspicuous gap left by the missing wrench.

Garcia searched the garage with deliberation. At one point, his flashlight beam picked up a curious gleam we almost missed. He beckoned me and together we bent over a hacksaw with fresh scratches that showed up under the light as silver lines. It lay atop a pair of light canvas work gloves with grease-smeared fingers.

"If we take the saw and gloves now, they'll be inadmissible as evidence," he whispered. "I'll ask Richardson to come back with a search warrant." He took a picture for insurance.

We found nothing else to arouse suspicion. Garcia extinguished his light, retrieved his jacket, and we tiptoed away.

Back in the car, Garcia said, "When Rubio works, he's a mechanic on foreign cars. He seems to be a lazy bum but maybe he's been busier than we thought."

"And more evil," I mused.

We rode in silence. I remained wrapped in my own thoughts until Garcia pulled up in front of Char's house.

He turned to me. "The only concrete clues we have are the hacksaw and gloves, and they point directly to Rubio. Or Tomás."

"But they don't have anything to do with Victor or Rita's deaths, only with the attempt on our lives."

"Well, we do have a picture of a black hole where a missing wrench should be, whatever help that might be, a wrench that could have been used to kill Rita.

"What about Randa?" I asked. "I haven't seen her yet. Is she holding up?"

"No. She's disintegrating right before our eyes. She did agree to see a psychologist." He sat silently for a moment. "Richardson is hell-bent on convicting her."

"Do *you* think she's guilty?"

He drew a deep hesitant breath before answering, "No. Of course not."

I understood his hesitation. He probably asked himself the same questions I asked myself, but his delayed response disturbed me.

Sensitive to that unsettling ripple in consciousness, he rushed on with his inventory.

"What about Tiahna? Did you learn anything on the reservation?"

I filled him in on Tiahna's confession that she and Rubio had hung the doll in an attempt to get money and included my reading of the subtext: she was manipulated by Rubio. The doll hanging, from which Tiahna fled, set up Victor's wild chase after her and in search of money, which in turn culminated in his death. She claimed not to have killed her father even though she felt guilty and disturbed about it. Given the highly-charged spiritual circumstances of the tribal ceremony, I believed her.

"I wonder if Father Quejada could be a key figure in all this." Garcia's question was rhetorical so I didn't bother to reply. He was thinking aloud, bouncing ideas off me.

"Father Quejada could have killed Rita, but he had no connection to Victor's death unless the saintly Father was in on the drug smuggling as well as immigrant smuggling. What if he or drug men in his organization were looking for me at the spa when they were caught by Victor?"

Garcia had come full circle to his original theory that the whole thing had been set up to discredit Skylark.

"At first, everything seemed so disconnected, but I have a gut feeling each part will wind up fitting into a horrible whole."

"Yeah, like my picture of a black hole?" Garcia indulged in a bit of mocking humor.

I let myself back into the house at one thirty in the morning. Our foray, in just an hour and a half, cleared up some confusion and gave me a sense of being proactive in our search for answers.

In the morning, after my run and shower, which I took very carefully because of my healing bones, Char and I talked for a few minutes. Busy with insurance claims, death benefits, suspicions and accusations, she still had time to worry about Randa. In an attempt to help her in the same way I had been helped, through action, I said, "Let's call Rita's cousin, Father Quejada. Maybe he could tell us something about Rita's life we don't already know."

Father Quejada immediately agreed to see us, the sooner the better. We made an appointment for early afternoon.

An insurance man arrived at the house just before ten. I excused myself and went to the kitchen so he and Char could talk in private. I sat at the kitchen table writing notes when a neighbor arrived with a pan of hot cinnamon rolls. I tried to avoid them. I really did, but their homey smell intruded upon my senses. I had just taken my first bite, my eyes closed in appreciation, when Randa and Garcia arrived.

"Whoa," Garcia said. "Talk about being lost in space."

"Oh, hello," I said, startled. "You must have picked up my message—ESP—I was just thinking about you."

"Taking a bite out of crime, hmmm?"

I laughed. There had been a pitiful shortage of laughter lately. "Say, you two. How about a hot roll?" I invited. "They're delicious."

"I'm not hungry," Randa said. She looked thin, faded and nervous. Her hair was dry and lackluster.

"Honey, you should eat something," His concern for her was in his voice.

Garcia bit into a roll with healthy gusto. Randa took one bite, then put her roll on a napkin and began pulling it apart with a fork.

My heart went out to her. "How do you feel, Randa?"

She answered with a withering look. Tears glistened in her eyes as she stabbed and smashed the cinnamon roll.

Char walked in. "Oh, Randa. How did it go with the therapist?"

"Okay."

"What did he say?" Char pressed.

"He said depression is a sign, telling you when something is wrong in your life."

"Well. I guess if we weren't depressed at a time like this, we'd honestly be nuts."

"Yeah."

"But did you like him? Will you keep going?"

"Mother, please leave me alone." Randa walked away.

We all watched her retreat to another part of the house, aware of her turmoil but not allowed to share it. She'd left her roll a heaped-up mass of sticky crumbs. Garcia rolled it up in the napkin and threw it away as if he couldn't bear to look at it. Char followed Randa, unable to refrain from offering sympathy.

Garcia and I remained in the kitchen, the mystery on our minds.

"Have you seen Richardson yet?" I asked.

"Yes. He got a search warrant, and we went to Tomás's house first thing this morning."

"How did Tomás react?"

"Not well. Shocked. But he didn't try to stop us," Garcia said. "A whopping big oiled wrench filled that black hole. But I took another picture."

"Did you tell Richardson why?"

"Yes," Garcia answered with grim satisfaction. "We looked at it on my iPhone and then downloaded it at the station."

"What about the hacksaw and the gloves?"

"They were still there. They impressed Richardson, but he doesn't want to give us much credit. He thinks we knew where to look because we know people around here. But he did take them in to compare with the tie rod from my car."

Char and I went to our appointment with Father Quejada after lunch. He invited us into his office. His resemblance to Rita was stronger than usual for cousins. The Father was short and rotund, quick and cheery with her same snappy brown eyes, except his looked tired. It was easy to see her murder on the steps of his church had taken its toll.

We told him the chaotic violence was threatening Randa's sanity and our main objective was to help her.

He expressed sympathy, not only for Randa's state of mind, but also for the emotional upheaval Char had been forced to endure.

"Mrs. Cooper, all I can tell you is that Rita called me and wanted to come to confession. She said she had a terrible summer. Since your husband's death, she couldn't sleep. One of my parishioners came by and stayed ten or fifteen minutes. Later, about ten thirty, I went out onto the front steps." He rubbed his hands over his face. "There she lay in a heap, dead. It could only have been a matter of minutes after my parishioner left. If only I had walked out with him, maybe I could have prevented it."

"Don't reproach yourself, Father," Char said. "Sudden violence catches us off guard. None of us are prepared for it."

"Thank you." He drew a deep breath. "I know that's true, but I can't help going over what I might have done."

"Did Rita come to confession every week?" I asked.

"No. Not to me. She may have gone to her parish priest every week. I think she called me this time because I'm family."

"So it was somewhat unusual?"

Father Quejada's tired eyes acknowledged his own conviction that Rita had something preying on her mind. "I hope you won't read too much into the fact she called me. Confession does not mean one has done great evil." He smiled. "A priest usually just hears about daily difficulties. Confession helps to keep one's spirit sweet."

"Yes," I agreed. "But those same daily difficulties sometimes cause people to kill each other."

"I don't know what she had to tell me. I'd like to help you, but even if I knew anything, I couldn't tell you." His shoulders lifted in an eloquent shrug.

Char and I stood outside the door after we'd said goodbye. A bridal party waited to move inside. A bride in white satin, hovered over by attendants like bright butterflies, emerged from a car. Smiling and radiant, she looked about seven months pregnant. The lighthearted scene, bursting with color and life, contrasted sharply with Rita's painful, lonely murder in the dark of the night on the same spot.

Char and I walked around the happy bridal party and crossed the street.

"Why would anyone want to kill Rita?" I wondered aloud. "Was it because she knew about the money taken from the safes? Was she a threat to someone?"

We arrived at Char's car. "Let's go to Tlaquepaque. We can sit outside one of the restaurants and talk," I suggested. "I'm meeting Tomás there in a few minutes."

We sat on a sunny patio and ordered iced tea. "Char," I said, "Tell me all you know about Rita."

"For starters, the nickname 'Rita' doesn't do justice to her impressive name," Char answered. "It was Marguerita Patrizia Consuelo de Vargas Avila. She grew up in Santa Fe. Her family has been there for centuries. It's a widespread family now, with members in every economic level from sheepherders to senators. Tomás grew up in Arizona but went to the University of New Mexico. They met there. Between them, they are related to half the Hispanic people in New Mexico and Arizona." Char sighed. "She did a marvelous job for me, took excellent care of my gallery. She was a good friend. I miss her."

We sat in silence for a moment. Then Char continued. "Tomás told me when he went to school as a young boy, his lunch shamed him. His grandmother sent burritos in his lunch bag, beans and chilies in a tortilla, and a little jar of hot sauce. The Anglo kids had peanut butter and jelly or lunch meat with mayonnaise and mustard. Before long, when the other kids discovered what Tomás had, they all wanted to trade, so Tomás ate bologna." She paused, and then smiled. "He ended up with a hot enchilada, though. Rita. She was full of beans and hot sauce."

After another period of silence, she said, "I can't believe she's gone. I can't believe Victor's gone." Her voice caught back a sob. "But they *are* gone. The best we can do for them now, and for me, is to find out why."

"Marguerita Patrizia Consuelo de Vargas Avila," I said. "It rolls off the tongue with a regal sound."

"We're the interlopers here, you know, among the Hispanics and Native Americans. I believe on some subliminal plane, Rita resented us, resented having to work for an Anglo," Char's voice was once again calm and introspective. "We must seem like volcanic lava to them, flowing over everything in our path, too hot to handle." Char had wandered away into the subject of ethnic sorrow. She must have been thinking in depth about it lately. "But we Anglos just want to be, well, just *to be who we are*, too, you know."

I cringed inside at burdening Char with my search for justice and motive. Well, actually it was *our* search, but her grief was still too fresh. I dropped my eyes, breaking the flow of wordless communication. I wondered how to pull Char back out of emotional quicksand.

Char, always quick, picked up the shift. "Well," she wiped her eyes, leaving a dark smudge of eyeliner, "Maggie, I'm worried about Randa. I'm afraid she's going to crack."

"How often is she going to see her therapist? It will help to pour her thoughts out into objective ears."

"She's going every day this week. This morning's session didn't sound like a breakthrough, though." Char finished her tea. "What time did you say you were meeting Tomás?"

I glanced at my watch. "We're meeting in the plaza in fifteen minutes."

"If you need me later, I'll be at the gallery for the rest of the afternoon."

"Good. I'll ask Tomás to drop me off at the house, or else I'll walk over to the gallery to meet you."

While I waited for Tomás, I thought about Randa. She, like Tiahna before her ceremony, had deteriorated. Perhaps she could have handled Victor's violent death better if she hadn't been filled with anger before the violence. That anger kept her as a suspect in his murder. That, and the fact Richardson hadn't found anyone else to charge. In just the last few days, she'd grown hollow-eyed, thin, and even more fragile. I hoped Randa's "medicine man" could help her recover her center as Hatathlii had helped Tiahna.

I had wanted to go to Tomás and Rita's home to express my sympathy and to see if I could be a friend to him and his family in their sorrow. He was the one who suggested we meet somewhere else. I wasn't sure if there was anything I could say or do, but I wanted to make the gesture.

Tomás approached, a changed man: sad, distraught, and uncommunicative. He didn't want to talk about Rita, and I didn't have the heart to persist. After just a few dispirited minutes, we said goodbye.

I walked to the gallery. It had been a day that included a lot of talk with few specifics. However, I had arrived at the conviction the two murders were related, and I also believed Rubio, behind his jaunty demeanor, concealed dark secrets. Just how he fit in, I did not yet know. One other little fact, I reminded myself, was that Tiahna, Doria, and I were not here in Sedona on the night of Rita's murder. More importantly, no one else had an alibi, not even Tomás.

After a day spent with grieving friends, I felt sad and gloomy. My resolve wavered. For the nth time, I wondered about my own involvement in these murders. I could just go home and leave it to the professionals. I was not under suspicion and I could leave any time I wanted to. This could drag on for weeks, months even, since all the evidence was circumstantial. But loose ends still nagged at me. I vacillated. Stay or go?

Had my promise to Char been made too impulsively? Doubts about my usefulness dragged me down. Maybe what I needed was another visit to the energy vortexes. By the time I had reached the gallery, I was struggling with an unusually somber mood.

At dinner, I told Char I felt useless and wondered if I should leave. Her face fell. Even though she had begun painting again, partly for therapy, but mostly because painting was her livelihood, she was still shocked and grieving over Victor's death.

"I know you can't stay forever, Mag. You have your life to get back to, but your being here has helped us a great deal. You'll never know how much."

By the next morning, I had remembered my little drawings of turquoise nuggets, and my usual optimism had bounced back. Over coffee, I said to Char, "I've still got a few questions I want to ask and a couple of places I want to check out. Can you recommend a decent jewelry shop?"

"Rita had a cousin with a jewelry shop in Tlaquepaque. We've used him for years. I'll call him. He'll take exceptional care of you." She rose and called the jeweler right then.

In the jewelry shop, I introduced myself to Rita's cousin and expressed my condolences. Rita's family must have had some deep roots. I found myself looking at yet another cousin who resembled Rita. The jeweler talked affably with me. After a few moments, I showed him the card on which I drew my impressions of two turquoise nuggets, the one I saw in the cold plunge and the nugget missing from Randa's concho belt. I spent almost an hour in his shop, and when I left, I carried a gift-wrapped box containing a bracelet for my granddaughter and a nugget of useful information about turquoise-studded jewelry, the two pieces with missing stones in particular.

THIRTEEN

C har told me while I was at the jewelry shop, Randa's therapist, Dr. Warren, had called. He reported that, so far at least, Randa was maintaining total silence. He wanted Char to know that due to her inability to open up and express her feelings, Randa's therapy did not look promising. In fact, he felt it was at a standstill.

"I've talked with Randa about family therapy," he told Char, "and she has agreed to have you come in with her. Your involvement might help her open up and express her feelings."

That afternoon, Char went with Randa to her therapy session and later described to me, as an artist would, how it played out. I had a clear picture in my mind.

Randa reclined on Dr. Warren's couch and waited quietly, her eyes closed.

"Randa," the doctor began.

"Yes," she answered without opening her eyes.

"Whenever you're ready."

After a pause, she said, "Did you know when an owl catches a mouse and eats it, the owl's digestive system reprocesses the leftovers into a little mouse package? The head is intact, and the hair is wrapped around the bones. Even the tail is still there. The little package is deposited back on the forest floor. One day when I was walking in the hills behind the spa, I found one. Very strange."

"No, I didn't know that. What made you think of it?"

"I don't know. I was just thinking about owls and life and death and nature and stuff. Maybe I feel like I've been shot at and shit on. I don't know. What do you think?"

"I don't know why, either. Maybe after we've talked some more we'll see a reason. Did you start a daily journal as I asked?"

"Yes."

Dr. Warren waited. Randa waited. Silence reigned. Char, too, tensed up. Five minutes passed. No one spoke.

At length, Randa burst out. "You're the expert. Say something."

Dr. Warren said, "Randa, only you know what is in your mind."

"I just told you what is on my mind, and you didn't have any comment."

Imperturbable, he had spoken in a calm voice. "You chose to come here. You can spend your time in silence anywhere. The purpose of coming here is to talk about what is troubling you. You don't want generalizations from me nor I from you."

Another five minutes passed. Then she burst out, "Why would my father be so insensitive? Why couldn't he see what he was doing to me?"

"Tell me what your father did to you."

Randa described her feelings of jealousy and frustration, her need for her father's attention, her wish that life would go back to the way it had been before Tiahna. According to Randa, her anger, sense of rejection, depression, even her car accident stemmed from Tiahna's arrival in her life, and from the way her father had overreacted to Tiahna.

"Did you ever think your life could have been too easy before Tiahna?"

Silence again. After thirty more minutes. Dr. Warren's secretary buzzed to indicate an hour had passed. Randa rose and left the office without another word.

After she had gone, Dr. Warren spoke to Char.

"Believe it or not, today turned out to be the best day we've had," he said. "Your being here must be a catalyst. Could you come again for another day or two and maybe we'll get the floodgates open?"

Char, in mother hen mode, had said to him, "I must have a blind spot where Randa is concerned. I never realized before today how brittle and rude she can be."

"Her abrupt manner comes from her pain." Dr. Warren spoke to Char with gentle conviction. "And, too, perhaps you have always overprotected her."

Later, when Char asked Randa how she felt about her session, she snorted, "He told me only I can know what is in my mind."

Char sighed. "Maybe he won't always seem so obvious."

Randa's rage had been visible to Char. "How can he say my life 'had been too easy' before Tiahna?" She made quotation marks with her fingers. "It's the only life I've ever known."

But she continued to attend sessions with Dr. Warren with his warm brown eyes and voice and Char went with her. Randa had told Char she could share the sessions with me.

I had decided to use more of my accrued leave. I felt that I had to know how all Char's and Randa's struggles were going to work out, and who the killer was. I could learn it secondhand, but I felt too involved now to give up. I was feeling much more positive since my momentary downturn. I would stay until the mystery was solved or my leave ran out, whichever came first.

Char kept me abreast of developments with Dr. Warren. After a couple more days, she reported that Randa had arrived at a point where she could say to him, "I guess my life has been easy. But who would welcome a situation like Tiahna caused, just so their life could stop being easy?"

"Did Tiahna *cause* the situation?"

Randa, Char said, had to admit she'd known that truth already in some level of her mind. Tiahna, herself, was not the cause of Randa's anger and sorrow.

Dr. Warren had reminded Randa in her private pain her vision narrowed, and certain larger truths crossed cultural barriers. That challenge was more valuable to her, indeed to everyone, than ease. Regardless, she couldn't have remained daddy's one and only little girl forever. The day he told her that, she actually laughed, and said,

"Guess what I wrote in my journal last night? GROW UP!"

"Did you, on any level of your mind, wish your father harm?" His probing question caught her by surprise.

Silence surrounded them all again. It was obvious Randa needed time to think that one through. Because of that, they bore her silence with ease. Before she left his office that day he said, "Randa, this is where you begin to make a new life. Don't fight the changes that will come with honest answers."

While Tiahna had knelt at her grandfather's feet for nine nights of a mystical cleansing ritual, Randa struggled through hours and days of being forced to accept responsibility for her own life.

Meanwhile, the search for their father's killer went on.

Once again, I felt that I had to go to Page for a few days to catch up with mail and bills. Before I left Sedona, I called my friends, each one a possible suspect, to say goodbye and I hoped to see them soon. I listened with a fine-tuned ear to every response, hoping to hear innocence.

Randa said, "Thanks for being here with us, Maggie. We'll miss you."

Garcia said, "Hell, Maggie, I just started to depend on you and now you're running out on me?"

Tomás seemed too unhappy even to flirt. He said, "Goodbye and thanks for calling. Have a good trip."

Of course, I did not have Rubio's telephone number, so he remained incommunicado. I didn't consider him my friend, anyway. I called Tsosie who told me we were going to drum together someday.

In answer to a nagging interior voice telling me to "Just do it," I called Father Quejada.

He surprised me. "I just remembered something Rita said to me on the telephone when she called. Will you stop by on your way out of town?"

When I left the house, Char hugged me hard and said, "Maggie, don't be surprised if you get a call for help from us."

Father Quejada met me in the foyer of the church with his nugget of remembered information. At the end of his conversation on the telephone with Rita, she had suddenly lowered her voice and said, "I've got to go. Tomás just came in. *He doesn't want me to come to see you.*"

After I left Father Quejada, I stopped at the police station and asked to see Detective Richardson. He was in and agreed to see me.

"What can I do for you, Ms. McGinnis?"

"I thought you were calling me Maggie now."

"Okay, Maggie." He laughed. "What can I do for you?"

"Could you wait another week before making an arrest in the 'Love Nest Murders' as the papers call it?"

"What if we wait and there is another murder?"

"I'm sure you're keeping close tabs on Randa and Garcia. How could they kill anyone under that kind of surveillance?" I challenged him. "Besides, they're not guilty. Give me another week and I'll prove it."

"All the evidence points to Randa Cooper with or without Garcia," he said. "We can't arrest her yet, but as far as I can see, it's all over but the shoutin'."

"Doesn't the fact they called the police and didn't make any attempt to hide make you wonder?"

"They had to call. Her mother showed up."

"All right. They had a weapon and opportunity. What about motive?"

"I can see two scenarios, either one of which would have resulted in Victor Cooper's death. The only reason we're holding off is because we're not sure which version actually took place."

"Would you tell me your two theories?"

"Sure. Why not? Number one—they killed him in cold blood, in cold water."

"What motive?"

"Hatred and jealousy. Randa thought Victor behaved with insensitivity to her feelings, no doubt about that. He might have deserved a rude awakening, but death by drowning?" Richardson spread his hands and shrugged.

I sighed. "So what is the other point of view?"

"Accident. Maybe they went to investigate the strange noises in the night, attacked in the dark, and then recognized who they had 'done in.' So they put him in the cold plunge, fabricated the story about running footsteps, and called us after Randa's mother appeared on the scene."

"You say it might be another couple of weeks before you make an arrest?"

Richardson nodded.

"Have you questioned Tiahna?"

He nodded again, but gave nothing more away, forcing me to keep asking questions.

"Is she a suspect?"

"No."

I'd come to share the few facts I knew, but after struggling with his off-putting manner, I changed my mind. We sat in silence a moment, staring at each other with antagonism.

Richardson must have felt as I did, that we were wasting time, because he cleared his throat and said, "Okay—you have a few more days. Why not? We're not ready to make an arrest yet, anyway."

That astonished me. I'd been thinking him an arrogant poop when, without warning, he gave his consent for me to keep on searching. Yahoo! My opinion returned to my first impression: *What a hunk!*

In an effort to stay as noncommittal as he, I said, "Thank you," in as ladylike a way as I could.

Richardson's response put a new spin on my decision to leave because he'd given his approval for me to stay and snoop. I returned to Char's house, told her about my visits with the priest and the detective, and moved back in. Then I called Garcia and brought him up to date.

"What Rita said about Tomás is significant. What do you make of it?"

"Father Quejada strikes me as a logical man," I answered. "He looks tired, as if he has been affected by all this. I can think of at least two reasons why: either he has suspicions about Tomás, or he wants to cast suspicion away from himself. What do you think?"

He looked at me. "I'll get back to you."

FOURTEEN

Richardson looked over his bifocals at Garcia and me. "Check out Father Quejada?" he asked. "On what grounds?"

"Same grounds you have on Randa and me," Garcia replied. "He had an appointment with Rita; he was on the scene of the crime; he found her body."

"What else? You know something I don't know?" He glared at me. Our relationship seesawed back and forth between friendliness and suspicion.

"Maybe," I replied. "I talked to Father Quejada this morning."

"And?"

"Father remembered Rita said Tomás didn't want her to go see him. Tomás didn't want Rita to confess."

The dumbfounded look on Richardson's face gave me a small jolt of joy. "How did you arrive at that interpretation?"

Garcia stepped in. "Several possibilities occurred to us. Maybe Tomás suspected Rubio of being involved and wanted to protect him, or maybe Tomás suspected Father Quejada and wanted to protect Rita. Maybe Tomás is the murderer we're looking for. Doesn't seem credible, but no more incredible than Randa and me as suspects."

"Hmmm. So?"

"So both of them should be investigated. Tomás wanted Rita to keep quiet, and Father Quejada could be trying to deflect suspicion away from himself."

"You don't trust the priest, hey?" Richardson asked.

"He's open about his involvement in a sanctuary movement for illegal immigrants. That may or may not have something to do with the murders."

Richardson's stoic expression gave away nothing of what he thought.

"Inspector," Garcia persisted, "you've got to know when a man in my position, a police lieutenant, is the chief suspect, he's going to make sure you check out everybody, even those who seem the most innocent."

"Garcia, sit down," Richardson commanded. "I want you to stop prowling the room and tell me everything you've learned. Don't try to act uninformed. I know you've got hundreds of contacts in this town, and I know you've been in touch with them. You and your . . ." he frowned, ". . . sidekick."

He turned his attention back to me, hesitated a moment then said in a baffled tone, "How did you manage to finagle your way into this investigation anyway? This is *my* case."

Garcia stopped pacing to look out the window, his back to Richardson. I could see his face. He winked at me.

I looked at Richardson and rolled my eyes. "Finagle, huh! You left out the part about leaping tall buildings and flying on a broomstick."

"I already knew that part," Richardson said.

After a moment of silence, not prayerful, Richardson cleared his throat. "I don't want to believe you're guilty, Garcia. Hell, we're colleagues. Just between the two . . ." he glared at me, ". . . I mean, *three* of us, let's overlook the facts that implicate you for the moment. Let's pool our information. I know you want to clear yourself, and your girlfriend if you can, and I'm willing to cut you a little slack. At least until I have absolute proof against you."

"That's fair," Garcia said. "I'll tell you all I can."

"I just want to check my findings against yours. What do you know about Tomás and his wife on the night of Victor's murder?"

Garcia outlined the movements of each person as we knew them.

"Victor and Tiahna left the reception together. Because of the doll hanging and the afternoon spent trying to find Tiahna, Maggie asked Tomás and Rita to follow them with her. They lost them and returned to the reception. Tomás and Rita went home together where, according to them, they stayed. Rubio claimed to have been in Phoenix, but no one has been found to corroborate his claim. Father Quejada attended the reception, but no one checked on him for that night. Randa's and my movements are well known, as are Char's, Tiahna's, and Maggie's. And that's what we know."

Garcia and I stood to leave the office. Richardson stopped us with a growl.

"Ms. McGinnis, I told you this morning you had a couple of weeks. Change that to a couple of days." He cleared his throat. "Why didn't you tell me this morning about talking to Father Quejada?" For such a tough guy, he sounded a little bit hurt. I shrugged, unwilling at that point to say that he was just too damned arrogant.

Later, in the car, we laughed because Richardson hadn't told us a thing even though he'd said he wanted to share. At least, he hadn't muzzled us.

I laughed again. "I wonder if he always clears his throat just when he's ready to act a little bit human."

A call to his grapevine revealed to Garcia that Richardson continued with his bluff. With the evidence from the Avila garage and with the new suspicions Garcia and I had raised about Father Quejada, Tomás, and Rubio, his case against Randa had sprung leaks.

Garcia's source said Richardson intended to arrest Randa within the next couple of days, on the theory if he got her while her emotions were unstable she'd incriminate herself and even draw Garcia in. He was waiting for a profile on Randa from a court-appointed psychologist.

"I want to talk to Tomás, but I wonder if it's too soon after he's just buried his wife," Garcia said. We rode in silence. I was still contemplating his last words when he continued,

"Char said Tomás had returned to work, trying to go on with life without Rita."

"That will be hard," I said. "Rita seemed to anchor him, but it would be good for him to take up some normal activities again. He'll have to find a new anchor."

Because time was short, Garcia and I decided to take advantage of the few days we had left. He wanted to talk to Tomás and Father Quejada in a friendly, relaxed atmosphere, so he called the priest and asked his opinion. Father Quejada suggested a golf game and said he would call Tomás,

"How about the course at Oak Creek Village?" the priest said. "I have an appointment there late in the afternoon, and I could just go to it after we play." Garcia arranged a tee time for the next day, then called to confirm he'd meet them in the pro shop at noon. When all the plans were made, he repeated their conversations to Randa, Char, and me.

Tomás, working again, said, "I have to go to the school for a Spanish Club fundraiser. We're selling *Huevos Rancheros* tomorrow morning to raise money for a trip to Mexico. I'll meet you there."

"Fundraiser?" I said. "Hey. I want to take you all out for *Huevos Rancheros* tomorrow. Let's go to the Spanish Club fundraiser and show our support for Tomás."

Saturday morning started out as a bright, crisp November day, perfect for golf, perfect for Spanish-style eggs and tortillas served with refried beans and salsa. A sizable crowd attended the fundraiser, and Tomás worked the frying pans. We weren't able to do more than wave and call "Hi!"

While Garcia went to Oak Creek Village for the golf game, Char went with Randa for a session with her therapist. He agreed for her to come in on Saturday because he felt she was poised for a breakthrough. Randa, although still tied in knots, still indifferent to the effect she created, wanted to put it all behind her. She, too, felt ready to break through. Char remained steadfast in her conviction of Randa's innocence, but even she knew Randa's strange reluctance to loosen up made her appear guilty. I got the report straight from Char.

"Randa," Dr. Warren had said. "The last week of November I will be away on a three-day wilderness campout in the Sonora desert south of Tucson. My purpose there will be to act as a guide for those who participate in a personal search for their center within. American Indian tribes call it a vision quest, which is a good description for seeking to uncover an internal vision by which to live. It's a matter of getting to know oneself. Some other groups call it dream time."

Randa's face had lit up with interest. "I wish I could go," she said.

"I'd like you to go. An internal adventure might be more useful to you now than anything, or anyone else."

Randa had become energized. With the promise of a desert adventure, a journey into the wilderness of her own soul, she surged to life.

"Did you kill your father?" Dr. Warren had asked.

In a torrent of tears, Randa confessed the guilt she'd been harboring. "I killed part of him. He was Tiahna's father as well as mine, and I refused to recognize that truth in him. I attacked that fact with all the viciousness I had in me. But no, I did not physically kill my father. But because of my bitterness and jealousy, I killed something inside him."

Later, seated around a fire in the family room, it was Garcia's turn to fill us in on the day's events.

He, Father Quejada, and Tomás arrived in separate vehicles at the beautiful course built in Oak Creek Village. They teed off at twelve fifteen in the afternoon.

Father Quejada, called Rafe in casual company, took a bold approach to the situation. He swung his club, hit it far out on the first green, and then said, "What's up, Garcia? We're not here for our health."

"Maybe we are, Rafe," Garcia replied and watched his ball roll to a stop not three feet from Father's.

Tomás swung, and his ball arced wildly right. "Looks like a day in the rough for me," he said. "Hope it gets better."

They started forward with their pull-carts. "Rafe," Garcia said. "Tomorrow, in the Sunday paper, your sanctuary movement is going to hit the front page. Everybody will be brought up-to-date about it."

"Good. We want the publicity."

"I understand your congregation is split down the middle on the wisdom of it. I thought maybe you'd tell me the theological or philosophical reasoning behind it."

"It's simple," Rafe said. "We want to help the poor and the hungry. This is such a rich country. New Mexicans and Arizonans have a blood link to neighbors south of the border. And it is our Catholic tradition. You know that. You were raised Catholic, and I'd be willing to bet you have blood relatives still in Mexico."

"Yes. But I'm an American lawman. What you are doing is against the law."

"Man's law and God's law are not always the same."

"You must know that drugs are being passed along your people pipeline."

Father Rafe's shaken expression had appeared genuine. Either he was full of unsophisticated fervor or full of bull crap. Garcia, even with a close watch, could not tell which.

"You have proof of that?" Rafe asked.

"Of course we have proof. Has Rubio been one of your drivers?"

"Yes."

"He's in it up to his ears. In fact, he's in over his head."

Tomás stood listening, his head down. He took a deep breath. "So why did you ask me down here?" he asked.

"I wanted you to know that the clock is ticking against Rubio. I don't want to think he killed his mother, but if you know something you haven't told me, now is the time."

Tomás shook his head and remained silent.

The golf game fell apart. November clouds and a strong wind came up. As other groups hustled in from the greens to the clubhouse, Garcia, Father Rafe, and Tomás did the same. After changing shoes and arranging for a rain check on the game, they walked outside to their cars. At his car door, Garcia said to Tomás, "Because of our personal ties, I'll give you a few hours to think about this. Make no mistake; the sky is falling on this. I'll call you tomorrow."

As he drove away, he looked back in his rearview mirror. Father Rafe and Tomás were huddled in deep conversation, Rafe with his arm around Tomás's shoulder.

"I'd have given a lot to hear what they were talking about." He sighed. "Overall, it wasn't a very productive afternoon." Garcia got up and began to pace. "It is looking more and more like Rubio is the key. To everything. Stupid kid. He makes me want to smack him upside the head just to see if I can knock some sense into him."

I suddenly remembered something important. "Randa, in the newspaper clippings of the reception, the ones your scrapbook, there's a shot of you and Garcia."

Randa nodded.

"The picture shows a turquoise stone missing from your concho belt *during the reception*."

"Thank God," Char breathed.

"Hmm," Randa said, "It must have fallen out there at the hotel, or on the way there, because all the stones were in place when I put it on. If they hadn't been, I wouldn't have worn it." She responded in such an unemotional tone I thought maybe she didn't understand the implications of my revelation.

At last she said, "Thank you, Maggie. You don't know the tension I've been under."

"I have a pretty fair idea just from watching your face these past weeks." I turned to Char. "I have another piece of news. Tiahna and Rubio hung the doll in your studio. Tiahna told me herself." I related then how the two set it up.

Randa's face tightened.

Char's face reflected feelings like a shattered mirror. "Why?" she exclaimed. "It was so destructive—so self-destructive." But then she blew out a deep breath. "I'm not truly surprised, though. I had a squirmy feeling she knew something about it."

Randa shook her head. "Why did they pull such a bizarre trick?"

"Rubio needed money—a lot of money and decided to try his hand at witching, hoping that Victor would give Tiahna money to help her."

Randa exploded, "After all you've done for Tiahna—and for Rubio!"

Char sat in pained silence.

"But of course it didn't work out the way Victor hoped." I paused. "Someone else got to your money first. It might have been Rubio, but Tiahna didn't get it."

"How can you be so sure?" Randa demanded.

"Because Tomás, Rita and I followed her and your dad the night they opened Char's safe. We watched them come up empty-handed." Both Char and Randa looked surprised. "I'm convinced she had no idea evil energy might come back on her from the doll hanging. She fell apart. She spiraled down into worse shape than you were in, Randa."

Garcia held Randa's hand. She began to speak again, "Well, she just—"

"Come on, Randa," Garcia shook his head, "you weren't the only one hurting. Give her a break."

Randa had the grace to look embarrassed.

Garcia turned to me and said, "And once again, Rubio is at the center of it all."

The telephone, on an end table near Garcia's elbow, rang. He answered then handed the receiver to me. "Tomás."

"Hello, Tomás."

"Maggie," he sounded old and exhausted, "I'm just wrung out. I'd like to talk to you face to face about Rubio. I could pick you up, say forty-five minutes or so. I know a great place for *Chile Rellenos.*"

"Sure," I said. "I'll get ready. See you soon."

I hung up and looked at Garcia. "He wants to talk to me alone."

"Huh," Garcia said, "I wonder what he has in mind."

I didn't know the answer to that.

I showered and dressed in slacks and sweater. I debated about shoes—would I need running shoes? A shadow of fear tugged at me, but I dismissed it, reminding myself that Tomás, a lonely, bereaved man, didn't know how to cope with his son. I cast the premonition aside, and chose sleek pumps with slender three-inch heels. With a woolen coat around my shoulders against the November chill, I waited for Tomás.

We entered Tlaquepaque through an archway on the western side. Most of the shops were darkened and locked for the evening. We passed the jewelry shop of Rita's cousin and saw him inside, although most of the lights were out and the doors were locked. He looked up, recognized us, and beckoned us to wait.

He opened the door and said, "Tomás, I finished your watch. With all that has happened since Rita brought it in, I just didn't get to it. Anyway, I had to wait for the right color of turquoise to replace the stone you lost." Beside me, Tomás tensed up and I prayed the jeweler would say no more. No such luck.

"Ms. McGinnis," he went on. "After you came in the other day with the measurement of the stone you'd found at the spa, I remembered an old brochure I used to keep on the counter describing turquoise and the differences in quality and color. I've got a copy for you if you'd like to have it."

"Thank you. That's thoughtful of you." I slipped the brochure into my shoulder bag without looking at it, acutely aware of Tomás at my elbow.

No more than ten or fifteen minutes later, seated in a secluded booth across from Tomás, I wondered how I ever could have thought his brown eyes were warm. With icy intensity, he stared at me like a silent crouching cat staring at a cornered mouse, waiting to pounce. The hair on the back of my neck stood up. Fear clutched at my stomach as I tried to control my breathing. For a brief moment, our eyes locked. Mutual recognition of Tomás's murderous intent passed between us.

"So you found a turquoise stone?" Small talk. "You know, hundreds are lost every year."

"Of course," I agreed too quickly.

"But you found this one at the spa? Would it happen to be in the cold plunge? People do tend to remove their jewelry before they get in the water."

"Yes, they do." A platter of nachos arrived. My stomach clenched, on heavy-duty alert.

"So the stone could have been anyone's."

"Right. Anyone's." I knew I couldn't eat, but I didn't know if I could convince Tomás I wasn't worried.

No, I couldn't. I stared at the food.

"Eat." His voice had a hard edge. "You *turistas* are all alike. Wasteful."

"I guess I'm more tired than I thought, Tomás. Could you cancel the *rellenos* and take me home?"

"Of course." Sarcastic. "Why should the kitchen care?"

In a matter of minutes, we were in Tomás's car. His hostility radiated like a palpable presence. We started into the foothills, the road to Char's house. Then he swerved to take a different mountain road.

"Where are you going?" I demanded.

"What's the matter, Maggie? You like to snoop around, don't you? I want to show you something you missed at the spa."

The almost full moon glowed in the east; the clear night made way for its glory; the deserted road stretched ahead. Isolated with Tomás on this shining cold night, I could see no help in any direction.

As if reading my mind, he said, "You have only yourself to blame."

"To blame for what?"

"For anything that happens to you."

If anything is going to happen to me tonight, now is the time to find out why.

"I can understand why you killed Victor. He must have discovered you robbing Randa's safe." I said. "But Rita?"

"She panicked, wanted to confess."

"When did you get the money from the gallery safe?"

"I didn't. Rita took it before she locked up Friday afternoon. Rubio had been to see her earlier in the week."

"I saw them talking together."

"He begged her to help him get money. They, whoever 'they' are, threatened to kill him. Rubio was Rita's baby and always would be, no matter what."

Tomás had every intention of killing me at the spa—why else would he tell me everything? But I had a subliminal intuition, the eerie feeling an angel rode with me on that moonlit mountain road. So I kept asking the questions that had haunted my thoughts for weeks.

"Did you already know Rita took the money when the two of you went with me to follow Victor and Tiahna?"

"No. I learned later, after the reception, when Rubio came to the house to get it. But there wasn't nearly enough. He had to have twenty-five thousand." He sounded incredulous. "Twenty-five thousand dollars. And that was just a down payment on what he owed."

"So you went to the spa?"

"Yes."

"And Victor stumbled in on you, so you killed him?"

"Yes!" he exploded. "Oh God, how I hated doing that. My life is ruined. And you. Why didn't you just mind your own business? Now I've got to silence you, too."

"Well, if you intend to 'silence' me, first I want to know everything that led you to this."

"God, you are tough. You remind me of Rita."

Rita, who you killed in cold blood.

Aloud, I said, "Why did Rubio hang the doll if he knew his mother was getting the money?"

"Rubio planned the doll hanging to be a double whammy, insurance to push Victor into getting the money in case Rita couldn't, and to steer things away from him and Tiahna." His nonchalant disclosures were beginning to unnerve me.

We went past the spa, no longer guarded, no longer bright with lights, closed, shuttered, deserted, with windswept leaves piled up against the walls. A CLOSED sign was posted on the uprights. Randa had moved in with her mother until a suspect was apprehended and Victor's murder went to trial.

Tomás turned in on a side road and stopped.

When he saw I was looking at him, he said, "This is the back way to the spa. No one will see the car."

"Oh," I said.

He put the car in park and reached for the key.

I threw open the door, leaped out and ran. The headlights blazed around me but before I veered out of their halo, a bullet whizzed by and smacked into a nearby tree.

"Come back," Tomás snarled.

I walked slowly back to the car, my legs trembling.

He got behind me and prodded with the barrel of the gun. Panic welled in my throat, almost bursting out in a scream before I clenched my teeth together to regain control. My classy little heels slipped and slid on the rocky, rutted path as I stumbled through the woods ahead of Tomás. A coyote howled in the hills above us, a long, eerie shiver of song. I jumped. Even Tomás started. Answering howls came from the mountain. Dogs began to bark. The wild chorus reverberated in the cold, moon-bright night.

We moved fast. Stealth was pointless now that the police guard was gone. Tomás was in a hurry.

"Tomás, why are you doing this?' I tried to keep myself from sounding pitiful. "Garcia knows everything I know."

"I already talked to Garcia. He thinks Rubio killed his mother." He snickered. "That boy wouldn't hurt a fly."

Obviously Rubio was Tomás's baby, too. He harbored a significant blind spot where his son was concerned.

"I thought you liked me, Tomás."

"I liked you until I realized you were like all the rest of the *turistas*. I despise people like you who come to Sedona and pretend they own it— silly, talentless women who come to paint the natives with *dignity*. How egotistical to think native dignity comes from their paintbrushes."

The loathing in his voice convinced me I was going to have to do something to save myself. Terror gripped me.

A sudden misstep sent me sprawling. I fell on my broken wrist and cried out. Tomás jerked me up.

"Don't try your female tricks on me. You are going in the water just like Victor." His civilized veneer was gone, ripped away in a witching atmosphere of his own making. He jerked me to my feet. His light, his good, his loving nature, if they were ever there at all, had given way to the darkness within him. Evil and hatred controlled his actions.

"How could I have misjudged you so?" I wondered aloud.

"Easy," he snorted. "Your Anglo arrogance. It prevents you from seeing the real people under the masks we wear."

We stood outside the cold plunge enclosure. "Open the door," he commanded.

I obeyed like an automaton.

"Now climb."

Tears blinded me and I nearly choked on racking sobs.

"Oh, shut up," he snarled. "You should have gone home like Rita's note told you. It would have saved us all a lot of trouble. Rita liked you but wanted you to quit snooping around, too."

I stared at him through my tears, accepting too late what had seemed implausible just a few days before. And then something loosed inside me.

"Go on," he prodded.

"No!" I yelled, "Help!" and pushed him.

He staggered back but recovered quickly, swinging his gun around at me. I threw up my good arm.

The butt of the gun glanced off my left temple. Fireworks went off in front of my eyes and bright pain shot through my head. I fell back and hit my head hard against the tiled rim of the cold plunge.

Semiconscious, I was aware Tomás picked up my feet and pulled me around. Then I tumbled heels overhead into the icy water. My skin contracted. Cold water rushed into my nose and mouth. I kicked frantically. Oxygen, as it escaped from my lungs, forced more water into my nose. My waterlogged woolens held me down.

An explosion in my head sprayed out splinters of light. Thunder pounded against me in roaring waves. Then it all subsided into ripples of lapping water.

Soft, silent dark engulfed me. I sank. Did I only imagine the haunting serenade of a coyote?

FIFTEEN

"Poor Maggie. Two black eyes. Bandaged head. Casts on both arms."

"But you should see the other guy," I murmured.

"Can't. We buried him yesterday."

My eyes popped open then squeezed shut in the bright light. "You buried Tomás? What happened?"

"You'll have to tell us," Garcia said. "The wire we taped to you shorted out and didn't kick back in until you were already out at the spa. We nearly didn't get there in time. If it wasn't for Tsosie, we wouldn't have."

"Tsosie?" I asked.

"Your friend, Tsosie, tracked you, stayed right behind you all the way."

"Really?" A sound reverberated inside my head. "Did I hear Tomás's gun go off."

"You did. Tsosie grabbed him from behind. Tomás got off a round. That's when we arrived."

"We?"

"Me and Richardson."

Weakness flooded over me and tears ran out from under my closed eyelids.

Garcia's voice softened. "Please, forgive me, Maggie. I would never have wanted you to suffer. But you did help us catch the murderer."

"I thought wearing the wire was all we needed. I didn't expect . . ." I was so tired. "Tomás wouldn't have been dangerous if the jeweler hadn't informed him I was asking about the missing nugget in his watch."

Garcia looked surprised. "The jeweler? So that's what set him off. You know, Maggie, if you knew you were in trouble, you should never have gotten in the car with him."

"I thought I could handle it. I so wanted that confession. I remembered Oprah's first rule too late."

His brows knit together. "You'll have to explain that to me someday." Garcia sighed. "It could have been a disaster. Thank God for premonitions. Have you ever had one, one you couldn't rationalize away?"

"Ha! Me and my rational mind *ignored* terribly real promptings."

"What were they?" Garcia asked.

"Someone or something whispered to me, *running shoes*. I chose heels instead."

"Well, Char, Randa and I each had bad feelings about what you were doing with Tomás and when the wire failed, I called for reinforcements. Obviously, Tsosie had mystical warnings, too."

"What happened to Tomás?"

"After Tsosie grabbed him from behind, he shot himself before we could get his gun."

"I thought that explosion came from my bursting lungs."

"You were brave, Maggie, and foolish. If Tsosie hadn't been there, Tomás would have killed you."

"Bless Tsosie. What an inspiring, intuitive friend he is."

"Yes, isn't he? Every law enforcement agency in Arizona wants him, from city police to state police to the Shadow Wolves. He told me he doesn't want to give up his art, but he does want to help the Wolves as much as he can."

A tall black, nurse with kind eyes, and a great smile stuck her head in the door. "You need to leave now, Lieutenant. The lady needs her rest."

He smiled, squeezed my good hand and promised to come back later.

I was feeling better when he came back after a few hours.

"Garcia, I thought of something. Char joked that Tomás was a lady-killer, but I didn't pay any attention. We all thought him such a charmer."

"He could be devilishly charming until Rubio got into drugs in junior high, then began dealing and thieving to support his habit. That was when their family malignancy started to grow."

"At the end, said he despised me and everyone like me because we overrun Sedona."

A strangely uncomfortable expression crossed Garcia's face. "Many of us natives have trouble dealing with that, Maggie. It's an ancient problem of class and minorities. Please don't take it to heart. You have done a lot to help this city, and whether anyone else knows it or not, I do."

I kept silent, remembering that Char had tried to discuss the subject of race relationships in Sedona, and I had turned her away from it to spare her grief. I sighed and said, "The hatred emanating from Tomás smothered me. I've never felt anything like it before. He wanted to annihilate me. Victor probably felt that same bitter loathing directed at him."

"Victims feel that force of implacable fury all the time. Criminals who've felt betrayed by society and vent their societal rage on the innocent seem to focus all their viciousness on one small, powerless victim at a time, perhaps because they feel powerless in society as a whole."

I felt vulnerable and in pain, so I cried. The nurse bustled in and said to Garcia, "You again? Look what you've done. You'll have to go now, sir."

"No, no," I protested. "Garcia isn't upsetting me."

"But I do need to go. I'll see you tomorrow, Maggie." He walked toward the door.

"Just a minute. Where is Rubio now?"

Garcia's shoulders sagged. There was something mournful about him. "The most ironic thing happened. About the same time Tomás shot himself, the guys who had been following Rubio shot him and threw his body on the banks of Oak Creek in a kind of gangland warning. Tomás never knew it. It's a sad ending for that family."

He started out of the room again "Garcia? What about José, the body at the gallery?"

With a grim expression, he shook his head. "José was my undercover recruit on Skylark. His cover was blown. We don't know how. His death, retribution for helping us, also targeted Skylark. Drugs caused that and Rubio's death as well¾both gangland killings. Two days ago, there was a shootout between rival coyote smugglers on Interstate 10. We've found expensive, upscale houses that have been rented by innocent owners and turned into drop houses crammed full of starving illegals in filthy conditions. What an inhuman way to treat a fellow Mexican national. Skylark is just a tiny drop in the bucket of drugs and illegal human trafficking, but each little drop is crucial if we hope to eliminate it. I'll admit I got carried away with my theories. Victor's and Rita's deaths had nothing to do with any of that, except in the sense that they were connected through Rubio and Tomás, and for me to think they did shows how arrogant I can be. Can you ever like me again?"

"Oh, Garcia, I like you a lot. You can't tell me you don't recognize that simpatico vibe."

His eyes twinkled. "By the way, you've made a conquest. Richardson thinks you are one supremely sexy woman. Smart, too."

"I have to admit I think he's a hunk. What am I turning into, a fool for love, a sellout for sex?"

"Aren't we all? I know I am. It's that old, irresistible A & E syndrome."

"A & E? What is that?"

"You know, Adam and Eve. Blame it on ancient ancestry."

I got lucky to have such a comfortable relationship with Garcia. He's easy to talk to, nonjudgmental, and smart.

The nurse came in with a medication tray and shooed Garcia out again. She gave me an antibiotic to guard against lung infection from the near drowning and a sleeping pill. I drifted off, still weak, and almost overwhelmed by the dark memory of the homicidal hatred I had survived.

I felt life surging back when I woke up to flowers and cards. A sunny Thanksgiving arrangement and card from my office in Page: "Hurry and get well. We miss you."

Richardson paid a visit during the morning. Out of uniform he looked more diffident. He had to clear his throat before he began.

"Ms. McGinnis."

"Please call me Maggie."

He hemmed and hawed a bit then said, "Maggie. I've got a little ragbag here I want you to burn. In triumph. You were right, and I was wrong." He handed me a plastic bag with the paint rags from the spa. A single Peace rose, the soft blush of pink on the edges of the creamy yellow petals, bobbed from the top of a vase concealed by the rags. "I want you to know that wasn't easy for me to say."

"Well, thank you for saying it, Inspector." I tried to smell the rose, but the mayonnaise on the rags was rancid and interfered with the charm of the moment. I think I managed not to wrinkle my nose.

"You can call me Jed, short for Jedediah," he confided, revealing more of the real man under the façade than I ever expected, or even thought I wanted, to see. "I want to be your friend."

"Why, thank you, Jed. I'd like that."

"Maggie, are you ever in the Phoenix area? Or Tempe?" he asked. "If so, will you go out to dinner with me when you're feeling better?"

"Hey, Jed, I'm already late for a hugely significant date—my granddaughter's birthday party in Tempe. When are you going back to Phoenix?"

"My case is closed. I'm on my way back right now as soon as I leave here."

"I'll be going down soon. Why don't you give me your phone number and I'll call you when I'm there."

"Promise?" The man was persistent. I liked that, but I couldn't help remembering Garcia and I laughed at him just a few days earlier.

He went on. "I have tickets to the ASU, U of A football game next week. You want to go?"

"Hmmm—who will you be cheering for?" I asked.

"Well—U of A?" He grinned and ducked his head with beseeching charm, that age-old, momentary humility men use with devastating effect from the cradle to the grave.

"U of A fans are rabid," I observed.

"I know. Can you overlook that?"

"That's asking a lot of an ASU grad." Then I let him off the hook. "I'd love to go to the game. I'll be there."

After Jed had gone, Garcia and Randa came in. Randa, looking less like a crushed flower, bloomed again with a calmer, more mature radiance. Her hair, in a new upswept hairdo with tendrils everywhere, looked shiny and sophisticated.

"Hello, Mama Maggie." She hugged me, taking care not to jostle me. "How are you feeling?"

"Better," I said. "I'll be out of here soon. How are you? You look great."

"I am feeling great, with lots of thanks to you. What would we have done without you?"

"Don't ask me hard questions," I laughed, returning her hug with equal care. Then I asked, "What about you, Garcia? Will you be able to continue with your projects?"

"We closed one tiny loophole—the one Father Quejada provided. He didn't know they were smuggling drugs in with the people he offered sanctuary to. We haven't been able to close the border, but we made a significant drug bust and caught a few ringleaders. It's all in the newspapers." He handed me a bundle of folded newspapers. "Even though misguided, Rubio provided the breaks we needed."

"Thanks. I'll read them later."

"Guess what, Maggie," Randa said, glowing. "Garcia and I are going on the wilderness adventure Dr. Warren told me about in the Sonoran desert."

"And when we get back, Randa is going to complete the massage she started on me last month." Garcia waggled his eyebrows suggestively. "And then start a new one."

In my hospital bed, I read with interest the newspapers Garcia had brought. One of the articles concerned the Shadow Wolves. I was thinking about the unique expertise they provide when Tsosie walked softly on moccasined feet into my room. The moment I saw him, I started to cry. He stood at my bedside and watched me with an inscrutable expression.

"You saved my life," I sobbed.

He nodded. I cried. He stood still.

In time, I regained control of myself. "*Hyeh-Heh, Tsosie. Hyeh-Heh.*" All I could think to say was "Thank you." I felt, in his silent presence, that a flood of words would be sacrilegious, worse than a flood of tears. I could only hope my overflowing emotions carried the message of my heart.

When my eyes were dry enough to look directly at him, I could see understanding in his eyes. No words were necessary in an extraordinary communion of spirit. When his quiet presence had calmed me, he left.

Char arrived during afternoon visiting hours carrying an unwieldy package. I opened it and found the portrait of Tiahna, once ruined, now restored. The dark eyes mirrored a shadow of pain in their luminous depths. Speechless with delight, I looked at Char and she looked back, each of us with silent understanding. The same shadow she had painted into the portrait of Tiahna was in Char's own eyes. Maybe it was cathartic for her to at last have painted Tiahna as real. Char's elegance, never more evident than in this gift, filled the room. The gift was not only for me, but also for Tiahna and Victor and perhaps, in time, for Randa, when she arrived at the point where she could accept with grace what she could not change. Tears welled up in my eyes again.

"Maggie, why do you stay in Page?" Char asked apropos of nothing. "The kids are grown, and Ron is gone."

"I've asked myself that more than once of late. My house is paid for—that's something. I love the lake, the pink and blue scenery, and my friends. The people in my office sent me a card; they miss me."

"Why don't you move here and help me in the gallery? I know you enjoy your work, but you have enough years in to retire. I wouldn't demand much, two or three days a week. Would you think about it?"

"Yes, Char, I will. I didn't give serious thought to changing my lifestyle after Ron left because a counselor told me not to make substantial changes for at least a year. But you know, right now I'm in the mood for change. I could find a suitable apartment here . . ." I mused. "Let me think about it for a few days. And thank you so much for the painting. I love it!"

Just before visiting hours closed at eight in the evening, Tiahna slipped into my room. "*Yah te hey*," she said softly.

"*Yah te hey*," I answered.

"When are you going back to Page?" she asked.

"Soon. Do you want to go with me?"

"No, thanks. I'm going to stay here and finish school."

"What will you do when you graduate?"

"I want to work in the Navajo Arts Council."

"You are an extraordinary young woman, Tiahna. You were pressured from every side. Rubio wanted money and sex but didn't want to give of himself in return. Victor wanted you to absolve him from guilt."

"And he gave everything in return," she said.

"Yes. And your grandfather?"

"My grandfather didn't pressure me. He just did what medicine men do. He helped me."

"His pressure may have been invisible, but powerful nonetheless. He wants you to return to ancient traditions."

"I did turn to him when I needed help."

"Yes. You took healing from his medicine, but you added your own courage and spirit to make your decision. That is what is so remarkable in you; the blend of old tradition and modern spirit. Both are valuable." I paused. "Did you see what Char brought?"

Tiahna looked at the portrait for a long time and then she said, "I want to share talent and beauty the way Char does."

The lights blinked. Visiting hours were over. Tiahna rose to leave.

"Tiahna," I stopped her because I had just remembered something that had been bugging me for a long time. "I met the guy I called Geronimo. Do you know who he was?"

Tiahna shrugged. "I haven't got a clue. What did he look like?"

I described him with details that had grown increasingly vivid in my mind.

Tiahna laughed. "Oh, that's Tsosie Tsinniginnie. He teaches at the Art Center. Some day he'll be rich and famous, you know. We're getting married in the spring."

The next morning, the doctor released me from the hospital. Char picked me up and took me to her house where I packed my things and prepared to leave.

"I'm thinking long and hard about your offer, Char," I told her. "The U of A, ASU game is this weekend. I'll be in Tempe for Thanksgiving with my daughter then Christmas is just around the corner. A busy time but I'll be in touch. After the first of the year, who knows?"

I drove from Char's house, deciding at the last minute to visit the Bell Rock vortex. It wasn't my favorite of the vortexes. I liked them all, but it was close to the road, and I did have a serene spot where a twisted cedar tree and a natural pine bonsai tree grew side by side.

When I found my spot, in the shallow shade of my stunted trees, I sat on the rock outcropping and loosened up, unwound, untwisted, and unscrewed. Right then I knew the secret of the hold the vortexes had on me: they don't twist and squeeze me; they unwind me and let my spirit soar free.

SIXTEEN

I n Tempe, my family and I played catch-up for a couple of days. I had second thoughts about calling Jed Richardson. In our limited acquaintance, he had only demonstrated two of the top five on my list of preferences in a man. My top five are: gainfully employed, talks with ease, quick sense of humor, wide-ranging interests, and masculine vitality. He is gainfully employed and has a strong, masculine presence, but I didn't know him well enough to judge his humor and interests; so far, they had escaped me. To call or not to call?

But I am a woman of my word, so I called Jed Richardson from Jennifer's house the day before the traditional football grudge match pitting ASU against the U of A. From the suppressed laughter in his extremely sexy telephone voice, he was truly happy to hear from me. He sounded like the Marlboro Man looks, which did nothing to ease my "lonely lady's" libido problem.

November in Tempe was football heaven. The home games were played in the early evening. Jed said, "The game starts at six tomorrow. How would you like to go to a tailgate party with a bunch of my buddies about four?"

I laughed with sheer joy. "That sounds positively fantastic to me. What should I bring?"

"Nothing but yourself," he said. "Everything is already taken care of. What kind of beer do you like?"

"Sorry. I don't drink beer. But I love a good white wine."

"You got it. Where and what time should I pick you up?"

"You know what, Jed? If you have the day off, I would honestly like to get to know you better. Could we get together early in the day and just talk?"

"Sure thing," Jed answered. "I know a quite charming little place where we can talk. How does ten o'clock in the morning sound?"

Honestly, I had every reasonable intention of just talking until I saw him. He arrived at Jennifer's house just before ten wearing a dark blue U of A polo shirt and tan shorts revealing muscular, hairy legs, slim ankles, and an Arizona suntan. He carried a plastic shopping bag with "ASU" printed on the side. He had brought me a white ASU polo shirt, with the familiar maroon and gold Sun Devil logo. He was so cool to think of bringing me the shirt of the opposing team.

The "charming little place" turned out to be his townhouse south of Phoenix in Ahwatukee. It was compact with an appealing entry way and a tiny patio in back. I walked through with him and when he went into the kitchen, I walked back to the front door and opened it. I knew myself too well. I was not staying there to be charmed out of my skull.

Jed walked out of the kitchen with a tray with grapes, apples, and a pitcher of iced tea. He looked questioningly at me standing at the open door.

"Sorry, Jed. I thought maybe we could go to the Paradise Grill for iced tea. Forgive me, but this is too intimate for me at this particular moment of my life."

His eyes crinkled. He smiled and I could see he knew exactly what I was talking about. He also looked a bit sheepish as if he was aware I'd caught him red-handed planning this intimacy.

"You knew what you were doing, didn't you?" I asked.

He nodded.

"Being alone and together like this is not what I meant when I said I wanted to get to know you."

"It's not? What did you mean?"

"Oh, I guess I want to know where you come from, where you've been, and where you're going—something like that."

"What changed your mind?" he asked.

"Must have been that little Garden of Eden in the back."

"Didn't I tell you that I had a nice little place to talk?"

"And was talking what you had in mind?" I asked.

He was silent for a few moments, and then he answered me honestly. "Sex is serious. It's life. I don't want cheap sex. I don't believe in it. But you turn me on, Maggie, not just with your body, but with your intelligence and your sassy personality. I've been out of my mind with wanting you for a while now, and when a couple gets to that point, what better way is there to get to know somebody intimately? I hope you feel the same way."

"I do feel the same way—and I would still like to get to know you better, but go slowly, please."

He did. We spent nearly all day drinking iced tea and talking about everything under the sun. Around three, we left for the tailgate party where I met a bunch of his friends.

My eyes were still underlined with fading bruises; I was wearing a cast on one arm and an ace bandage on the other.

One of Jed's friends said, "What happened to you?"

When I answered airily, "Oh, someone tried to kill me . . . twice," no one believed me and we all laughed. Jed's blue eyes sparkled with laughter, and when he winked at me, I winked back. Just a couple of exchanged winks again gave me a brief glimpse of his sense of humor and almost catapulted me into meltdown. Three out of five and looking good, Jed.

After six weeks, it was time to go back to work. I'd taken my two-week vacation, and thirty days of accumulated sick leave. I had to get back to Page and decide what to do with the rest of my life. So much had changed in the past six weeks that my past seemed flat, stale, and unlivable. I was ready to move on. Even though I had found in Jed a friend and a possible future, it was prudent to make changes a little at a time. I had been single long enough to value my freedom to make choices without considering others.

There's an old adage: The way to tell a girl from a woman is the girl loves the gift; the woman loves the giver. Like a lot of old sayings, I do not agree entirely. I loved Jed's gift of friendship and promise, but was it a lifetime thing? I thought Ron was for a lifetime and look what happened. The silly thing is I had never filed for a divorce from Ron. I must have been crazy—did I think he would come back? *Did I even want him back?* No.

Here's the thing. We were blessed with a sexual nature designed to make us all slightly nuts. Deal with it.

When I got home to Page, I finally filed for divorce and began the process of cleaning out the accumulated debris of my past. A year had passed since Ron left. Good riddance. It was about time I took care of myself. What would happen with Jed in the future was yet to be seen.

In May, I received a square, cream-colored envelope in the mailbox at my new apartment in Sedona. *Someone is getting married. How exciting.* I opened the envelope and read:

Mrs. Doria Zahne
Requests the pleasure of your company
At the traditional marriage ceremony of her daughter
Tiahna Zahne
And
Tsosie Tsinniginnie
On Saturday, May twenty-first, two thousand and thirteen
At ten o'clock in the morning
In Navajo Canyon at the hogan of
Hosteen Hatathlii
Reception following the ceremony
At six o'clock in the evening
Chapter House
Willow Water, Arizona

I read the invitation with its unusual combination of ancient and modern marriage customs and felt a sad shiver of regret for the passing of the old Navajo ways and for the passing of old friends. But I felt, too, a delicious tingle of anticipation for the future.

I decided to ask Jed to make the trip into Navajo Canyon with me.

The End